THE COUPLE UPSTAIRS

SHALINI BOLAND

Published by Bookouture in 2021

An imprint of Storyfire Ltd.
Carmelite House
50 Victoria Embankment
London EC4Y 0DZ

www.bookouture.com

ISBN: 978-1-83888-150-4
eBook ISBN: 978-1-83888-149-8

This book is a work of fiction. Names, characters, businesses,
organizations, places and events other than those clearly in the
public domain, are either the product of the author's imagination
or are used fictitiously. Any resemblance to actual persons, living or
dead, events or locales is entirely coincidental.

THE COUPLE
UPSTAIRS

BOOKS BY SHALINI BOLAND

The Secret Mother
The Child Next Door
The Silent Sister
The Millionaire's Wife
The Perfect Family
The Best Friend
The Girl from the Sea
The Marriage Betrayal
The Other Daughter
One of Us Is Lying
The Wife
My Little Girl

For Pete
xxx

PROLOGUE

Icy rain streaks down my face. My pyjamas are soaked through, clinging to my frozen skin. My throat is raw from screaming, fists bruised from battering the back door repeatedly to no avail.

'Let me in!' I cry for the hundredth time. 'Open the door! Please.' My voice is carried away on the moaning wind, drowned by the creak and swish of the trees. I curl my fingers into a fist once more and pound the wooden door.

The flat within is dark. I don't even know if he's still in there. I can't work out which is worse – the thought that he's inside listening to my pleas, yet choosing to ignore them, or that he's left without telling me.

A sharp crack of thunder judders through my bones. A flash of lightning as bright as daylight illuminates my reflection in the kitchen window. I look like a ghost. A spectre of misery. Hair plastered to my head. Face pale as death. Eyes wide.

What should I do? What can I do? I step away from the back door and gaze up at the flat above. It too lies in darkness. But as I squint through the driving rain, I'm startled to make out a shape through one of the windows. A silhouette.

Someone is staring down at me.

CHAPTER ONE

I take a deep breath and offer Zac the keys. 'Do you want to do the honours?'

He accepts them with a nervous grin and inserts the gold Chubb key into the lock, followed by the Yale into the slot above.

I drink in the front of the property – *our* property – swooning over its gorgeous exterior. The mix of brick and white-rendered facade, the wisteria around the pale-blue front door, the gravel drive and mature trees. Even now, in the third week of September, with everything dying back, with the chilly rain and grey skies, it still feels magical.

I catch a movement from one of the upstairs windows. A twitch of curtain. A shadow. It must be the people in the upstairs flat getting a sneaky look at us, their new neighbours. The estate agent said they were a couple in their early thirties, same as us. Hopefully, they're nice.

Zac was wary of buying a flat. He'd rather have had a small house in a not-so-nice area. Something about having neighbours in such close proximity put him off. But this place isn't like that. It's one big house split into two apartments. We've bought the downstairs flat – 15A Mistletoe Lane. Included is the front driveway, a large private rear garden, and a fantastic outbuilding – my new office and storeroom.

The upstairs flat has its own entrance around the side and a private parking spot, but no garden. So even if the neighbours aren't our cup of tea, we'd barely have to see them. Obviously, it would be great if we all got on. Even better if we became friends. This feels like a fresh chapter for Zac's and my relationship – new place, new opportunities. A chance to leave the past behind us. It's exciting.

Even from three roads back, I can hear the roar and pound of the waves. It thrills me to be this close to the beach. Zac wanted to be nearer to the town centre, but I've always loved this part of the coastline, having spent time here as a child. Friars Cliff in Dorset is quiet without being boring. It's beautiful without being too much of a tourist trap. Zac's mum, Sandra, said that living by the sea is a con invented by estate agents – that it's always windy, the salt air wrecks the house, and the sand gets everywhere. Not to mention the fact that your money doesn't get you half as much. But, even though I love Sandra, on this matter I disagree with her one hundred per cent. To me, it's perfect. Everything I ever dreamed of.

'Nina? Are you coming in, then?' Zac's warm brown eyes beckon.

I realise I'm standing on the doorstep in a dream while Zac has already stepped into the hallway. Suddenly, I'm giddy with nerves and excitement. I can't wait to get inside, but I'm also a little anxious. The one and only time we saw the inside of the flat was three months ago before we put in the offer. I knew we had to move fast to secure it. Property gets snapped up so quickly in this area. I hope it lives up to my memory.

I follow Zac into the hallway. We walk into the living room on the right with its open fireplace and high ceilings.

'It's nice,' he says, running a hand through his dark blonde hair and grinning at me.

'It's amazing.'

'Come on.' He reaches for my hand and pulls me back into the hallway and through to the other large room at the front of the house.

'Our bedroom.' I twirl around, arms outstretched.

'Let's set up the bed first.' Zac takes my hand and pulls me close, starts to kiss me. 'Or maybe we don't need the bed.'

My body responds, but I'm too impatient to see the rest of the flat to be seduced right now. Too distracted. I pull away gently. 'Later,' I promise and pull him out of the bedroom without checking his reaction, which I know will be disappointment.

There's a small, plain bathroom next door, then at the back of the house are a good-sized second bedroom, a gorgeous dining room with French doors out to the garden, and finally a basic wooden kitchen – not my taste, but we can change it.

'Okay, so if we're not going to christen the bedroom right now, shall we start getting everything in?' That's the thing about Zac – he doesn't stay down for long.

He's a self-employed plumber and heating engineer, so luckily we've got his van to move our things from the rental flat. We don't own a lot of furniture, so it should only take a couple of trips. He's always super busy, but has managed to book a few days off for the move and it's great to get to spend some time together. Even if it has been somewhat hectic and stressful.

'Hello?'

We raise an eyebrow at one another before turning towards the sound of a man's voice, followed by a knock at the front door, which we must have left open. I run my fingers through my brown wavy hair, and smooth a hand down my leaf-print shirt and bottle-green cargo pants.

We leave the kitchen, and I follow Zac into the hall where a tall dark-haired man in jeans and a grey sweatshirt is peering through the front door, clutching a bottle of red wine.

'Hi.' I give a tentative smile.

He doesn't respond to me at all. Instead he looks at Zac. 'Hello. Just thought we'd pop down to say hi. We live upstairs at 15B. I'm Chris Jackson, and this is my wife, Vanessa.'

I smile again, trying to catch his eye. 'Is it still raining out there? Come in. It's so good to meet you. I'm Nina Davenport. This is my boyfriend, Zac Ainsworth.'

Chris gives me a fleeting glance and steps over the threshold. He's followed by a small woman with short ash-blonde hair. She's carrying a Tupperware box, holding it in front of her as if it were a bomb about to go off.

'Hi.' Zac shakes Chris's hand. We all stand facing one another in the hallway, and it's ever so slightly awkward for a few seconds.

'This is for you.' Chris steps forward and presents Zac with the bottle.

Zac glances at the label. 'Very nice. Thanks, mate.' Zac's more of a beer drinker, but it's a lovely gesture.

'Oh, and Ness made you a cake.'

'Wow, thank you so much.' I step forward and take the proffered Tupperware box from Vanessa. 'That's so kind.'

She gives me a brief shy smile and rests a hand on her rounded stomach.

Chris notices my gaze. 'Ness is five months pregnant. It's our first.'

We congratulate them before I remember my manners. 'Would you like to stay for a cuppa and a slice of your cake? I'll just have to grab the kettle and mugs from the van.' I take a step in the direction of the front door. Thankfully, I packed a separate container with items I knew we'd need straightaway.

'No, that's okay, we won't keep you,' Chris says. 'Just wanted to say welcome, and if there's anything you need, please give us a knock. Our front door's round the side.'

'Cheers,' Zac replies. 'Likewise.'

The Jacksons wave goodbye and leave. Zac and I give one another a look.

'They seem okay.' He walks into the kitchen and sets the wine bottle down on the counter.

'It was lovely of her to make a cake. And it's so nice that they're welcoming. Did you notice she didn't actually say anything? Chris did all the talking.'

'Maybe she's shy. Shall we get this stuff in?'

We spend the next two hours unpacking the contents of the van before deciding to stop for a tea break. Zac and I gratefully dig in to Vanessa's chocolate cake. It's so good we polish off two slices each. Refuelled, we make the final trip to our old flat, load up the rest of our belongings, and make the return journey to our new home.

The first time I saw the place, I knew it was the one. *Love at first sight.* Can you say that about a property? Well, I can… After that first viewing, I was a goner. Unfortunately, Zac wasn't quite as certain. He needed to be wooed. To have the good features pointed out. To be reassured that the electrics could be upgraded. That the overgrown back garden could be tamed into a beautiful private oasis. That the original sash windows were a bonus – who cared that the place might be draughty? No one wants to live in a sealed-in box, right?

My wooing eventually paid off, and here we are after months of rejected offers and mortgage applications, of surveys, and meetings with financial advisers. Of trying to calm Zac as he asked if all this shit was worth it and why we couldn't just carry on renting. I despaired of Zac and I ever reaching this point.

During the five years we've been together he's always been a free spirit, an eternal traveller, so to get him to commit to a mortgage was quite a big step, especially as he's never been great with money. He's definitely more responsible since becoming self-employed, but it's me who usually sorts out the financial side of things. I think Zac thought that working for himself would give him more freedom than it actually does. Who knows if he'll ever commit to marriage and babies. Good thing I'm not ready for that either. Not yet anyway.

Owning our own place has always been my dream. I thought we'd be renting forever. It's taken years of saving to get here and, even now, I can't believe it's actually happening. I keep expecting someone to come along and tell us *it's all been an unfortunate mistake* and *of course you don't own it*. I try not to think about the size of our mortgage and our monthly repayments. No. Today, I'm going to enjoy the feeling that we've come this far all by ourselves.

As the van trundles along, the wipers swishing back and forth, I let my mind drift towards the future. Towards what this move means for me and Zac. Although I'm already thirty-one, I feel like this, right now, is the start of my life. I'm going to be working from home on my start-up online fashion store. I created my business just over a year ago, but I had to change the original name as it was too similar to a competitor's. There was some unpleasantness with them and they threatened to sue. It was stressful and horrible. Zac came up with the idea to rename my company Mistletoe Lane after our new street once we'd exchanged contracts on the flat. It was a total pain to change the name and branding, but I love the new image – it conjures up cosy vibes, luxury and treating yourself, which is what my brand is all about.

This is something I've been wanting to do for years, but it's only now starting to get off the ground, thanks to an investor who sees the potential in me and what I'm trying to do. It's all quirky curated pieces made ethically and sustainably. I'm also trying to use up-and-coming new designers. I want it to feel fresh and new.

Zac interrupts my thoughts. 'I think I ate too much of that chocolate cake.' He changes gear and puts a hand on his stomach which growls so loudly I can hear it over the engine.

'It was quite heavy.' His mention of the cake has made me feel queasy. I take a breath. I'll be glad to get out of the van. I don't think the motion is helping.

'I don't feel too good, Nina.' All of a sudden, Zac swerves into a layby. The driver in the car behind sounds his horn and throws us an angry glare as he drives past. Before I can ask if he's okay, Zac flings open his door and staggers out into the driving rain. He's now throwing up on the grass verge.

Just watching him makes my stomach protest in sympathy. A hot flash of nausea sweeps over me. Oh no. I think I'm going to be joining him. I unclip my seatbelt and edge around the van to another area of grass where I'm violently sick. I can't remember ever feeling this bad. Not even when I had gastroenteritis from a dodgy shrimp salad in Portugal a few years back. Ugh, why am I even thinking about that?

Once I've stopped retching, I look over to see Zac staggering my way.

'What the hell was in that chocolate cake?' he croaks.

I shake my head and groan. 'Cali said there's a bug going round.'

'Whatever it is, I feel bloody awful.'

'Same.'

Zac puts a hand on my shoulder and we stare mournfully at one another as cars speed past, and cold rain spatters down our faces.

Of all the ways I imagined today going, this isn't one of them.

CHAPTER TWO

It's been two days since Zac and I have been able to eat anything other than dry crackers. I'm trying not to take it as a bad omen about our new apartment. It's just one of those things – bad timing, a story that one day we'll look back on and laugh about. But I feel so frustrated by what a waste of time this sickness bug has been. Zac's due to go back to work tomorrow, and we haven't even made a start on any of the things we said we were going to do, let alone tackled the unpacking. The unopened boxes in every room are just mocking me right now.

I leave Zac sleeping, heave myself out of bed and wobble into the bathroom for a shower. At least we've stopped throwing up. Hopefully, we'll start to feel better soon. We can't be sure whether it was the Jacksons' cake or a nasty stomach virus that's caused our sickness but, either way, I don't think I'll ever be able to look a chocolate cake in the face again.

As the hot water pounds my body and sluices through my hair, I hear the faint sound of a doorbell. I think it's ours, but can't be certain. My immediate thought is to turn off the shower, grab a towel and answer it, but the water feels so good, so reviving. Maybe Zac will get the door. I stand under the jets for a few more seconds before reluctantly turning them off and reaching for my towel. I crack open the bathroom door and listen.

A draught sweeps down the hall from the open front door, making my skin turn to gooseflesh.

'Mum…' Zac's voice is still groggy with sleep.

'Sorry, love, did I wake you? How are you feeling? I've come to give you a hand.'

I relax my shoulders. It's Sandra. Zac texted her yesterday to say we're ill, and not to come round for lunch as arranged. But it looks like she's turned up anyway.

I rearrange my towel, open the bathroom door and step into the hallway to greet her.

'Nina, love! How are you? I'm so sorry you've been feeling poorly.' Sandra looks up at me from beneath her blonde windswept hair, her soft features pulled into a concerned frown.

'Hi, Sandra. It's lovely to see you. Sorry we didn't get anything in for lunch.'

'Don't be daft. I brought you round some clear soup, and picked up something from the pharmacy to help settle your stomachs.' She waves a couple of carrier bags at me and Zac, then pushes the front door closed behind her. The air settles. 'It's blowing a gale out there. Summer is well and truly over.'

I nip back into the bedroom to get dressed in joggers and a sweatshirt, while Zac takes a shower, then I join Sandra in the small kitchen where she's already started unpacking boxes.

'You don't have to do that.' I gesture uselessly as Sandra unwraps mugs and plates, setting them down on the counter.

'I want to,' she insists. 'I've cleaned out these two cupboards, so I'll start putting things away.'

'Thank you. You're so kind.' I was actually looking forward to finding a home for all our things myself, but right now I don't have an ounce of energy, so it's lovely to have Zac's mum take over. Sandra's what I think of as a proper mum – she's warm and friendly, a hugger, a nurturer. I can't help comparing her with my mother, who's more polished and considered. Aloof, I guess you'd say. Mum loves her family, but she holds back, concerned with how she comes across. It makes me wonder what I'd be like as a mother…

Zac eventually joins Sandra and me in the kitchen, where she's already warming up soup in a pan she brought with her.

'I think this is the first time I've felt hungry since we were ill.' Zac leans back against the counter. 'That smells great, Mum.'

'It really does,' I add.

'Not too much room in here,' Sandra comments on the three of us squished into the compact space. She looks up from the cooker. 'But the view through the window is nice. I think you might have a few fruit trees out there. Looks like plums, pears and apples – lovely. You'll have to get that grass cut, Zac. You can borrow my mower if you like. That's if the rain ever stops. Have you met any of the neighbours yet?'

I tell her about our visit from Chris and Vanessa upstairs. I make a mental note to do something reciprocal once Zac and I are better. It would be great if the four of us could become friends. I have hopeful visions of us sharing fun dinner parties and summer barbecues.

'We think it might have been their cake that made us sick,' Zac adds.

'I shouldn't think so.' Sandra takes two clean bowls from one of her bags and starts ladling out the soup. 'It's probably that bug that's going round.'

'I hope you don't catch it, Sandra. Maybe you shouldn't have come over.'

'I'm tough as old boots. Never catch anything.'

'Mum's right. She's never ill.'

I take one of the bowls from Sandra. 'Well if it really is a bug, I hope we didn't give it to the neighbours. Vanessa from upstairs is pregnant.'

'Is she? That's nice. You'll have a little one up there. Hope you've got thick ceilings.' Sandra chuckles. 'I remember you used to scream your head off all night, Zac. Then sleep all day. It was terrible.'

'Sorry about that, Mum.' He gives her a cheeky grin.

'Never be sorry about that. You were my little treasure.' Zac's dad left Sandra while she was pregnant, so it's always just been the two of them. 'So now you've bought a home, when are you two planning on having kids? I want grandchildren while I'm young enough to enjoy them.'

I hope Sandra's question doesn't send Zac screaming for the hills. He's already jittery about commitment. I don't look at either of them in the hope that the question will somehow fade away.

'Give us a break, Mum. We've only just moved in.'

Sandra tuts and hands Zac his soup. 'No kitchen table? Maybe you could fit a couple of stools in here.' She glances around. 'Hm, maybe not.'

'We've got a dining room.' Zac tips his head, indicating the room next door.

We troop through and Zac and I sit at the white table that's much too small and modern for such a grand room.

'Oh, it's lovely in here,' Sandra coos, wandering around the room. 'Look at that fireplace. You'll make use of that this winter. Looks like it's going to be a cold one and this place is quite draughty.'

'It's not that bad,' I reply.

'No, but once winter sets in you'll notice it's much colder than your last flat. There's a lot to be said for double glazing.'

I know Sandra has our best interests at heart, but I can't help feeling protective over our new pad.

While we eat our soup, I can feel the energy returning to my body. 'This is absolutely delicious, Sandra.'

'Mum's magic soup.'

Sandra ruffles Zac's hair before dropping a kiss on his head. The doorbell chimes. 'Who can that be on a Sunday?' She frowns. I go to stand up, but Sandra holds out a hand. 'Finish your soup, love. I'll get it.' She bustles off towards the front door.

'Thank goodness for your mum.'

'You don't mind her coming over, do you?' Zac asks. 'I know she can be a bit much sometimes.'

'No, course not. She's lovely. You feeling any better?'

'Loads.' Zac puts down his spoon. He's already finished his bowl. 'Who d'you think's at the door?'

We twist around, trying to listen. Sandra returns. 'Another set of neighbours,' she mouths, 'from next door.' She points left. 'Shall I tell them to come back another time? Looks like they've brought you some flowers.'

I get to my feet. 'No, it's okay. We'll go and say a quick hello.' I don't want to appear rude, and I'm pleased the neighbours are being so welcoming. It's nice that the neighbourhood is just as perfect as I'd hoped it would be.

Zac rolls his eyes.

I give him a look and lower my voice. 'It's better to say hi now, then we can relax.'

Sandra puts a hand on her son's shoulder and fixes me with a firm look. 'Zac's right, love. Let me tell them to come back another time.'

I adore Zac's mum, but she can be overprotective at times. 'It's fine, Sandra. I'd rather we introduced ourselves now.' I drop my gaze to Zac. 'You stay here if you don't feel up to it.'

He drops his shoulders. 'No, it's okay, I'll come.'

Zac follows me to the front door where a couple in their fifties are standing on the doorstep.

'Hello.' The woman is small, brunette and fidgety. 'We just popped over to welcome you to the neighbourhood. I'm Tricia Middleton, and this is my husband Rob.'

Rob nods and smiles. He's wearing cycling gear, carrying a helmet in one hand and a bottle of cava in the other. 'Brought you some bubbly to celebrate your new pad.'

Tricia also hands me a bouquet of yellow and white flowers.

'These smell gorgeous, thank you! How kind.' I know I should invite them in, but the place is a mess and I still feel pretty out of it. I can tell Zac is still quite woozy too.

'Have you met Vanessa and Chris from upstairs yet?' Tricia asks. 'She's a sweet girl. Quiet though. They're having a baby. She's about five months pregnant now. And then there's Marion Lindstrom on the other side of you. She's in her eighties. Still got all her marbles. Very independent is Marion, if a little on the gloomy side.'

'She's not that bad,' Rob chips in.

'And then you've got Barry and Sue immediately opposite.' Tricia points to a mock-Tudor house on the other side of the tree-lined avenue. And Mr Linklater lives next to them in the bungalow – poor man lost his wife last year, so we've all been rallying round.' Tricia rattles off more names, but I can't take them all in. The street is wide, the houses separated out, not squashed together like the previous road we lived in, and the abundant greenery gives it all a lush feel.

Rob must notice our glazed expressions. 'They don't need to know everyone in the whole neighbourhood, Trish. Let them settle in first.'

'I'm just giving them the low-down so they feel more settled. I don't think we caught your names.' She turns to Zac. 'Sandra who opened the door, that's your mum, right?'

'Uh, yeah. She's just visiting. I'm Zac, and this is my girlfriend Nina.'

'Lovely. Well, like I said to your mum, Zac, we're just next door, so if you need anything, just knock. I'm a social worker, so I work all hours. Rob's a project manager at JP Morgan. Our street has a WhatsApp group so if you let me have your mobile numbers I can add you both.'

'You okay?' Rob asks me. 'You look very pale.'

'We know how stressful moving can be,' Tricia adds.

'Thanks,' I reply. 'We're just getting over a stomach bug. It hit us on moving-in day so we've been too wiped out to do anything.'

'That's bad luck.' Rob's brow crinkles with concern.

Tricia takes a step backwards onto the driveway. 'A stomach bug? Oh, you poor things. Well, we'll leave you in peace.' She wipes her hands down the sides of her jeans and ushers her husband away.

'Hope you feel better soon,' Rob calls over his shoulder.

'Thanks again for the flowers and the wine,' Zac calls after them. But they've already disappeared back out onto the street.

CHAPTER THREE

I lean back into the dining-room chair and stretch my arms above my head. So many emails to catch up on. I guess it's good that I'm busy, but I hope I can keep on top of all the paperwork, as well as everything else. I'm working in the dining room until I get my garden office sorted. At the moment, everything's just stacked against a wall, and my stock is really building up, which is why it was so important for us to buy a place with a dedicated outbuilding. It was either that, or rent space in a warehouse.

I take a sip of peppermint tea and gaze out the window at yet another cold rainy day, the wind pummelling the trees. It definitely feels stormier here, near the coast. More exposed. I'm hoping next summer will make up for it. I can already picture us walking down to the seafront carrying nothing but a towel and a paperback. Long, lazy days on the beach followed by barbecues with friends in the evening. Of course, this doesn't take into account my massive workload. But I'm allowed to daydream.

Thankfully, Zac and I are both fully recovered from our stomach bug and have already managed to unpack most of our belongings. The place doesn't quite feel like ours yet, but we're having a flat-warming party on Saturday, so I'm hoping that having familiar faces round will help us get more settled. Nothing like eating and drinking with friends and family to make you feel at home.

I haven't seen anything of the neighbours since Sunday, when Tricia and Rob from next door came to introduce themselves.

None of the others have been round, but we're planning on inviting them all to our flat-warming so we can get to know them better. Knocking on their doors is on my to-do list for today.

I turn down the radio for a moment and cock my ears. Footsteps creak across the boards upstairs and I hear the low murmur of Chris and Vanessa talking. Or maybe it's their radio or television. The soundproofing isn't as good here as it was in our old place. I think back to what Sandra said about when their baby's born. I really hope we don't hear it crying all night. I think their bedroom is directly above ours, so it's probably quite likely. Maybe we'll have to switch bedrooms and make the smaller back bedroom ours. I put the thought out of my mind – no point worrying about something that hasn't even happened yet.

I stop trying to eavesdrop on the neighbours and switch the radio back on. I shouldn't be listening, and I also shouldn't be daydreaming. I don't have time. That food poisoning, or whatever it was, has really set me back. I need to clear these emails and then check today's deliveries. But I'm still feeling fragile and more anxious than usual. Probably an after-effect of being ill.

My business has always worried Zac. Don't get me wrong, he's supportive and encouraging, but he's a straightforward kind of guy and he just doesn't get why I chose to do something so hard. So consuming. So *risky*. He worries that I'm beholden to an investor who's injected thousands into the company. He hates that I get stressed about the workload, and about whether the company is going to be a success or fall flat on its arse. But I can't help that this is who I am. I'm ambitious and competitive and I want Mistletoe Lane to be a household name. I want people to associate my brand with feeling great about themselves. I want their friends commenting on the clothes and accessories and asking where they got them. I want bloggers buzzing with the name, and Instagrammers hashtagging it.

But I have to admit it's been hard keeping on top of it all. Harder than I initially thought. Zac's more of a realist while I'm a straight-up optimist. At least I always have been. But I can already feel little bits of that optimism being chipped away by the day-to-day stresses.

Now that we've moved in and are over our sickness, I hope things will really start to take off. I kind of wish I'd never arranged the flat-warming – it's a time-suck I could really do without. But Zac's looking forward to it. He's invited all his mates. I guess it'll be good to catch up with everybody.

I give myself a shake, finish my peppermint tea and really focus on the screen. I've managed to negotiate a better price on my packaging, so that's a good bit of news to include in my next investor report.

A crash from upstairs startles me from my work. *What on earth was that?* I turn off the radio and push back my chair. Getting to my feet, I stare up at the ceiling, as if I'll be able to see through the plaster and floorboards into the flat above. It sounded like a huge piece of furniture tipping over. I think the walls actually shook. I hope no one's hurt up there. I should go and knock on their door. Check to see if they're okay.

I glance around for my keys, but Chris's voice stops me in my tracks – at least, I'm assuming it's Chris. He's shouting something, the words deep and rumbling. There's violence in that voice.

'No, you're not!' he growls, followed by a stream of something unintelligible and then, 'For fuck's sake, Vanessa. What did I tell you?'

I hear a high, pleading tone in her voice, but it's too quiet to make out any actual words. I realise my heart is beating too fast. My whole body is jittery. I'm horrified by this outburst. By the confrontation. Not knowing if it's a simple argument or something more sinister. That crashing sound… what was it? Could Vanessa be hurt? She's pregnant so surely such a heated argument can't be good for the baby. But I'm probably letting my imagination run away with me. All couples argue. But do they argue like *that*? Zac and I certainly never have. And I hope we never do. I just pray this isn't a regular occurrence. I don't fancy living with that type of upset going on over my head. I don't want to interfere, but what if Vanessa's scared? What if—

'No!' Chris yells, his voice booming from above.

I jump out of my skin and reach down for my mobile phone. I'm going to call Zac and tell him what's going on. There's a loud house-juddering thud as a door upstairs slams. The faint sound of footsteps coming down a set of stairs and then another slam of their front door. I rush round to the lounge and peer out from behind the open curtains. I flinch backwards as Chris comes into view, striding down their section of driveway and out onto the pavement where he marches away up the road. He's not even wearing a coat and it's pouring out there.

I'm still clutching my phone. I could call Zac, but now that Chris has gone, maybe it would be okay to go up there and see if she's okay. I don't want to interfere, but what if she's upset… or hurt? I can't just sit here as though nothing's happened. If it was just the shouting, that's one thing, but that huge crash…

I take a breath and swipe my keys from the hall table and my coat from the hook. Before I can change my mind, I leave the flat, my breath taken by the icy wind, my face already damp with rain. I pull up my hood and glance out at the road, but there's no sign of Chris returning so I hurry along the side of the house towards their ugly half-glazed UPVC door that's not in keeping with the house at all. I ring the doorbell and hear a distant chime.

I wait, my heart still hammering, nervous that Chris might return at any moment. If he does, I'll just say that I wanted to ask Vanessa round for a coffee. In fact, that's what I'll say anyway when she answers. That way, she can tell me about the argument if she wants to, but it won't be so awkward. I won't let on that I heard them at all. Now that's decided, I feel less fraught. More confident. A proper grown-up who knows what to do in these kinds of situations.

I listen at the glass, but I don't hear the sound of approaching footsteps. I press down on the bell again and hear the chime, so I know it works. Maybe she's too upset to answer the door. Maybe she's hurt. What should I do? I'm reluctant to ring the bell again. If she's not up to talking to anyone then I don't want to make her anxious. I wait a moment more, then trudge back around to my beautiful pale-blue wooden front door – such a contrast to Chris and Vanessa's.

Letting myself back in, I close the door behind me and stand in the hall for a long moment, my coat dripping wet. The flat feels cold and empty. Did we make a mistake moving here? *No.* It'll just take some time to settle in, that's all. Zac and I need to create good memories here. We need to laugh and make plans and have fun. I need to stop thinking about the couple upstairs and concentrate on my life. On my relationship with Zac, and on making my business a success.

Overhead, I hear the creak of floorboards, the faint sound of music – a radio's been switched on. Okay, Vanessa's fine. Maybe it was just a regular argument after all. It's definitely fine. I let out a breath and smile at my overreaction. At my daftness at letting my imagination run away with me. Suddenly the flat feels warmer, brighter. I think the clouds may be clearing a little out there. At least I hope so.

CHAPTER FOUR

THEN

I stand next to my brother outside the study, which has recently become Dad's bedroom. The closed door – once white – is now cream and flaking with age, just like the rest of the house. Mum warned us months ago that this day might come, but I didn't believe it then and I can barely believe it now. It can't be happening. It just can't.

The knot of dread in my chest has been growing heavier and heavier this past week as various nurses have been in and out of the house, as my mother's eyes have grown progressively redder, the house messier, the fridge emptier.

I tried to talk to my brother about everything, but he's been simmering with pent-up emotion for weeks, unwilling to talk to anyone. Least of all me. And I can't talk to Mum, because every time I say anything, she tuts or inhales or tenses up as though I'm an irritation. As if she'd rather I wasn't here at all.

The door opens and the nurse slips out with her bag, giving us teenagers a fleeting, pitying glance. Mum said that Dad was in terrible pain. We heard his cries from down the hall. It was awful. Sickening. I wanted to go in and hug him, but at the same time I wanted to run as far away as possible. Now the nurse has been in to give him morphine to help with the pain. Mum said that this is it. The last time we'll be able to speak to him. She said he doesn't have long. What a monstrous thought.

The lump in my throat is so big, I don't know if I'll even be able to choke any words out.

What if I'm unable to tell him how much I love him?

What if he dies without knowing?

CHAPTER FIVE

The doorbell rings, saving me from the stilted conversation in the living room. Zac flashes me a look of envy as I move to answer it. It's the night of our flat-warming party and, so far, the only people to show up are the neighbours – Tricia and Rob from next door, Marion from the other side, Sue and Barry from over the road, and their neighbour, Mr Linklater, a widower who looks a little lost. Vanessa and Chris from upstairs have also just arrived, and let's just say that things are taking a while to get going. Thankfully, since their argument earlier in the week, I haven't heard a peep out of the couple, aside from a few nods of greeting in the driveway, and they seem perfectly fine with one another today, so hopefully it was just a one-off.

Zac and I have spent every evening this week getting the flat ready for the party – unpacking the last of the boxes, cleaning and tidying, arranging the furniture. Of course, there's plenty more to be done, but at least it all looks presentable.

I check my reflection in the hallway mirror, loving the fifties-style emerald-green dress I chose to wear tonight. It shows off all my curves, flattering my figure. I tamed my chestnut waves so they gleam, and my make-up still looks fresh. Satisfied, I pull open the front door.

'Nina, we made it! You look amazing! That dress really suits you. Goes with your eyes.' My best friend Cali gives me a hug and I squeeze her back. It feels like forever since we last caught up, even though it was probably only a few weeks ago.

'Thanks, Cal. Gorgeous to see you too. Glad you like the dress.'

'I love it.'

'It's a local designer, I'll show you the whole range later. You look stunning, by the way. Glad to see you're wearing Mistletoe Lane.'

'Wouldn't wear anything else to your party, hun.'

I nod approvingly at her plum-coloured shift dress. It goes perfectly with her pale skin and jet-black hair. 'You look like a model.' I turn to her husband. 'Ryan, how are you? Zac'll be glad to see you.'

'Hey, Neens, I'm good thanks. What about *me*? Do I get a nice comment about my outfit?' Ryan leans in to kiss my cheek.

'Of course! You look handsome as ever, Ry. Sharp suit.'

'Cheers, that's better.' He grins and glances around the hallway. 'Nice pad.'

'Thanks. I've been praying you guys would get here soon.' I lower my voice. 'Right now, it's just me, Zac and the neighbours in the living room. I need my besties to liven things up.'

Cali and Ryan Jensen are the reason that Zac and I got together in the first place. We all met five years ago at Bournemouth Airport in the check-in queue for a flight to Crete. I was travelling with Cali and a few other friends, and Zac was with Ryan and his group of friends. Cali got talking to Ryan, and the two of them hooked up at the start of the holiday. If it weren't for them getting together, Zac and I may never have got talking. Ours was more of a slow burn. We both really liked each other, but it took a few drinks before we plucked up the courage to actually speak to one another.

I'd never been out with anyone like Zac before. Someone unpretentious and honest who wears his heart on his sleeve and never tries to act cool. It was refreshing and liberating to be attracted to someone like that. Someone who didn't see money and status as the holy grail. Who didn't put on a front. Nothing like my previous boyfriends, who were all too focused on wealth and image.

'Nina!' Amy Cavendish, my other best friend, comes tottering up the driveway in her trademark crazy high heels, her dark curls whipping around her face. She got divorced earlier this year, but she and Steve are both happy about it. They agreed they got married too young, so there's no bad feeling. She steps inside and gives me a hug. 'This place is beautiful! I can't believe how close you are to the beach. I'm coming to stay with you next summer, okay? What's the guest bedroom like?'

I laugh and tell her she can stay if she helps me to sort out the garden. Amy throws me a look of horror; she hates manual labour.

The evening finally feels as though it's getting off the ground. Our friends are a sociable bunch. They don't stay in a clique, but mingle and chat to all our neighbours, even to Marion, who's in her eighties and is – like Tricia warned me – a fairly gloomy lady. She's sitting in my navy peacock chair nursing a glass of prosecco and digging into a bowl of crisps on the side table. She was talking to Amy a minute ago, but my friend has flitted away so I go over to see if she's okay.

'Can I get you anything else to drink, Marion?'

She purses her thin lips and shakes her head of thin white curls. 'No thanks, dear. I've still got this glass of fizz.' She grips my arm with a bony hand. 'You know I've lived on Mistletoe Lane for almost fifty years.'

'Wow, that's longer than I've been alive.' I catch the scent of her perfume – sweet and talcum-powdery.

Marion nods. 'When we first moved here, we always thought it was a wonderful name for a street.'

'I know! It's just so lovely. Almost magical. I've actually named my company after it.'

'Have you indeed?' She fixes me with a smile. 'But do you know what mistletoe actually is?'

'It's a plant, isn't it? Something to steal a kiss under at Christmas.' I try to reclaim my arm, but she still has it so firmly in her grasp that I'm worried it's going to bruise.

'Mistletoe is a *parasite*.' She says the word triumphantly, as though she's trying to shock me.

'I don't—'

'Which means it has to glob on to other plants to survive. It grows in round clusters that sprout from the branches, leaching all the nutrients and water from the tree that it grows on, making it weak.'

'Oh.' I swallow, wishing she hadn't told me that. *Way to kill the party atmosphere, Marion.*

'I thought it was an interesting fact for you to know about the street we live on. Actually…' She finally lets go of my arm and waggles a bony finger in front of my face. 'The man who used to live here in this house told me that very fact when I first arrived as a new bride.'

Marion is the least bride-like person I've ever met. But I guess she must have been young once. 'You knew the person who used to live in our flat?'

'It was one big house back then, owned by the same family for years. Such a shame they converted it. But that's the way of the future, isn't it? More money to be made in flats.'

'I suppose there are more people and not enough properties. We live on such a small, crowded island.'

'You're probably right.' She sighs. 'Look at me, rattling around on my own in a huge five-bedroom house. I imagine my children will turn it into flats after I'm gone.'

'You have children?'

'Two of them. A son and a daughter. Grown up now, of course, with children of their own. Both living abroad.' Marion's expression darkens.

'Oh.' I frown. 'That must be hard for you – not seeing them very often.'

'Hmph.' She shifts in her chair. 'I see that Vanessa's expecting her first child.'

I realise she's switched subjects and is talking about the woman upstairs. 'Yes, she's five months along, I think she said.'

'I like my peace and quiet,' Marion grumbles. 'I like to potter about in my garden listening to the birds. I can do without a baby crying all day and night. Be worse for you, though, won't it? Living underneath them.'

'I don't mind.' I don't want to admit that I'm nervous about the very same thing.

'Do you have any more snacks?' Marion scoops up the last handful of crisps from the bowl next to her. 'I thought there'd be food here, so I didn't have any supper – I get Meals on Wheels, you know, or whatever they call it nowadays. Looks like I made a mistake. Should've had my steak and kidney pie.'

'Oh no, of course. We've got all sorts laid out in the kitchen and dining room. Hang on. Let me fetch you a plate of something.'

'That would be lovely, dear.'

I turn to go and walk smack into Belinda Evans, my brother Henry's fiancée. 'Hi, Belinda, are you okay?' I rub my shoulder where we collided, and she does the same.

'Goodness, Nina, you've got solid bones! Lovely to see you.' She kisses the air next to my cheeks with her slick, pouty lips. 'Henry and I can't stay long, unfortunately, but we wanted to drop in to see your new place. It's such a trek over this way, isn't it?'

'Is Henry with you?' I look around, but can't spot him. I love my brothers, but they're always so busy that I rarely get to spend time with them.

'Yes, he and George have taken some bubbly through to the kitchen. We shared a lift with your parents.'

George is my eldest brother, a corporate lawyer like my dad, but single because he's a workaholic. I'm secretly hoping to match him up with Amy, but I don't know if that will ever happen. George is hopeless with women, and Amy's quite full-on. But I somehow think it would work if they eventually got it together. They might balance each other out.

Henry is an investment analyst and was snared by Belinda three years ago. He didn't stand a chance. Once she'd set her sights on him, that was it. Game over. I went to school with her and she was always a high flyer, a straight-A student. Which would be fine if she were a nice person. She studied history at university, graduated with a first, got a job as a teacher and hated it. Now Belinda has left all that behind her and owns a couple of designer boutiques imaginatively called *Belinda's*. One in Westbourne and the other in Wimborne. I'm ninety-nine per cent sure they were funded by Henry.

She gives me a fake look of concern. 'So tell me, Nina, how come you ended up in Friars Cliff of all places, and didn't stay in BH13 with the rest of us? We'll miss you now you've moved all the way out here.' She knows very well that Zac and I couldn't afford to buy in Branksome Park, where I grew up.

'We love it here. This part of the coast feels more laid-back, less busy.' *Less pretentious* is what I really want to say. 'And it's only half an hour's drive away from Mum and Dad's at the most – hardly the other end of the world.'

'Maybe not the *other* end of the world, just the *end* of the world.' She laughs at her feeble joke.

'Let me just…' I grit my teeth and take a breath. 'I said I'd fetch my neighbour something to eat.' I nod over at Marion who's now talking to Tricia and Rob. 'I'll be back in a second, all right? Are you okay for a drink?'

She nods and holds up her almost-full glass.

I make my escape. Somehow, Belinda always succeeds in making me feel both inadequate *and* bitchy. Not the best combination. But I can't let her spoil my evening. I head to the kitchen and start putting a plate of food together for Marion, choosing a selection of sandwiches, little canapés, vegetable sticks and some crisps.

Not for the first time, I wonder what Henry sees in Belinda. How is my least favourite person going to end up being my sister-in-law? Oh well, as long as he's happy, I suppose that's the main thing… But *is* he actually happy? I get the feeling that Belinda might have railroaded him into their relationship. Henry's a super-intelligent guy when it comes to his work, but his love life doesn't have the greatest track record. I try to forget about the fact that Belinda's going to be at every single family event from now on. That I'd better get used to her being in my life.

As I reach across the counter for a napkin for Marion, I catch an opened bottle of red wine with my elbow. I jump back and watch in horror as it topples, spilling its contents across the worktop and over several food platters, streaming in crimson rivulets down the side of the counter and onto the floor. 'Damn!' I'm not usually so clumsy. I realise I'm on edge. I need to calm down and try to enjoy myself. After all, this is a party. I take a breath. First I'm going to have to mop up this mess.

CHAPTER SIX

After cleaning up the red-wine disaster and giving Marion her plate of nibbles, I search out the rest of my family who, along with Belinda, are being given the guided tour by Zac and have now reached the dining room. I catch Zac's eye and he winks at me across the table.

Zac gets on brilliantly with all my family except for my mother, who's always perfectly nice to his face, but doesn't think he projects the right image for the family. Zac isn't stupid. He knows how she feels, but is always ultra-charming, nonetheless. I need to have it out with her, but the thought of telling off my mother makes my knees quiver. Joanna Davenport can be horrifically intimidating.

Of course, she thinks the sun shines out of Belinda's backside, and is always telling me how wonderful her boutiques are, and how I should partner up with her rather than taking the risk of setting up on my own. I love my mother, but she doesn't have much faith in me. Dad, on the other hand, is a sweetie.

'Nina ballerina!' Dad catches sight of me and opens out his arms.

I grin and walk over, letting him envelop me in a bear hug. I'm tall and full-figured, but Dad always makes me feel like a tiny little kid in his arms. I breathe in his comforting smell of soap and *dadness* – a smoky warm scent that makes everything seem better somehow.

My brothers come over and mess up my hair, poke me in the ribs and make me squeal like I'm nine years old again. They may be respectable adults, but they always revert to treating me like their kid sister.

'Henry, get off my hair! George, stop it! Dad, tell them.'

Belinda stands smugly next to my mother, who's looking at the three of us in exasperation.

'Goodness me, you three, calm down, there are other people here.' Mum narrows her eyes in my direction and nods. 'Nina, you look like you've lost weight.'

'Stomach bug, so it won't be permanent.'

She tuts. 'The house is very nice. I think you could do a lot with it. I was talking to your gay friends a few minutes ago.'

I try not to roll my eyes at the way she says 'gay friends'.

'Nice fellows – Ben and Smith, was it?'

'Ben and Kit. Their surname's Parker-Smith.'

'That's it. They were saying that you should knock through from this room to the kitchen. Open it up in here.'

I nod. 'They're architects, they're always designing.'

'Hmm, are they any good? I might take their details.'

Mum's always on the lookout for 'good' people – architects, designers, landscapers and the like. She and her friends collect them like vases, discussing their merits and shortcomings over canapés. I need to warn Ben and Kit before she collars them. They arrived while I was talking to Belinda, but I somehow lost sight of them.

'Help yourselves to snacks and drinks, I'll be back in a minute.'

I find Kit chatting to Ryan and some of Zac's work friends. Kit stands there tall, blonde, tanned and confident, telling them something hilarious by the sound of their laughter. Kit and Zac were best friends at school, but lost contact for a while. They got back in touch a few years ago. Kit didn't come out until his mid-twenties, but now he's living his best life, married to Ben, and we adore them both and try to catch up at least once a month.

'Nina, get your juicy arse over here.' Kit makes a grabbing motion with his fingers.

I shake my head and go over to give him a hug. 'Looking like a god, Parker-Smith.'

'If I'm a god, then you're Venus.'

'Where's your dishy husband?' I ask, looking around.

'Last seen decimating the buffet.'

'So?' I gesture around the room. 'What do you think? Do you still love it?' Ryan and I brought Kit with us on our viewing to get his opinion. He gave us the thumbs up. Told us it would be a great investment.

Kit nods. 'It's better than I remember. You'll have to knock that kitchen through, though. I'll find you a picture of the sliding doors you should have.'

'I'd love to, but it sounds pricey. Plus I'm not sure how happy the upstairs neighbours would be about the noise of a renovation. She's having a baby.'

'It's only a stud wall. Zac could do it over a weekend. Be cheap as chips.'

'Your version of "cheap as chips" is a little different to mine, Kit. Oh, and just to warn you, my mother's sniffing around. She wants your details. I've managed to keep you and Ben a secret for years, don't get suckered in by her elegant ways.'

'I spoke to her earlier. She's amazing. I think she's my spirit animal.'

'No, she's not. It's an act. She'll reel you in, set you to work and then you'll see what she's really like.'

'We're used to tricky clients, Neens.'

'Not like this, you're not. Listen, when I was growing up, we had a constant stream of builders and decorators walking out on various jobs – all because she was so demanding. No one could stand it. I heard them talking about her when she wasn't around, and the stuff they said would make your ears bleed.'

I squeal as a pair of hands grab my waist. I turn around to see Kit's husband. 'Ben!'

'Hey, Nina. Love the dress,' Ben drawls. He's more low-key than Kit.

'Thank you. It's so good to see you guys.'

'So when are you coming on the show to talk about Mistletoe Lane?' Ben asks.

In addition to owning their architecture practice, Kit and Ben also run a successful YouTube channel as well as social-media pages dedicated to their projects. Their reputation as influencers has been steadily building over the past couple of years. Ben keeps asking me to come on the show as a guest but I'm not that confident in front of the camera. I know it'll be good publicity though, so I need to get over my fear and just do it.

'Okay, okay, I'll call you soon to sort out a date.'

'I'll hold you to that.' Ben grins.

We chat some more, until I spy Zac's mum across the room looking lost. I go over to say hi and reintroduce her to Rob and Tricia who she met briefly earlier in the week. It turns out they have some friends in common and so I leave them happily gossiping and return to my family in the other room.

The time is whizzing by and I realise there are a few other guests I haven't spoken to yet. I already said hello to Chris and Vanessa when they first arrived, but I didn't spend much time with them. I still feel awkward after hearing their row earlier in the week. Every time I see Chris, I think about the way he yelled at Vanessa. She's standing at his side now, sipping a glass of orange juice, her other hand cradling her bump. Chris is swigging from a bottle of pale ale, glancing around the living room with what looks like a critical eye.

I should go and speak to them again, but I'm not thrilled by the prospect. As I finally dredge up the courage to approach them, I breathe a sigh of relief when I'm joined by Zac. At least he'll help to get the conversation flowing. 'Can I get you anything else to eat or drink?' he asks.

'We're fine thanks,' Chris replies.

'Vanessa, would you like anything?' I ask, annoyed by Chris's assumption that she doesn't want anything either.

'No thanks. I can't eat much in the evenings – morning sickness, or rather evening sickness.' She graces me with a small smile. Her voice is quiet, almost childlike, but not babyish. Just… there's something vulnerable about it.

'Sorry to hear that,' I reply.

'It's fine. I don't mind. It's worth it for this little one.'

'I was wondering if our flat layout is similar to yours?' Zac asks.

Chris scowls and a worried expression clouds Vanessa's face. There's an awkward pause before Chris answers. 'It's not too dissimilar. I think our kitchen's bigger, but we don't have a separate dining room. So we have our dining table in the living room.'

For a moment, I wonder if they might invite us up for a look, but no invitation is forthcoming. Zac asks Chris what he does for a living. Turns out he's a structural engineer.

'Have you met our friends Kit and Ben?' Zac asks. 'They're architects, maybe you'll have some people in common. I'll introduce you.'

'That would be great.' Chris and Zac clink bottles. 'What is it you do?' Chris asks.

'Plumber. Self-employed.'

'Good to know,' Chris replies. 'I think I've got a few jobs I can put your way.'

'Cheers.'

'What do you do, Vanessa?' I try to draw her out.

She shakes her head. 'Not working at the moment.' I may be mistaken, but it looks as though her eyes are filling with tears. She stares at her shoes.

Chris clears his throat and says they'd better be going. That Vanessa's looking tired.

I really want to say that I'm sure Vanessa's capable of speaking for herself. But I haven't worked out their dynamic yet. I don't want to cause any problems, so I just nod, smile politely, and thank them for coming.

'Don't worry, we'll turn down the music,' Zac says, ever thoughtful.

'Cheers, mate.' Chris pats him on the shoulder.

As I watch them leave, unease stirs in the pit of my stomach. There's something not quite right there, but I can't put my finger on what it is.

The other neighbours drift away after a while and I manage to spend some more time chatting to George, mentioning that Amy's newly single. But he doesn't seem to pick up on my matchmaking attempts. I'm going to have to be less subtle. I tell him to go and get her a drink, but before he can act on it, Belinda comes over and pulls him away.

'Hen and I are heading off now, George. If you want a lift, you'd better grab your coat.'

I take George's arm. 'Stay longer if you like. You can get a taxi, or crash in the spare room.' I nod in Amy's direction, hoping he'll take the hint.

He shakes his head. 'No, that's okay. I've got a lot of work to catch up on tomorrow. Better not have a late one.'

I nod, defeated. I should've got them together earlier in the evening. I follow him and the rest of my family out into the hall, sad to see them leave. Belinda's right, we may be only half an hour away from them, but it does feel like we're at the end of the world here. I stand in the hall for a few moments after my family has gone, feeling strangely sad. A peal of laughter from the living room reminds me that I still have guests to socialise with.

Two hours later and it's just me and Zac alone in the flat. Cali, Ryan and Amy stayed to help clear up, but now I hear car doors slamming outside and the sound of an engine starting up and fading away.

'That was fun.' Zac puts his arms around me.

'Yeah, it's a good party flat.'

'You look hot in that dress.'

'Thanks. You don't look too bad yourself.'

'Yeah?' He nods slowly and closes his eyes. 'I'm so drunk.'

I giggle. 'Me too. And I'm bloody starving. I never got to eat any of the food. Is there anything left?'

'Should be. Me and Ryan stuck most of what's left in the fridge.'

We take a plate of leftovers into the lounge and I sit cross-legged on the sofa. Zac sprawls next to me, feet up on the coffee table.

'Kit suggested knocking the kitchen through,' Zac says.

'I know. What do you think?'

'It's a good idea, we should do it.' He picks up a dry-looking sandwich, examines it and puts it back on the plate.

'Did you get much of a chance to talk to Chris and Vanessa?' I ask, digging into the remains of the rice salad.

'Yeah, he seems like a good bloke.'

'Do you think? I thought he was a bit… I don't know. He didn't let Vanessa get a word in. Didn't you notice? Just before they left he said she looked tired and they should go home. Like he was making the decision for both of them.'

Zac shrugs. 'She's pregnant. He's probably just worried about her.'

I purse my lips for a moment, wondering if I'm being over-sensitive. After all, things have been so hectic with the move, I'm probably not thinking straight. 'I guess that makes sense. You're probably right.'

Zac frowns and puts a hand behind his ear. 'Sorry, what was that? You think I'm *right*?' He glances around the empty room. 'Hey, everybody, Nina Davenport thinks I, Zac Ainsworth, am *right*.'

'Ha, ha, very funny, Ainsworth. But, seriously, maybe we should invite them down for dinner one evening, get to know them better.' Even as I say it, I know it's not something I want to do, but part of me is holding out hope that it's still early days. That a friendship might still grow.

'Yeah, good idea.' He stretches his arms out in front of him and lets out a noisy yawn. 'I'm going to bed. You coming?'

'In a minute. Let me just finish this salad and I'll be there.'

'Okay.' He kisses my forehead, eases himself off the sofa and walks towards the door.

'Hey, Zac…'

He turns and raises his eyebrows.

'We've got a good relationship, haven't we? Kind of… equal, yeah?'

He moves his head from side to side. 'I guess so.'

His reaction gets my hackles up. 'You don't sound very sure.'

'I'm knackered, Neens. And drunk. Of course we've got a good relationship. We've just bought a flat together, haven't we?'

I nod, unwilling to push it further. My senses tell me this line of conversation is likely to go south very quickly. I want to believe it's tiredness and alcohol, but I get the uncomfortable feeling that Zac's not quite as happy as me. I already know he's anxious about the mortgage payments, and about living in an apartment in an expensive location rather than a house in a more modest suburb. He's also worried about the long hours I work. I know our relationship isn't perfect, but whose is? Ours is better than most. Our differences are what makes things interesting.

'Hey, Nina.'

I look up.

'I love you.'

I exhale and relax my shoulders. 'Love you too, Zac.'

CHAPTER SEVEN

I shove the table up against the door, its legs scraping across the floorboards with a screech. I can hear them out there, trying to get in. Trying to get at me. *Where's Zac?* He should be here by my side but he's not. I don't know where he is! What if I never see him again? What if they've already got him? This table isn't going to be enough to keep them out. I tip the wooden bookcase forward so all the books slide onto the floor and I'm able to push the empty shelves up against the table. As if it will do any good. The door is already opening, bashing against the furniture, shifting it gradually so the gap in the door widens. My heart pounds, my throat is dry. I don't know what to do. There's nowhere for me to run. There's no more furniture to pile up against the door, which keeps smashing against the table. *Bang, bang, BANG!* And now silence. The fine hairs on my arms stand up as a pale hand comes around the door frame.

I wake up, my heart still pounding, body damp with sweat, bathed in remnants of the nightmare. Someone was out there, trying to get me. I can still see their white hand coming around the door frame. It's fine. I'm fine. I'm here in my bed. There's nobody beyond the door. I reach out a hand to feel Zac's solid shape lying next to me, his soft snores like a lullaby soothing my fractured nerves.

I swallow. My mouth is dry, sour. A thump from above freezes the blood in my veins. Raises the hair on the back of my neck.

Am I still dreaming? I blink several times, the dark room a mass of shapes and shadow. It all feels so unfamiliar. I remember back to this evening – our house-warming party. But now everyone's gone. It's the middle of the night.

I reach for my phone, knocking my glass off the nightstand with a clank, followed by the glug and trickle of water. Too bad. I'm so thirsty right now. I turn on my phone and wince at the too-bright light. It's 3.20 a.m.

Another noise from above has me sitting up. It sounds like someone scraping something across the floor. Fragments of my dream come back to me once again – a table, a bookcase, a white hand.

'Zac,' I hiss. 'Zac, are you awake?' I give his shoulder a shake.

He mumbles something and turns over, away from me.

There's a rumble from above like something heavy being wheeled across floorboards. Another thud. Each sound has me catching my breath. What's going on up there?

'Zac.' I say his name more forcefully this time. 'Wake up.'

'Huh? *What?*' He lifts his head slightly.

'Did you hear that?' I whisper. 'They're making weird noises upstairs.'

'Upstairs?' His head sinks back into the pillow. 'Don't worry about it. Go back to sleep. They're probably having a shag.'

'No, it's not that. It's like furniture being dragged across the floor. Listen…' I hold my breath, waiting for the noises to start up again, but the house is silent.

'I can't hear anything.' Zac turns and reaches across for me, his hand pulling me closer, his mouth searching for mine. I wish I hadn't knocked my water over, I'm so thirsty, but his hands and mouth take me away from everything for a while as we have sleepy sex.

Afterwards, Zac falls asleep and I get up to use the bathroom and get myself some water. The house feels chilly and damp, the autumn wind finding its way in through the single-paned windows. I give a shiver, wishing I'd taken the time to put on my slippers and dressing gown.

As I stand in the cold, dark kitchen gulping down my water, I give a start at another series of thuds from above. What is going on? Surely they're not moving furniture in the middle of the night. Maybe they're insomniacs. Maybe they like doing DIY in the early hours of the morning. I yawn and refill my glass. I suppose it could be pipes creaking, or the house settling. A deep groaning, scraping noise confirms to me that it's definitely not pipes. No way. That sounds like someone pushing a wardrobe across the floor. *This is ridiculous.*

I unlock the back door, slip into a pair of Zac's trainers and step out into the garden, my thin pyjamas flapping in the wind. At least it's not raining. I pick my way across the dark patio using the light from my phone to see where I'm stepping, and I look up at the Jacksons' flat.

The curtains are closed but the light is on in one of the rooms. *What are they doing?* It's too soon for Vanessa to be having the baby.

Suddenly the curtains twitch. One side is pulled back and I find myself staring directly at Chris.

I almost scream in shock. My hand flies to my chest and I stumble closer to the house, out of view. My heart is pounding. How does he know I'm outside? He must have heard the back door opening. As I recover my senses, I realise that he might not even have seen me as he's in a bright room and I was standing in the dark with nothing but a phone light.

But what if he did?

This is crazy. I need to stop worrying about the neighbours and go back to bed. It was them who woke me up in the first place, and I'm entitled to go out in my garden, day or night. As I open the back door and step into the dark kitchen, I scream as I come face to face with a man.

He grabs my shoulders, and a jolt of terror tears through my chest.

'Jesus, Nina! It's me. It's Zac, calm down.'

'*Zac?*' I can hardly breathe.

'Who else did you think it was? You're freezing.' He gives my arms a rub before walking over and switching on the light. We both blink and squint in the brightness. 'What were you doing outside?'

'Why are you up? Did you hear the neighbours too?' I step out of Zac's trainers, not enjoying the ice-cold tiles beneath my feet.

'What? No. I was just getting some water.'

'I heard all these weird noises from upstairs, so I went out to look up at their flat.' I shiver. 'Can we get back into bed? I'm bloody freezing.'

'Not surprised. Let me just get some water. I'm coming, okay?'

Once we're back under the covers, with the lights turned off, I tell him about the weird sounds I heard.

'Maybe they couldn't sleep, and decided to get up and do stuff,' Zac suggests.

'At three in the morning?'

Zac shrugs and yawns. 'I dunno. Good job it's Sunday tomorrow. I'm knackered.'

'Same.' I snuggle into his side and risk putting the soles of my feet against his calves.

'Bloody hell, Neens!'

'Let me warm them up? *Please.*'

'The things I do for you.' He puts his arms around me and kisses my forehead.

I give a smile and snuggle closer. I love how Zac has never been embarrassed to be affectionate. Even in our early days of going out, he would always put his arm around me, hold my hand or pull me into his lap. He didn't worry that I might not like it. He never held back or seemed concerned about possible rejection. That was the difference between us back then. I would never want to lay my heart on the line, whereas he offered his heart up to me. His openness made me more confident in our relationship. Something I'd never felt before. It made me fall for him almost instantly.

'Don't worry,' Zac adds, rubbing a hand up and down my back. 'Things only seem weird because it's a new place, but it'll feel more normal once we get used to it.'

'I hope so.' Despite his reassurances, I still feel pretty shaky inside, unable to shrug off my worries.

'And things are always creepier in the middle of the night,' he adds.

'I know. I thought I was going to have a heart attack when I saw him up there looking down at me, and then I walked straight into you in the kitchen. Surprised my hair hasn't turned white with the shock of it.'

Zac yawns and mumbles drowsily. He's obviously falling back to sleep, but my mind is still wide awake. I lie next to him, gradually thawing out, wondering what Chris and Vanessa were actually doing up there.

CHAPTER EIGHT

THEN

I follow my brother into the room. It's a sunny afternoon and the light streams through the windows, illuminating shafts of swirling dust motes. Dust to dust, that's what they say, isn't it?

My brother is already sitting on Dad's office chair next to the hospital bed that was delivered to the house only a few weeks ago. The metal bed makes the once-cosy room seem like somewhere else. Dad's desk has been dismantled and leans forlornly against one of the bookcases.

Mum stands next to my brother, her hand on his rounded shoulders as they stare down at Dad. There doesn't seem to be any room for me in that small triangle of pain. I edge closer until I catch sight of my father's shrunken face. He was never a big man, but now he's tiny. Like a shrivelled bird. He opens his eyes and sees my brother, my mum, and finally me. His smile lands on me alone. He tells me to come closer. For the first time in days, his words don't seem to cost him. There's no pain behind his eyes right now. What does that mean?

His expression seems to convey that he understands what I'm think-ing. That I'm hoping he's better now against all the odds. That the cancer has finally gone. But we all know deep down that it's not the case. This is simply a short reprieve. His eyes are full of love and pity.

I gasp and sob. Tell him I love him as the tears slip down my cheeks, slide onto my chin, and drip down my neck. He tells me not to be sad. Says that he loves me so, so much. That I'm the light of his life. His little princess. That he knows I'll go on to have a wonderful life, a family of my own. That I'll watch my children run and play in the garden of our family home like he did when he was a boy. That it will all be all right.

I think of how little time I've given to my father this year. How self-absorbed I've been with school and trying to fit in and make friends. How I told my parents not to come to the school fete with me, even though I saw the hurt on Dad's face.

I wish I could rewind the months and be a better daughter.

CHAPTER NINE

'So what do you think?' Zac asks, his gaze wandering around the kitchen. 'Should we do it?'

I follow his gaze. 'I'd love to, but only if you're up for it too.' It's been a week since our flat-warming party and we've just said goodbye to Kit and Ben, who've been over for a coffee and to discuss opening up the kitchen. 'Like Ben said, it will add value to the place, so we won't lose anything in the long run.'

'True. But it's probably going to be more expensive than we think. It's not just a case of knocking down a wall – there's a new floor to lay, new kitchen to build, new doors out to the garden, decorating and the rest.'

'But it will be lovely once it's done.' I stare wistfully around the small space, picturing what it could be like. 'Anyway, we don't have to decide right away.'

'No…' He chews his bottom lip. 'But if we are going to do it, I'd rather get it done sooner than later, so we can enjoy it. I can do most of the work myself. It's just the cost of the materials.'

'So…?'

'Sod it, let's go for it.'

I give a squeal of excitement.

'You sure it's not going to be too chaotic, on top of all your Mistletoe Lane stuff?'

'It'll be fine.' I have a habit of underplaying things around Zac. He can be quite a worrier about work and money – mainly because it makes him feel restricted – so I try not to make a big deal of things, even when they're getting on top of me. 'When should we make a start?'

'I've got a lot on at the moment.' Zac starts putting our coffee mugs in the washing-up bowl, squirts over some Fairy Liquid and turns on the tap. 'We'll have to do it gradually over a few weekends.'

'Do you think it'll be done by Christmas?'

Zac turns and raises an eyebrow. 'Easter maybe.'

We're interrupted by a faint knocking sound. I frown. 'Is that someone at the door?'

'Could be.'

'I'll get it.' I leave Zac washing up and head into the hall.

It's Tricia from next door, her shiny brown bob ruffling in the wind.

'Hi, Tricia, how are you? Do you want to come in?'

'No thanks. Your doorbell doesn't seem to be working.' She presses it a few times to demonstrate. It chimes on the third attempt.

'Oh, okay, I'll check the batteries. Or maybe it's a loose wire.'

'Must be why the delivery man came to me instead.' She purses her lips. 'We took in some parcels for you. They're stacked up in our porch. There are quite a few, so are you able to come and fetch them now?'

'Oh, I'm so sorry. I work from home – they're stock items for my business.'

'Oh? What business is that?'

'It's a fashion brand – Mistletoe Lane. You can look it up online.'

'Oh, well, that sounds interesting. I'll certainly have a look. But in the meantime, can you take the parcels, please?' She fixes me with a beady-eyed stare.

I blink. 'Yes, of course. I'll get Zac to come help.'

'Thanks, I'd appreciate it. I usually like to have quiet, uninterrupted Saturday mornings.' She leaves abruptly without saying goodbye.

Nice one, Nina. Way to piss off the neighbours.

I explain to Zac what's happened and he follows me next door where we're confronted with about twenty packages piled up in the Middletons' porch. No wonder she's fed up with me. There's no sign of Tricia or Rob, and their front door inside the porch is firmly closed.

'Should we knock, or just take them?' Zac asks.

'Let's just take them. I'll come back to apologise later.'

We each grab an armful and make our way back home. As we reach our driveway, I drop several packages onto the puddled gravel. 'Shit.'

'Here, let me get those.' I look up to see Chris. He crouches and gathers the fallen packages.

'Thank you.' I'm grateful for his help, but I feel a little awkward since last weekend, in case he saw me in the garden in the middle of the night, staring up at him. 'Delivery guy thought we were out so he dropped them round at the Middletons'.'

'Trish won't be happy.'

'She wasn't.'

Chris gives me a sympathetic smile. This feels new. Maybe he's not as bad as I thought.

Zac's already taken his packages inside and is coming back to fetch more. 'Hey, Chris, let me take those from you.'

We leave them in the hallway and return next door to get the rest. Chris gives us a hand, so it only takes us one more journey.

'How's Vanessa?' I ask as we drop the remaining packages in the hall.

'She's fine. My sister's been staying for a couple of days so Ness has had some company while I've been at work.'

'Oh, nice. How long's she staying for?' I think back to the last few days, but I don't remember seeing anyone coming or going. Then again, I've been busy working.

'She's gone back to Somerset now, so Ness is down in the dumps.'

'Why don't you guys come down for dinner this evening?' Zac offers.

My heart plummets. It's one thing being friendly in the driveway, but quite another having to pass several hours together. I suppose it depends on whether we're going to get friendly Chris or moody Chris.

'That would be great,' Chris replies. 'If you're sure. I don't want to put you to any trouble.'

'No trouble,' Zac replies blithely.

Meanwhile my brain is now spinning with how much tidying I need to do, what we're going to eat, what I'm going to wear…

'Great,' Chris replies. 'What time do you want us?'

'Seven-ish?' Zac looks at me for confirmation.

'How about seven thirty?' I offer.

'Great, we'll see you then.' Chris gives a short wave and leaves, pulling the front door closed behind him.

'Where do you want this lot?' Zac asks. 'In your office?'

'That would be great.'

He bends to gather up a few.

'I wish you hadn't invited them tonight.'

'*What?* It was your idea in the first place.' Zac looks offended.

'*My* idea?'

'You suggested it after the party.'

'Oh.' I think back to the previous weekend. Now that he mentions it, I do have a vague recollection of saying something to that effect. 'Well, I was a bit drunk.'

'You were. But we can't exactly uninvite them.'

I grab an armful of parcels and follow Zac through to the kitchen and out the back to the office. 'We need a wheelbarrow or something. I can't keep ferrying parcels back and forth down the garden.'

'Or one of those old-lady trolleys.' Zac smirks.

'They're actually quite fashionable now. You can get some good designs. I might source some for Mistletoe Lane. I reckon they'd sell quite well. Anyway, I wish the Jacksons weren't coming round tonight. Chris creeps me out.'

'Shh.' Zac jerks his head in the direction of the house.

'What? They can't hear us out here.' But I lower my voice just in case.

'They might have a window open.'

Zac and I finish unloading the parcels. I'll have to deal with them tomorrow, now that the rest of the day is going to be taken up with organising this evening's dinner. Zac and I go back inside and plan a simple menu of Thai curry with jasmine rice. It's easy to make but always goes down well and we've already got all the ingredients. While Zac nips out for some kind of pudding and more wine and beer, I do a quick tidy round. The place is already pretty clean thanks to our frantic tidying session this morning before Kit and Ben's visit.

'Stick the kettle on!' Zac's back from the shops. 'Guess who I found outside.' Zac grins and plonks a couple of carrier bags on the counter.

I glance past him to see his mum. She gives me a tentative smile.

'Hi, Sandra!' It's always great to see Zac's mum, but right now I'm up to my eyes in organising tonight's dinner.

'Hi, love. Hope you don't mind me showing up. I was meeting a friend in Christchurch and thought I'd pop round as I was so close. Do you need a hand with anything?'

'That's so kind, but no, I'm fine. Do you want a cuppa?'

'I can make it.' She shrugs off her coat and starts bustling around the kitchen.

I open one of the carrier bags and ease my way past Sandra, trying to find space in the fridge for all the cans and bottles that Zac bought for tonight. He hands me a box containing a ready-made black-cherry cheesecake.

'That looks amazing. Can we have it now with a cup of tea? Or, better yet, we could skip dinner and go straight for wine and pudding.'

'No, I'm not going out again for another dessert. You'll have to wait.' Zac shakes his head, a half-smile on his lips.

Sandra reaches past me for the milk. 'Zac mentioned you're having the neighbours down for a meal tonight. What are you making?'

'Thai curry,' Zac replies.

'Might be too spicy if she's pregnant. Why don't you make them a comforting chicken casserole instead? I can help you make it if you like? Zac loves my casserole, don't you?'

Zac nods. 'It's the best.'

'I think I've had it,' I reply. 'Is it the one with the sweet potatoes?'

'That's it. What do you think? I can nip to the shop and get the ingredients if you like?' Sandra's face is open and hopeful.

The casserole was lovely, but quite stodgy. I'd rather make the Thai curry, but I don't want to hurt her feelings. 'Sandra, that's so kind of you, but we already had you cooking for us last time you were round.'

'I don't mind at all. It's my pleasure. It won't take long and then I can teach you how to make it.' She reaches for her coat.

I put my hand on her arm. 'Why don't we go into the lounge and have some tea and biscuits instead?' I turn to Zac. 'Tell your mum to come through and put her feet up. We can fill her in on our plans for the flat.'

Sandra pauses in the midst of her tea-making and then gives a nod. 'Okay, you've talked me into it. Tea and biscuits and a natter. Sounds good. What are these plans, then?'

Thankfully, that's the last we hear of Sandra's casserole. We take our drinks through to the living room where we tell her all about our idea to open up the kitchen. She sounds dubious about Zac knocking down the wall himself, but she's always been quite a cautious person. When I'm around her, I always feel as if I'm leading Zac astray. Even though she's never said anything to make me feel that way, it's just an impression I get.

She eventually rises to her feet and declares that she'll leave us to get on with our evening. I'm already anxious that time is slipping away and we haven't even started preparations yet. We hug and kiss goodbye, then Zac and I wave from the doorstep as she drives off down the road.

'That was nice,' I say, meaning it. I know for a fact that my mother would never show up unannounced and offer to help us cook for friends. The very thought is preposterous. However, much as I enjoyed seeing her, I'm also guiltily relieved that Sandra's gone. I know she likes me, but I'm not sure if she thinks I'm daughter-in-law material. I love my work too much and I'm not keen enough to have babies. I'm sure Sandra thinks my life should revolve around Zac. Maybe it's a mother-and-son thing.

'Mum might've had a point about the Thai curry being too spicy for Vanessa,' Zac says, closing the front door.

'It'll be fine. We'll make a mild one.'

As Zac and I work together in the kitchen, I get a warm feeling, like the flat is actually starting to feel more like home. Finally, everything's prepared, the dining table is set, the music queued up. All that's left is for Zac and I to get ready. The Jacksons will be here in half an hour.

As I jump in the shower, music from upstairs filters down through the ceiling, a bassline thump of something I don't recognise. Must be their getting-ready music. I smile to myself, feeling more positive about this evening. Chris was actually quite nice today – he helped us with the parcels and spoke politely to me. Maybe I had the wrong impression of him before. I could have just caught him at a bad time. All couples argue. I know how difficult it is to act nicely to people around you when you're going through a bad time. I decide that tonight is going to be a clean slate. I'll welcome them with an open mind.

I step out of the shower and start drying myself. The music upstairs has stopped and instead I can hear the sound of Chris's voice, loud and heated. My stomach drops. Not another argument. I pad barefoot into the bedroom where Zac is sitting on the end of the bed, his eyes wide and disbelieving.

'Are you hearing this?'

'I couldn't hear them until I switched off the shower. Has it been going on for a while?'

'About two or three minutes.'

'What are they arguing about?'

He bends down to take off his socks. 'No idea. Chris is doing most of the shouting.'

'Do you think they'll cancel tonight?' I sit on the bed next to Zac, now unsure whether it's worth getting dressed up.

'I don't know.' He frowns up at the bedroom ceiling for a moment as the rumble of Chris's voice vibrates through the building.

I try to make light of things as Zac heads to the bathroom for a shower. 'Maybe they're just going through a bad patch. You know, with the pregnancy and everything. It must be stressful. I mean, all couples argue and at least it isn't happening every day.' But inside, I'm worried about it too.

So far this hasn't been the idyllic move I was hoping for.

Far from it.

CHAPTER TEN

'Do you think they'll still come?' Zac asks, putting on one of his playlists. 'I mean, that wasn't exactly a little tiff, was it?'

'They better bloody come after we've spent half the day getting ready for them.' Although I won't be disappointed if they call to cancel. I light a couple of candles on the dining-room table, and another on the sideboard.

Zac stares up at the ceiling. 'That was just…'

'I know, right. I tried to tell you how bad that last argument was – the one they had while you were at work.'

'Sorry. I didn't realise. And also how *loud* they are. I mean, the soundproofing in this place is shit.'

Uh oh. The neighbours' drama is really turning Zac off our new place. I need to make this evening's dinner a success. I don't want him to regret buying the flat any more than he already does.

Seven thirty swings around and there's a knock at the door. Zac and I glance at one another. 'Maybe it's Chris come to cancel,' I say.

'I'll get it.'

Zac leaves me in the dining room hoping they're not coming. But my hopes are in vain. I hear Zac telling them to come in. I wonder if we should go into the living room first for a few drinks, but Zac's bringing them into the dining room so I'll just go with it.

'Hi!' I give them a cheery smile that feels forced. 'So nice to see you again, Vanessa. Hi, Chris.'

Vanessa is pale, her hair still slightly damp from the shower. She's wearing dark jeans and a long powder-blue sweater. She has small pearls in her ears and a thin sheen of pale-pink lipstick. Her blue eyes are dull, but she manages a smile.

'Hi, Nina.' Back to his surly self, Chris doesn't even manage a smile. But I'm not surprised after hearing his earlier anger. I don't suppose it's something you can easily switch off.

'Come in, sit down.' I gesture to the table which is laden with picky things – olives, fancy crisps and dips.

Zac pours the drinks and we all sit. Chris and Vanessa sit diagonally across from one another. I'm directly opposite Vanessa and Zac is opposite Chris. Which means I'm sitting next to Chris.

'It was nice of you to invite us,' Chris says to Zac.

'No worries. Nice of you to come. You okay, mate?' Zac points to a scratch on Chris's cheek.

'Mountain biking. There are some good trails round here, but I had a bit of a wipeout this afternoon.'

'Damn.' Zac shakes his head. 'I've had a few of those myself. Where do you ride?'

The two of them launch into a detailed conversation about bikes and trails while Vanessa and I remain mute. I rack my brain for a topic of conversation.

'So how's the bump?' I ask.

'Yeah, good thanks.' She takes a sip of her mineral water.

'Please, help yourself to crisps and olives.'

'Thanks.' She nods unenthusiastically and reaches for a single, tiny crisp.

Zac and Chris haven't noticed our discomfort. They're chatting and laughing away like old friends. I'm glad they're getting on, but I wish the conversation was flowing like that between me and Vanessa. Or if not flowing, then at least trickling.

I try again. 'I've made a Thai curry for tonight. I hope that's okay?'

'Um.' Vanessa looks panicked, and then she looks as though she might cry.

'If not, I can make something plainer.' I do a mental check of what else we have in the fridge and cupboards, realising there's very little aside from tonight's meal. I should have taken up Sandra on her offer of the casserole. 'I made it very mild,' I add.

'Normally I'd love it,' she says, tucking her hair behind an ear. 'But it's this morning sickness – I can't take anything too flavourful or spicy.'

'Of course. I'm so sorry, I should've thought.'

'Don't apologise,' she says quietly. 'Is there rice with it?'

'Yes'

'Plain rice would be perfect.'

'You can't just have rice. I'll make you something else. Tell me what you'd like. A piece of plain fish? A veggie burger?' I try to think what else is in the freezer.

'No, rice sounds great. The plainer the better.'

'Are you talking about Vanessa's morning sickness?' Chris asks.

'Yes, I feel terrible that I didn't ask if Thai curry would be okay.' I catch Zac's eye and give him a mortified stare. Thankfully, he doesn't give me an I-told-you-so look.

'I should've mentioned it when I saw you earlier,' Chris says.

Vanessa looks down at the table. 'It's fine, I'm having rice.'

I think this is possibly the worst dinner party I've ever hosted. They've only been here five minutes and I'm already wishing the evening were over. I take a gulp of wine and decide that I'm going to make it my mission to get Vanessa to open up. To find out something about her. *Anything*. I lean forward.

'So, I think I remember you saying that you're not working at the moment. Are you on maternity leave?'

'I was actually made redundant just before I got pregnant.' She rolls her eyes. 'Really bad timing.'

'Terrible timing,' I agree. 'What was it you did?'

'Nothing that exciting, just an admin job in an insurance company. But the people were nice and the hours were flexible. I'm going to have to find something else after the baby's born. Luckily Chris earns enough to keep us going for now.'

'Will you look for the same type of job?'

'Probably.' She shrugs and starts fiddling with her paper napkin. She doesn't ask me any questions and Zac and Chris are still involved in their dinner party for two.

I'm not usually the type of person to start talking about myself without any prompting, but we have to talk about something and she's not giving me any lead-ins. 'I've been trying to set up a company of my own.'

'Chris told me about all the parcels. Is that something to do with it?'

'Yes.' I tell her about Mistletoe Lane, but her reaction is muted so I can't work out what she thinks. Her clothes are nice but quite plain, so maybe fashion isn't her thing. Or maybe her lack of enthusiasm is down to her and Chris's earlier argument. I bet that's it. That's obviously why she's so quiet. It may even be why she's feeling too sick to eat. I give her a look of what I hope is compassion and solidarity.

After ten more minutes of torturous, stilted conversation, I get up to fetch the hot tureens of rice and curry. Zac asks if I need any help, but I tell him I can manage.

In the kitchen, I grip the sink and stare at the dark steamed-up window. I hate to admit it, but ever since we've moved in here, there's been an air of melancholy about everything. The flat is damp and chilly, even with the heating on. The rooms feel gloomy. *Sad.* I try to picture the bright, airy flat we saw during our first viewing, but I can't equate that place with this. Not at all. Even though it's the same flat. It's as though that viewing was an illusion; a trick to conceal the flat's true nature.

That's ridiculous. I need to shake myself out of this gloom. It's Vanessa's mood – it's rubbing off on me, that's all.

As I return to the dining room, Zac is pointing enthusiastically to the stud wall between the kitchen and the dining room. 'Yeah, that wall there. So I apologise in advance if there's some crashing and banging for a few weekends.'

Although they can't exactly complain about crashing and banging, I think to myself. Not with the noises that have been emanating from their flat. I wonder what they'd say if I asked them about it. Not that I would. I put the tureen of rice in front of Vanessa and tell her to help herself.

'So you're knocking through to the kitchen?' she asks.

'Yes,' I reply. 'The kitchen's quite small so it'll be great to have some more space.'

I head back into the kitchen for the curry. Everyone loves talking about renovations, perhaps the conversation will get going now.

'It's such a shame when people knock the character out of houses.' Vanessa's voice carries through from the dining room. I return to join them, sitting opposite her once more. She points out the picture rails and the fireplace, the wooden floors and sash windows. 'Once they're gone, it's hard to get them back.'

'We'll keep all the original features, we just want a bigger space,' Zac says. 'A more sociable kitchen.'

Vanessa gestures to the dividing wall. 'But wouldn't you rather keep all the kitchen clutter hidden from view?'

'I see your point,' I reply with a laugh. 'It looks like a bomb's gone off in there.'

'Exactly!' She nods, her eyes coming to life for the first time this evening.

'It's not really our business,' Chris says to Vanessa. 'If Nina and Zac want to knock a wall down then they're quite within their rights. It's their flat, after all.'

Vanessa flushes and looks down at her empty bowl.

'Please, help yourselves.' I gesture to the bowls and serving spoons, trying to gloss over the suddenly awkward atmosphere.

Vanessa has clamped her mouth shut and Chris has started talking to Zac once again. They're laughing about something Chris said about one of his work colleagues.

As the evening progresses, I try my hardest to draw more conversation out of Vanessa, but she's clammed up. I think she might be scared of her husband, or at least intimidated by him.

Zac catches my eye and gives me a smile. He's sitting next to Vanessa and so can't easily see her tight expression like I can. I need to put her back at ease, but things already feel stilted and out of line, like I'm inhabiting a completely different universe to the Jacksons. Perhaps dessert will liven things up. The atmosphere between me and the neighbours surely can't get any worse. Zac and I clear away the main course and he brings out that glorious black-cherry cheesecake which I've been looking forward to since he first showed me it.

'Vanessa,' Zac says, holding the serving slice over the cake. 'A big piece or a little piece?'

'I'm so sorry, but I don't think I can eat cheesecake. I'm not sure, but there are certain cheeses you're not supposed to eat when you're pregnant.'

'Oh, no! I'm so sorry.' Zac puts down the serving slice. 'I think we might have some ice cream in the freezer…'

'No, really, I'm full up anyway.'

I look at her tiny frame and thin face. Despite her pregnancy bump, she's so petite. I'm going to feel like a hog eating dessert while she sits opposite me sipping at her water.

'This cheesecake is amazing,' Chris says after his first mouthful. 'You're really missing out, Ness.'

She shrugs.

If I knew him better, I'd call him out for being an insensitive jerk.

We stumble on through dessert – Chris ends up having two huge slices – and finally the Jacksons make their excuses and get to their feet, thanking us for a *lovely* evening.

Really?

'Oh, I don't suppose you have my Tupperware container, do you?' Vanessa asks. 'The one I brought round when you first moved in?'

I place a hand on my throat as vivid memories of that rich chocolate cake and our sickness bug make an unwelcome return. 'Yes, sure, I'll just get it. Sorry, I meant to get it back to you earlier.' I disappear into the kitchen to retrieve the old-fashioned blue tub from the cupboard. Normally I'm good at returning things promptly, but I'd been putting off knocking on their door.

'Thanks.' Vanessa takes it from me. 'It was my mum's so I'd hate to lose it.'

'It was kind of you to make us the cake.' I try not to catch Zac's eye.

'You're welcome. It was my grandmother's recipe. I can let you have it, if you like.'

'That would be great,' I lie, certain that I'll never eat another slice of chocolate cake as long as I live.

As the door finally closes behind them, I walk into the living room, flop onto the sofa and heave a huge sigh. 'Thank goodness that's over.'

Zac stands in the doorway. '*What?* Didn't you have a good time?'

'Uh, *no*. Didn't you see how uncomfortable Vanessa was? She barely said two words and when she did, Chris shut her down. He's a bully.'

Zac looks at me as if I've lost the plot. 'I thought the evening went really well. I guess she was a little quiet, but maybe she wasn't feeling too good – you know, the morning sickness.'

'It was definitely more than that. She looked like she hated being here.'

'Oh.' Zac's face clouds over. 'Maybe she was still upset from their argument. Chris seemed fine, though. He seems like a really nice bloke. Why do you think he's a bully?'

'Didn't you hear what he said to her when she was talking about us knocking down the wall?'

'Yeah, he told her it was our flat and we could do what we liked. Which is true.'

'Hmm.'

'Do you want to help me clear up, or shall we leave it till tomorrow?' Zac asks through partly clenched teeth. I've somehow annoyed him.

'You okay?'

'Yeah, just tired.'

'Okay, good.' I get to my feet again, conscious of the weird atmosphere between us. 'Maybe we should clear up now. It'll be a pain to have to wake up and do it tomorrow.'

'Fine.' He leaves the living room and heads into the kitchen.

I go into the dining room and start clearing the table. A whiff of Chris's aftershave catches in the back of my throat, lemony and heavy. I blow out the candles and the aftershave is eclipsed by wispy threads of burnt wax.

All that effort spent on cooking a nice meal and tidying the house for an evening that was a total disaster. I still have a bad feeling about Chris, and I especially don't like the way Zac is taking his side over mine. Not that there are sides exactly, but… Oh, I don't know. Maybe I'm just tired.

I'm starting to think that maybe Zac was right about buying this place. But I don't want to think that way. No, I simply need to smooth things out with him. Get our relationship back on an even keel. Most of all, we need to take a break from seeing the neighbours.

CHAPTER ELEVEN

As we pick our way along the slippery garden path, I take deep breaths and try to talk myself into an upbeat frame of mind. I've already met James Kipling a few times before – he represents my investor, Mr Newbury, and now he's here for a catch-up meeting and to see my new workspace. I must say that I didn't expect they'd be so involved. I thought they would simply invest the money and then leave me alone to get on with things. But it hasn't been like that at all.

James is maybe a couple of years older than me. He's always dressed immaculately in a suit and tie, and his navy BMW is always gleaming – even in the rain. I think he must use some kind of super-wax on it. Maybe the same kind he uses on his shiny, shiny hair. But that's bitchy. He actually seems like a nice guy. Very fair and extremely professional.

Every time I have a meeting with either him or Mr Newbury, I get terrible butterflies. A mixture of excitement that I have an *actual* investor who's put *actual* money into my *actual* business, and nerves that I might cock it all up. But I have every confidence in Mistletoe Lane. My investor has nothing to worry about, and neither do I. This is what I tell myself as I try to quell my hammering heart.

It was serendipity that I even got an investor in the first place. When I started the business last year, I announced it on social media and was almost immediately contacted by a local property company looking to diversify. At first I thought it might be some kind of scam, but I did my research and found out that Newbury Ltd had been going for six years and had a solid reputation. After a couple of meetings with James and Mr Newbury himself, I got a solicitor and we worked out a contract where Newbury Ltd would invest in my company over a period of three years, taking a percentage of the profits, with the option for both sides to review at set intervals.

'Excuse the state of the garden.' I look regretfully at the tall wet grass and the jumble of brown weeds and dead flowers. 'We haven't got around to tidying it up yet. We'll leave it until spring, I think.'

'There's a lot to do,' he agrees.

'The outbuildings are split into two,' I say as I open the black-framed glazed door which leads to my office space. I've transformed it since we moved in. The room was already weatherproof, kitted out with electricity, heating and broadband, but in recent years it had been used for garden storage rather than as an office so it was looking very tired and battered. I've painted the whole space white for now, and covered the scratched oak floor with a bright oriental rug. There's modern artwork on the walls, lots of plants and a low white bookcase. My white desk, red faux-leather chair, and two visitor chairs complete the space, which measures around twelve feet by fifteen. I've had oil diffusers and scented candles in here to make it feel even more welcoming, and also to cover up the lingering smell of paint.

'Looks good in here.' James nods and takes a couple of photos on his phone. 'We might put a few images on the website. More publicity for you.'

'Great. I'll show you the stockroom. It's still a bit of a mess, I'm afraid, but I'm getting the rest of the shelving put up later this week.' I direct him through a door at the back into another space that's twice the size of my office. This room is also weatherproof – it has to be as it's where I'm storing all my stock and samples. If the company grows like I'm hoping, I'll eventually have to rent a warehouse. But, for now, this is perfect.

James makes notes on his phone and takes a few more photos.

'Don't put any pictures of the stockroom on your website, will you? Not until I've made it look more presentable.' I give a nervous laugh. 'I'll send you some updated pics next week once it's looking smarter.'

'Sure. This is just so I can show Mr Newbury.' James nods as he gazes around, taking in the boxes and half-built metal shelving. 'I'm impressed with what you've accomplished out here so far.'

My heart gives a leap of pleasure. I'm proud of what I've done in such a short space of time, but I'm also impatient to get it all finished and set up properly. I wish James had left it another week before coming round.

It was actually James who tipped us off to this flat in the first place. He knew we were looking for outbuildings and, being in the property industry, he was able to get us in for an early viewing. Zac and I were worried, as it was out of our budget, but Mr Newbury's accountant said that as we were running the business from home, we could allocate some of the investment funds towards it. There were a lot of hoops to jump through with permissions from the local council, insurance and tax, but with James's help we got everything squared away.

The previous owners were a couple in their forties with a growing family who were making the move from their flat to a house. In fact, they'd already had a below-ask offer on the place, but we were able to beat that by offering the full asking price, thanks to the investment from Newbury Ltd.

James and I return to the office where I bring another chair round to my side of the desk so he can sit next to me and see my laptop screen. I bring up the latest figures and projections, even though he already has access to them via our shared accounting software.

'Do you want to talk me through it?' James pulls out a pair of wire-rimmed glasses from his top pocket and slides them on.

I don't remember seeing him wear those the last time we met. They suit him. Take the edge off his shiny exterior. I start talking him through the figures.

'So, you've already seen from my weekly graphs that we're growing steadily, and customer feedback is brilliant. Everyone's loving the products. I've only had half a dozen returns since we started, and they were for things like the wrong size, or the customer changed their mind – nothing to do with the products themselves. You can see on Trustpilot that we've almost got a five-star average.'

'That all sounds very good, Nina, however…' He leans back in his chair and takes a breath.

My heart drops at his tone.

'You haven't quite met the targets we set out in the contract.'

I was worried he was going to say that.

'No, but I'm not far off, and I'm pretty sure that soon we'll be exceeding those targets.'

'Yes, but "not far off" isn't the same as actually meeting them. Mr Newbury isn't willing to release the next block of funding until that target is reached.'

I swallow.

'We really need to increase revenue while your brand is building. It isn't quite hitting the mark yet. Mr Newbury would like to see a substantial increase over the next six weeks. Do you think you can pull that off?'

My stomach sinks with disappointment before rising again with panic. I really thought he'd be more impressed at how much progress I've made. Sure, I haven't quite hit the actual financial target that we agreed upon, but everything else about the business is so positive – its image, word-of-mouth, reviews, publicity. Surely he can see that the financial rewards are very close.

'Don't worry,' I say. 'The next couple of months will be amazing. It's the run-up to Christmas and I've taken out an ad in *Dorset Life* magazine. They're also going to do an editorial piece on the company.' I haven't taken out the ad yet, but I will.

'Great.' James stands. 'Well let's hope it translates into sales.'

'Absolutely.' My cheeks grow hot as I realise this business meeting was a warning to do better. To meet my targets, or else… Or else, *what*? Might he ask for his investment to be returned? Can he do that? I realise I don't actually know. I need to check the contract again. Don't panic, Nina. The business is fine, great even. And, like I told James, Christmas is on the horizon so it's peak buying season.

I walk James back through the garden, my mind churning with everything I need to do. He leaves via the side gate, rather than coming back through the house. I realise that I was so anxious about the meeting and showing James the new space, I didn't even offer him a cup of tea or coffee. Not so much as a glass of water! I'd even bought posh biscuits especially for the meeting. He must think I'm so inhospitable. Rude even. I hope he doesn't hold that against me on top of everything else. I almost want to call him back to offer him refreshments before he drives off. But that would be daft. Desperate. Never mind. Next time I see him I'll apologise.

I let myself back into the flat and stand at the living-room window to watch him leave. He's on the drive talking to someone – a man. They don't look as though they're having a very friendly conversation. Who is it?

I race to our bedroom to get a better view. *It's Chris!* Even through the glass, I can hear their raised voices, but I can't make out the words. Why would Chris and James be arguing? Do they somehow know one another?

I open the window a crack to try to hear what they're saying, but as I do so, James strides away up the drive and Chris turns and walks back to the house. I duck out of the way. Maybe Chris was rude to James. I hope he hasn't said anything to jeopardise James's and my business relationship further. Chris is a menace. I wish to goodness he wasn't our neighbour. Maybe they'll move when the baby arrives – discover that flat life isn't for them. After all, it'll be awkward going up and down the stairs with a pushchair.

What on earth could he have been talking to James about? I guess it doesn't matter. It's nothing to do with my business, and that's what's important right now.

I'm worried about how I'm supposed to increase sales in such a short space of time. I know I told James it's the Christmas period so everyone will start buying soon, but my Facebook adverts are competing with everyone else's. The cost-per-click is going up almost daily. I need to do something to cut through all the noise. I need to make Mistletoe Lane stand out more.

Or maybe I need to change tack. I head to the kitchen to make myself a coffee and I tear open the packet of posh biscuits I bought for James. I think I deserve two, because I might have just come up with a brilliant idea.

CHAPTER TWELVE

THEN

My brother is speaking. Stiff and formal compared to my messy, emotional outburst. He's telling our father that he doesn't want him to die. His voice breaks. Dad cuts him off and tells him to be a man. To buck up and look after his mother and sister. To stop crying and be brave. That he must take charge now. My brother listens and stands up straighter, blinking back any tears that might have fallen.

It's always been this way. Dad treats my brother harshly to toughen him up. To make him a man. But he spoils me, his little girl. Even as a child I knew it wasn't fair – this distinction. It makes my brother resentful. Mum has always tried to make up for Dad's strictness by being soft on my brother. By spoiling him and being tougher on me. As though she can balance things out. I don't think things work like that. And now my dad is dying. He won't be here any more. Does that mean Mum's love will spread to encompass me too?

She rubs my brother's shoulders. She doesn't look my way.

Outside, the sun is losing its brightness. I already feel colder inside. As if the whole world is about to become darker…

CHAPTER THIRTEEN

I peer out the lounge window for what seems like the hundredth time this evening. It's 8.30 p.m. and Zac still isn't home. It's all the more annoying because I'm dying to discuss my new idea with him. I check my messages, but there's nothing. I tap out a quick text to see if he's okay. After a few minutes, I start to worry that something might have happened. Finally, after another ten long minutes, he replies:

> *Sorry, thought I'd already texted you. Went for a drink after work. Leaving now. Home soon xx*

My shoulders relax. He's fine. At least I managed to get some extra work done while he was out.

Half an hour later, we're sitting in the living room eating bowls of pasta arrabbiata off our laps. Normally, we might watch an hour or so of TV, but tonight, I really want to talk.

'Top pasta,' Zac says, wolfing down his huge portion with extra cheese. 'How was your day? Did you land that new jewellery designer you were talking about?'

'Not yet. Still working on it. She's going to check out our website and get back to me.' I didn't tell Zac about today's investor meeting because I don't want him to worry. Mr Newbury is also a guarantor for the flat – it's the only way we could get a mortgage for such a large amount – so it's doubly important that I make this business work. Otherwise things could get very tricky both financially and in terms of keeping the flat. 'How was your day?'

'Busy as usual. Still doing the Hortons' bathroom. I should've finished today, but they've changed their minds about the chrome finishes; now they want brushed steel.'

'That's annoying.'

'Tell me about it. I've got a kitchen refit in New Milton starting tomorrow, so I told the Hortons they'd have to wait. That didn't go down well, so I ended up promising to go back one evening this week.'

'That's not very fair.'

Zac shrugs. 'They've got a lot of rich friends. I don't want to get bad-mouthed around town.'

I shake my head, annoyed on his behalf. Zac works really hard and is a total perfectionist. He's always in demand, but there are those clients who'll take advantage.

'Don't they realise you've got a life outside of your job?'

'Apparently not. Anyway, I'm not going to think about it any more this evening. I'm going to enjoy my food cooked by my beautiful girlfriend.' He smiles soppily.

'You're quite drunk, aren't you?'

He grins and tips an imaginary hat at me, making me laugh. 'Nutter.'

'That's me.' He shovels in the last mouthful of pasta. 'Any more going?'

'In the pan. Grated cheese is on the bread board.'

'Yes!' Zac gets up. 'You want some?'

'I'm good thanks. Still got loads here. Finish it off, if you like.'

Zac soon returns with another bowlful and I start telling him about my idea. I'm excited, but nervous about how he's going to react because I already have quite a heavy workload.

'So, you know those party-plan evenings Cali sometimes has as a side job?'

'Nope.'

'You know, where she sells those skincare products.'

'Oh, yeah, like one of those pyramid selling things?'

'Kind of. But not as bad as that. She sells nice products to friends and family.'

'Tell me you're not thinking about setting up another business on top of the one you've already got.' Zac puts his bowl down for a minute, a frown settling on his face.

'No, don't worry, there's no new business.'

'Thank God for that.' He picks his bowl back up.

'I thought it would be cool to have an evening here where I sell Mistletoe Lane stuff to friends and family at a reduced price. Say, ten per cent off. What do you think?'

'A sale?'

'Kind of. More like a kickstart to get some word-of-mouth going again. I've got so many great new lines. I'll tell everyone to bring their friends, then I can ask them all to leave online reviews and post on Pinterest and Instagram. What do you think?'

'Yeah, I guess. But I thought the whole point was that it was an online brand rather than an actual shop.'

'It is. But this is more about publicity. Start local and hopefully the word will spread. Aside from Cali and Amy, I haven't really publicised my stuff round here. Makes sense to start with friends and family.'

'Are you sure you won't be taking on too much? You're already knackered, working weekends and evenings.'

'I'm fine. It's just been overwhelming with the house move, and setting up the office. Now that's almost done, I'll have more free time.'

'Which you'll fill up with work…' He rolls his eyes.

'You know me. I love my work.' I poke him in the ribs.

'Okay. But how about you take on some help. A part-time employee? That way you can give all the basic tasks to someone else and then you can concentrate on the big stuff.'

I put my bowl down on the coffee table and lean back against the sofa cushions. 'That would be heaven. But I'm nowhere near the employing-people stage. I need to watch the pennies right now.'

'Oh. Right.' Zac stops chewing for a moment and looks cagey.

'What? What is it?'

'Okay, so don't be mad…'

'Why would I be mad? What've you done?'

'I haven't actually *done* anything. But I said I'd ask.'

'What are you talking about?'

'I thought you could ask Vanessa if she wants to work for you part-time.' Zac looks at me expectantly.

'Vanessa from *upstairs*?'

'Yeah.'

'Did you not see that quiet mouse of a person who came for dinner the other night? She's got terrible morning sickness, can barely hold a conversation, and I don't even think she likes me.'

'Course she likes you.' He gives a loud belch.

'Zac!' I give his shoulder a shove.

'*What?* In some cultures, burping is a sign of appreciation.'

'Not this culture though.' I laugh despite myself.

Zac sees this as a green light to pursue his ridiculous idea. 'It was actually Chris's suggestion.'

'Chris?'

'Yes. He said she wouldn't want much payment. She was made redundant recently from her job as an office manager—'

'She told me that the other night.'

'Exactly. Well, she's feeling down about it. It would be good for her, good for you, and she can't be that bad if she was an office manager.'

'She told me it was just an admin job.'

'Maybe she was being modest. Plus, she's only upstairs. On hand if you need her.' Zac leans forward to stack our bowls. He gets up to take them into the kitchen.

I follow him. 'Why are you so keen for her to work with me?'

'Selfish reasons.'

I give him a quizzical look.

'Well, you're going to go and do some more work in your office now, aren't you?'

I give a half-shrug half-nod of acknowledgement.

'Right. So I want to spend more time with you when I'm home. You literally only stop working to eat and sleep.'

'That's not true. We had a party, didn't we? And we had the neighbours round on Saturday.'

'I know, but that's rare. I want us to do more stuff together.' Zac puts the bowls into the sink and squirts washing-up liquid over the top.

'Well, what about you? You work long hours too.'

'Nothing like as long as you.' He turns on the tap and starts rinsing the bowls.

'Anyway, when did you speak to Chris about this?' I get a new tea towel from the drawer.

'I told you, we went for a drink after work.'

'What, *tonight*? You didn't tell me you were with him.'

'Yeah, he gave me a few good contacts who could put some business my way.'

'Did you just bump into him or something?' I start drying the cutlery.

'He messaged me this afternoon.'

I stop drying for a second. 'That's weird, isn't it? He lives upstairs. He could have dropped the contacts in any time.' It's starting to feel as though Chris is taking over our lives. He always seems to be there at every turn, in every conversation.

Zac frowns. 'What's weird about going for a drink with a neighbour?'

I'm just about to tell Zac about Chris and James Kipling having some kind of altercation in the drive today, when I remember that

Zac doesn't know about James's visit. I shrug and resume drying, trying to shake off my doubts. Maybe I'm overthinking things. Chris lives upstairs, which means we're bound to see a lot of him.

'So, what do you think about asking Vanessa to help out?' Zac pushes.

'I'll think about it, but we didn't exactly click, and it might be too strange to employ a neighbour. What happens if it doesn't work out? It'll be really awkward.'

'It's just a suggestion. I told Chris I'd ask, so now I've asked.'

'But now if I don't ask her, they'll both think I don't want her working with me.'

Zac finishes washing the dinner things and dries his hands on his work trousers. 'I don't think he'll mind either way. He just thought it might be a good solution.'

This is all I need – Chris will hate me even more now.

Zac leans back against the counter as I finish drying up. 'Chris also mentioned you had a visitor round today. Some guy…'

I reach up to put the bowls in the cupboard, hoping Zac doesn't notice my red face. Damn. I should've told him about James. I grit my teeth.

'What is he, some kind of spy?' I tell Zac that it was in fact James coming round for an investor meeting.

'Why didn't you say?'

'Sorry. I didn't want you to worry.'

'Why would I worry?'

'I know you don't really like that the business relies on someone else's money.'

'It's not that… It's just… It makes life more complicated. I like to know that what's ours is ours. Not someone else's.'

I nod. It's a conversation Zac and I have had many times. But Zac said he's come around to accepting that this is my dream. That I need investment if I'm going to make a proper go of things without asking my family for financial help. My dad would lend me the money if I asked, but then Mum would make it her business to get involved, and I couldn't bear that. Plus, I don't want people saying that the only reason I have a successful business is because of my family's money.

Zac works for himself. He built up his business from scratch without any loans or outside help. But it's a different type of thing to what I'm doing. His business is just him – a one-man band – and he likes it that way. He doesn't have any spare cash in his business. It's just a way of him working for himself to pay the bills. Whereas I want my business to be a big company with employees and premises and a name that everyone knows.

My blood pressure rises at the thought of our neighbour snooping on me. 'Why's Chris being so nosy anyway?'

'Well, they do live in the same building. It's not exactly nosy to pass someone in the drive as you're coming home. He said he thought there was a strange man hanging around. He was just looking out for us. Being neighbourly.'

'I'm not sure I believe that. James isn't exactly a hoodie casing up the joint. Anyway, it looked like Chris was having a go at James about something. It's none of his business who comes round here and why.'

Zac raises his hands. 'All right. Don't take it out on me. I'm just the messenger.'

'Sorry, you're right.' I lean forward to give Zac a kiss.

He accepts my olive branch and kisses me back.

I really don't like the way that Chris is insinuating himself into our lives in such a strange way. Especially as Vanessa seems to be hidden away upstairs all the time. I also don't like the fact that Zac is so enamoured of our neighbour. That he can't see how creepy Chris is. That he's becoming his friend. That Chris is worming his way into Zac's confidence, coming between us. I don't like it at all.

CHAPTER FOURTEEN

Zac left at stupid o'clock this morning to get a head start on his job. He said the clients are early risers and don't mind him starting at seven. I got up at the same time as him as I've also got loads to get on with. I'm excited to start planning my friends-and-family event. I think it'll be great.

I swallow my last gulp of tea and head into the bedroom to get dressed. Even though I work from home, I still make sure I dress as if I'm going to a public workplace. Before setting up Mistletoe Lane, I was the head of the jewellery section in a local department store. I always had to dress super smart, so I've continued with that routine, only now I can go a little crazier with my look. Rather than conservative dark suits and plain shirts, I wear bright colours and interesting combinations.

Today, I pick out a burnt-orange pencil skirt and team it with a cream-and-black striped sweater. The look is fifties French singer in a smoky nightclub. It's a shame I don't have any fun meetings with designers today. That's the part of my job I love the best – sourcing products, and getting to know the people who create them.

Once I'm showered and dressed, I sit at my art-deco mirrored dressing table and start applying my make-up. I know it might seem over the top to dress up to sit in a garden shed on my own, but who knows what today might turn up? Perhaps I'll have an impromptu Zoom with someone, or have to dash out to a meeting. Even if I don't speak to another soul all day, looking good lifts my spirits and energises me. I'll get to my office, turn on the radio and get to work. It's only half seven so I've got hours of productivity ahead of me. My stomach gives a flutter of excitement. I really do feel positive today.

A creak of floorboards from above knocks me out of my reverie, and I'm reminded of the neighbours. I wish I could forget they were there, but now I can hear their voices. What starts as a normal conversation soon picks up in tempo and volume. *Oh no*. They're arguing again.

A crash and a short scream makes me gasp. I look up at the ceiling. My heart starts thumping. I wait for the inevitable follow-up shouting match – the dark rumbling tones of Chris's voice, the quiet remonstrations from Vanessa. I strain my ears, but there's nothing – only silence, which feels worse somehow.

With trembling hands, I put my make-up brush back in its pot and get to my feet. My heart is racing. What should I do? What if Chris has hurt her? I pick up my phone and call Zac.

He answers after a couple of rings. 'Hey, Neens. Everything okay?'

'Not really.'

'*What?* What is it?'

'They're arguing again upstairs.'

Zac exhales down the phone. 'Is that all? I thought something bad had happened.'

'It *is* bad. I heard a crash up there. And a scream.'

'A scream?'

'Yes. A short, frightened scream. And now it's gone deathly quiet.'

'Maybe they knocked something over.'

'What should I do?'

'Don't do anything.' His voice goes faint for a moment. 'Be with you in a minute, Cath.' He comes back on the line. 'Look, Nina, I've got to go. My client… I'm in the middle of—'

'Yes, sure, sorry. You go.'

'Don't worry, all couples argue. They'll be fine, I'm sure,' he adds before ending the call.

I clutch my phone and strain my ears again. It's still quiet up there. Zac's right. This is stupid. I need to forget about the neighbours and get on with my day.

The doorbell startles me and I realise my heart is beating really fast. Maybe it's Vanessa. Maybe she's upset and needs my help. My nerves really are on edge today. I need to calm down. I take a breath and get to my feet. It's probably a delivery.

I make my way to the front door. Standing in front of me, leaning on a wooden walking stick, is my neighbour from number 13, her thin white curls bouncing around in the wind. She's wearing a navy anorak over a tweed skirt and wellingtons.

'Marion, hello. Would you like to come in out of the rain?' I hope she says no, because I have so much work to get on with.

'Yes please, dear. I didn't realise the weather was so awful.'

I stand back and let her in, wondering if I should take her arm, but I don't like to presume. As it is, she manages quite well without my assistance.

'That's better.' She pats the rain from her face and looks at me with watery blue eyes.

'Is everything all right?' I ask.

She glances around the hall and gives a little harumph as though she disapproves of something. Her attention eventually wanders back to me. She reaches into the pocket of her raincoat and pulls out a blue airmail envelope. 'I wonder if I could trouble you to put this in the letterbox for me. My hip is giving me bother this week and I don't think I can make it that far. Not in this howling wind.'

I look at the letter and then back at Marion, who's biting her lip. She does actually appear to be in pain.

'Of course! Would you like to sit down?'

'Very kind, but no. If I sit, I might not manage to get myself up again. So you'll post it for me today? I've already added the stamps.

It's to my son. He's in Australia. It's his birthday next month so I'm sending him a little something.' She's still proffering the letter.

I take it from her. 'You have a daughter too, right?'

'Hmph,' she replies.

'Well, I'll take it up there after lunch, if that's okay?'

She gives a brisk nod and turns around. 'Much appreciated.' She stops and turns back. 'Have you seen much of those two?' She raises her eyes to the ceiling.

'The Jacksons?' I think about their earlier argument. The crash and the scream. I debate whether or not to mention it, but decide against it. I don't want to be branded as the neighbourhood gossip. 'I haven't seen much of them, no. They came down for dinner the Saturday before last, but Vanessa's morning sickness was so bad she couldn't eat much.'

Marion seems quite uninterested in my reply. 'What about *him*?' She jerks her head upwards.

'Chris?'

She nods. 'Mm.'

'I didn't really get to know him. He got on quite well with Zac though, my boyfriend.'

Marion pauses and looks as if she might say something. I wait for her to speak, but instead she raises her hand in a half-hearted wave. 'Thank you for taking my letter. You won't forget?'

'Don't worry. I'm happy to post it.' I walk around her and open the door, holding it steady against the buffeting wind. 'Would you like me to walk you back? It's pretty stormy out here.'

'I can manage!' she calls as she makes her way out the door, jabbing her walking stick into the gravel as she goes.

I close the door and place the letter on the hall table before returning to the bedroom. I stop in the doorway and listen hard in case there are any other noises from upstairs, but it's all quiet. This is ridiculous, I need to stop obsessing about the neighbours. I turn on the radio and finish applying my make-up.

Once I'm done, I make my way along the wet garden path to my office. Inside, I let out a sigh of relief. This space feels like a haven compared to the flat. My own little sanctuary. I push out the thought that it's supposed to be the other way around – my home is supposed to feel like the space where all my worries disappear. I glance through my office window up at the house. Upstairs, the curtains are still closed. Am I a bad neighbour for not checking on Vanessa? Or a good neighbour for minding my own business? I'm not sure what I'm supposed to do in this situation.

I need to throw myself into work, but I can't seem to fight off the feeling that things are sliding away from me. That life is slipping out of my control.

I give myself a shake, take a breath and start by answering emails and responding to comments on my social-media ads – that's a full-time job in itself, but I'm determined to respond to each and every potential customer. I want Mistletoe Lane to be friendly, funny, approachable. Not stuck-up and aloof like a lot of high-end fashion brands.

Once I've caught up on all my messages, I make myself a coffee and call the Arts University in Bournemouth. I'm put through to the Head of Fashion, a woman named Sariah Jones, to ask if any of their fashion students might be up for modelling at my event. I try to make it sound as glamorous as possible. I talk about influencers and bloggers, mention my existing designers and give her the link to my website. In return, I offer the opportunity for her students to pitch me their designs for future inclusion on my website.

Sariah says she'll speak to her staff and students and get back to me. She didn't sound as excited as I'd like her to be, but at least I've got the ball rolling. I don't know what I was expecting, but I feel deflated. As though I'm just some amateur chancer who's trying to get something for nothing. But then, nothing comes easily in the beginning. I just have to put little roots down everywhere and hope that some find the sun and start shooting. I try not to worry too much. I've done what I can, and even if I don't manage to get any models, I can still make it a brilliant event.

I get on with the job of packaging up today's orders. It always gives me a thrill each time one comes in. I get a leap in my chest, a real buzz. I'd love to make the website give a little ping sound with each new order.

Once the parcels are all labelled and ready to be dropped off at the local collection point, I load them into my newly delivered zebra-print waterproof shopping trolley along with Marion's airmail letter to her son. I don't know how I managed before I bought my trolley, lugging all those packages up the road in enormous carrier bags. This is infinitely more civilised, especially now it's started raining again.

I shrug on my knee-length raincoat and wheel my trolley up the garden path, feeling somewhat like an air stewardess. I realise I should probably have worn trousers – this skirt is quite restrictive. Out in the driveway, I see Vanessa coming towards me. She's been out somewhere and her hair and clothes are damp from the rain. Her face is blotchy, as though she's been crying.

'Hi,' I say, giving a short wave.

She dips her head and keeps walking past.

I stop walking and turn. 'Are you okay, Vanessa?'

'What?' She looks back at me.

'I was just asking if you were okay.'

She nods and my heart aches for her. She looks so forlorn. So lost.

Without thinking, I open my mouth again. 'I was wondering… I'm run off my feet at the moment. Don't suppose you'd be interested in a part-time temporary admin job?'

Vanessa's eyes widen. 'With you, you mean?'

'Yes. I'm trying to get my new business off the ground, but there's just too much to do for one person. The thing is… I can't pay you much right now, but hopefully that will all change in a few months when things pick up. It would be flexible hours and—'

'Yes!' Vanessa's whole face lights up. 'That would be amazing.'

This is the first time I've seen her look genuinely happy.

I smile back. 'That's great news. Why don't you dry off and come down for a cuppa and a quick chat in about thirty minutes or so. I just have to drop these parcels up the road.'

'Okay, great. Thirty minutes, yes?' She's already acting like a different person, standing taller, her eyes brighter.

Maybe, while we're working together, Vanessa might open up to me and I can discover if anything untoward is going on with Chris. Or if he really does have her best interests at heart. After all, it was him who suggested I offer her some work. Maybe she's simply been feeling down after losing her job. Either way, now that we'll be spending some time together, I'll be able to do some digging and find out.

CHAPTER FIFTEEN

It feels strange sharing my workspace with someone else. Like I'm running a proper company. Which I know I am, but having an employee legitimises it even more somehow. It's not simply me and my laptop any longer.

Zac was absolutely right to suggest hiring Vanessa. I'm already loving this new situation. While she answers emails and parcels up the deliveries, I'm able to concentrate on preparations for the Mistletoe Lane party. For now, she's using one of the visitor chairs, made more comfy with a couple of cushions, and I bought a cheap desk from the local charity shop for five pounds and spray-painted it red, which looks really good.

It's her second week here. We've decided it will be easier to do it on a freelance basis, so she can simply invoice me for her time. She's only doing three hours a day, three days a week at the moment but, like I said, if it works out, I'll be able to increase her rate once the business starts taking off. I know I'm supposed to be watching the pennies, not spending on freelancers, but with Vanessa doing the basic admin, it will leave me free to concentrate on maximising profits. At least, I hope James and Mr Newbury will see it that way. I maybe should have let them know in advance. But I can't run every little thing past them. I need to be able to organise the business how I see fit. They invested in *me*. So they need to let me get on with it.

'How's it going?' I ask Vanessa.

'Good,' she replies, her blue eyes sparkling. 'I've caught up on the emails and social media and made a start on uploading the photos of those new items from that scarf design place, Grey Carousel.'

'Amazing. You're doing such a great job. I can't believe your last company let you go! Are they mad?' I grin.

She gives an embarrassed smile. 'Thanks. I love working here so far. It's way more enjoyable than my last place. I can't quite believe my luck.'

'The luck's all mine, believe me. Here…' I reach into my samples box and pull out a pale-blue satin top. 'I may not be able to pay you a decent hourly rate yet, but I can definitely shower you with samples. This will really suit you. It's one of our bestsellers. The most popular colour's green, but I think the blue would suit you better.'

'You're giving it to me?' She takes the top in both hands and holds it to her chest.

'Oh, and this will go perfectly with it.' I hand her a pretty silver dragonfly necklace, inset with tiny blue aventurine stones.

'Oh, wow, I love them both. Thank you, Nina.'

'Thank *you* for being such a great help.'

I don't want to get ahead of myself, but I really think I might have lucked out hiring Vanessa. Finally, things are starting to look up. Zac is already unbearably smug that it's working out so well. I actually don't know how I'd have managed these past few days without her help. The orders seem to be pouring in. Plus, she's a really good worker. She gets her head down and gets on with the job. If anything, she's too quiet. She never wants to stop for a break or a chat. Better that way around than being a slacker, but still. It would be nice if we could get to know one another properly.

I'd also like her to think she could confide in me if there's anything going on with Chris. If he's being verbally abusive or violent in any way. Hopefully that's not the case and it's just a fiery relationship. But Vanessa seems anything but fiery.

'Hey, Vanessa, it's after one already. How about going to that lovely little beach café for a quick bite to eat? My treat.'

'You mean Tides Bistro?'

'Is that what it's called? Yeah, let's go there.'

Vanessa lays the top and necklace on her desk. 'You don't have to do that. I'll just make something upstairs.'

'I'd like to. It'll be nice to chat. We're always so rushed, there's barely time to even say hello in the mornings. Of course, if you're tired or busy then no worries.'

She looks thoughtful for a moment. Maybe she doesn't want to socialise. But then she seems to relax. 'Okay, well, if you're sure. My morning sickness doesn't usually start up until the evening, so lunch would be great.'

'Brilliant. Let me just lock up and set the alarm. I'll meet you in the drive – in say, ten minutes?'

The two-minute walk down to the beach is bracing. The sky is a freshly washed blue with racing clouds that merge and separate. Vanessa and I talk about how nice it is to live in such a beautiful place. How she prefers the winters when the beaches are empty and the tourists are at home. She says she's looking forward to walks along the promenade with her baby in a sling or pushchair. Apparently, she's lived in the area all her life.

I tell her that I grew up in London and my parents moved here when I was a teenager. I loved Friars Cliff, but my mother hated it – said it was too quiet and far away from everything. We eventually ended up not too far away in Branksome Park, which suited Mum much better. But I'd always secretly yearned to move back here one day.

'And now you have,' she states.

'Yes.'

We smile at one another.

Tides Bistro is packed.

'Oh dear.' I frown at the queue snaking out the door. 'I guess I should have booked.'

'You can't book at lunchtime,' Vanessa informs me. 'It's always busy so they don't bother with bookings.'

'So we just stand in line?'

'It'll move quickly. The service is fast.'

Sure enough, after a short ten-minute wait, we're seated at a table by the window. I order a crab-salad baguette, and Vanessa has a bowl of creamy parsnip soup with a crusty roll. She tucks into her food with abandon and catches me staring.

'Sorry,' I say. 'It's just… the last time we were eating together…'

She puts her spoon down and flushes. 'Oh, I'm so sorry about that night. Evenings are bad for me. I can't keep anything down, so when we came to yours for dinner, I was literally trying not to throw up the whole time. It was nothing to do with your amazing food.'

'You should've said. We could have done lunch some other time instead of dinner.'

'Chris had already accepted the dinner invitation. I didn't want to be rude.' Vanessa gets back to her soup. 'It's so weird. I'm starving all day, and then six o'clock arrives and I just want to barf. I usually end up going to bed at eight, just so I can get to tomorrow quicker.'

'It's a shame you've been feeling so rotten.'

I wonder if that's why they'd been arguing just before they came down to dinner. Maybe she told him she didn't feel up to it and then he'd got annoyed. But it's not the kind of thing I can ask her. Not without sounding nosy – which I totally am right now.

'Are you settling in okay downstairs?' she asks, tearing off a chunk of her roll and dipping it into her soup.

'Yes thanks. Pretty good. Zac and I have had a few ups and downs recently, but we're looking forward to beach walks and trying out the lovely cafés like this one. It's tricky because we both work such long hours.' I'm hoping that if I tell her things between me and Zac aren't perfect, maybe she'll open up to me.

'Sorry to hear you and Zac aren't getting on too well at the moment. They say that moving house is one of the most stressful things you can do. I'm sure things will settle down soon.'

'I hope so. How long have you and Chris been together?'

'Oh, ages,' she replies. 'He went to my school, but we only got together when we were in our twenties. How's your baguette?'

'Absolutely delicious. I can't wait to bring Zac here to try the food.'

'The crab's caught locally,' Vanessa says. 'If you get down here early enough you can see them bringing their catch in.'

'Do you and Chris come down here much?'

'Not as much as I'd like.'

'How did you two meet?'

'Through a mutual friend.'

Everything I ask her about Chris is answered with a short sentence. It's obvious that she really doesn't want to talk about their relationship. If she won't even talk about the basics of how they met, then there's no way she's going to mention their shouted arguments or the mysterious thuds in the middle of the night. And I'm not blunt enough to ask her outright. I'll have to respect her privacy. Easier said than done with their noisy relationship encroaching into Zac's and my flat.

We finish our meal and the conversation peters out. Vanessa's eyes are heavy.

'Ready to go back?' I ask.

She nods. 'That was lovely, thank you.'

As we near home, Tricia from next door comes out of her driveway. She waves to Vanessa and then fixes me with what can only be described as a steely gaze.

'Hi, Tricia. How are you?' I give her a tentative smile.

'I've got more parcels in the porch for you.'

'Oh. Thanks so much. I'll come and—'

Tricia holds her hand up to stop me talking. 'Look, Nina, I'm not a sorting office. I can't keep doing this. I've already told the delivery man that I'm not taking in any more. This is a residential area, not an office block.'

'I'm so sorry, Tricia. Don't worry, I'll arrange a secure drop-off place for when I'm out.'

She sniffs and gives me a single nod. Her face softens as she turns to Vanessa. 'How are you, love? Feeling okay these days?'

'Fine thanks,' she replies.

'You know you're welcome to pop round any time. Any problems while Chris is out, you let me know, okay?'

'Thanks.'

Vanessa is giving her usual one- and two-word answers, but Tricia isn't deterred, asking question after question and following up with her pregnancy and parenting experiences. I really need to get back to work, but I don't want to be accused of being rude, so I remain standing awkwardly next to Vanessa while Tricia does an effective job of ignoring me, making her point that I'm still very much in her bad books.

After five minutes of feeling like a lemon, I decide to make my excuses and head back inside. I need to get back to work. I walk down the garden path making promises to myself that once spring arrives Zac and I will really get to work on these overgrown weeds. I unlock the door, let myself in and walk over to punch my code into the portable alarm. But it's not flashing. Strangely, it's already disarmed. Maybe I forgot to set it. No. I distinctly remember doing it after Vanessa left. I guess it could be faulty. I glance around the office. My laptop is still here and everything else also appears to be in its place. I go through to the stockroom and see that all looks to be in order too. Weird. But as long as nothing's missing and no one's been in here, I guess that's the main thing.

CHAPTER SIXTEEN

THEN

It's been less than a month since Dad died and I can tell my friends are already sick of my sadness. I've never exactly been the popular kid, but now I'm even more of a pariah. By contrast, my brother has seemed to bounce back. He's out there now on the school field kicking a football around with his mates, laughing and joking. He's never like that with me. At home, he shuts himself in his room.

I sit on the wall outside the English block, kicking at the bricks with my heels, scuffing the backs of my shoes. Mum will go mad, but I don't care. I hate everything right now. There's still thirty minutes left of lunch break. I'll just sit here until the bell goes. No one has come to look for me to see if I'm okay. They're glad I'm not bothering them with my sad face and watery eyes. It's as though my grief is catching.

My stomach feels as though there's a brick inside it. A heavy lump of sadness holding me down while the world moves on happily without me. No one understands. The teachers are too busy to notice, Mum gets irritated with me, and there's nobody else. I've never felt so alone. Dad was my one ally. The person I could always count on to make me feel good. To cheer me up. Now he's gone.

Is this how life is going to be from now on?

My hands are cold, but the sun warms my face. What would Dad say to me now, if he were here? He'd tell me to get up and find my friends. He'd tell me not to sit here moping. Not to cut myself off from everyone. To make an effort. Maybe I'll do that tomorrow. Yes, tomorrow I'll make more of an effort.

CHAPTER SEVENTEEN

The flat is even more crowded than the evening of our house-warming party. I've made an uplifting party-vibes playlist, turned the dining room into a temporary showroom and the guest bedroom has become a changing room. I've had to crank up the heating as the weather's turned unseasonably cold with a bitter northerly wind that's creeping in through the gaps in the windows. I'm wearing one of my bestselling items, in the hope of taking a few orders for it – a floral knee-length shift dress with long sleeves that I've teamed with tan boots and bare legs.

Zac has gone out for a few drinks with Ryan, Kit and Ben so he can leave me to my friends-and-family event which, even though I say it myself, is looking like it's going to be a real success. There's already a line outside the changing room, and less-inhibited people – like Amy – are stripping off in the lounge and dining room to try on all the wonderful clothes.

I managed to get four fashion students to model tonight – they're all various sizes, which is great as I get to show how flattering the styles are to all shapes of women. I also had the genius idea of photographing them in all the outfits they'll be wearing throughout the evening and writing the price next to each item. I printed these out onto little cards so people can see at a glance how much everything costs, and I've also posted the shots on Mistletoe Lane's Instagram page.

After my initial muted conversation with Sariah from the college, she called me back with more enthusiasm and said she had eleven students who were interested. I whittled them down to four by picking the most outgoing characters. That seems to have paid off, because the four of them are now laughing and chatting to all the guests, bigging up the clothes and saying how great they make them feel.

Almost everyone I know is here, including friends of friends. Tricia from number 17 left a note to say she couldn't make it. I wonder if she's still cross about the deliveries. Marion from number 13 was one of the first to arrive, but I'm not sure any of the items are to her taste. She made some disparaging comment about how she prefers classic pieces that don't date. Cali and Amy have brought ten friends between them and they've already got stuck into the Prosecco.

'More alcohol equals more sales,' Cali hisses to me as she tops up her friends' glasses.

Vanessa is standing in the living room talking quietly to a couple of women in their thirties. I go over to introduce myself.

'Hi, Vanessa.'

'Oh. Hi, Nina.' She gives me a shy smile. 'This is Caroline.' She gestures to the dark-haired woman. 'And this is Sally.' Sally has light-brown hair and a smattering of freckles across her cheeks. 'We all go to the same antenatal class.'

I say hello to each of them. 'Thanks for coming along.'

'Your products are lovely,' Sally comments with an open smile. 'Shame I can't fit into any of the clothes.' She grins and gestures to her bump.

'We've got some lovely flowy tops,' I say. 'And have a look at the accessories and gifts. There are some more in the dining room. Ness will show you.'

'Okay, great.' Sally nods.

'Have you known one another long?' I ask, looking between the three of them.

'No, not at all,' Caroline says. 'The first time we spoke was at our first antenatal class last week and Vanessa invited us along this evening.'

Vanessa's cheeks redden. I wonder if perhaps she doesn't have many friends.

'We're so glad you did.' Sally nudges Vanessa with her elbow. 'All our babies are due around the same time, so it'll be great for us to get to know one another before they're born.'

'I won't be able to stay long,' Vanessa says. 'My sickness isn't great in the evenings.'

'Poor you,' I reply, remembering our disastrous dinner. 'I appreciate you coming tonight.'

There's a short lull in the conversation.

'Well,' I say, clapping my hands together. 'I hope you enjoy the evening. Help yourself to drinks and snacks. Thanks so much again for coming. And please do ask if you have any questions about anything.'

Sally and Caroline thank me and I leave the three of them to their slightly awkward conversation. It was good of Vanessa to put herself out there and invite them along. I'm so glad I made the effort to get to know her. She's definitely come out of her shell more since we first met.

I'm heading towards the living-room door past one of the rails when I hear a woman talking about the clothes.

'Some of it's all right, but there's no way I'd pay any of these prices. I mean, you can get nicer stuff in the high street for about ten per cent of the price of this.'

I stop as heat floods my cheeks. Should I say something? My clothes are all beautiful quality. They're original and quirky pieces made from material that won't fall apart after a few washes.

'I know what you mean, Linda, but it's my son's girlfriend's business. I have to show my support, even if it's not my thing.'

Sandra.

I guess I already knew she wasn't my target customer, but it's still hurtful to hear her agree with Linda – whoever she is. Must be one of Sandra's colleagues from the bank. I guess I won't be seeing any sales from that quarter.

I answer the door again and this time it's my mum. She's standing on the doorstep with Belinda, who I didn't invite, so this feels somewhat uncomfortable. I stifle a grimace and welcome them in. I know I should have asked Belinda along, but she's always so judgemental. I really didn't want her looking down her nose at me all night, or bad-mouthing my stock to the other guests. Now that she's here, I can't help feeling mean that I didn't invite her.

'I thought you were an online store,' Belinda says, coming in and handing me her coat. 'I didn't realise you were a party planner too. Is it one of those pyramid schemes? You know, if you're struggling financially, I'm looking for a part-time sales assistant in our Wimborne branch. Although that might be too much of a schlepp for you. Probably spend all your wages in petrol getting over there!' She gives a tinkling laugh. 'Seriously, though. The offer's there if you need it.' She gives my arm a squeeze.

'That's so nice of you, Belinda.' Mum gives her a grateful smile before turning to me. 'Isn't that nice of her, Nina?'

'It's lovely of you, Belinda. I'll bear it in mind.' *For when hell freezes over.*

'Seriously, though,' she says, her eyes darkening. 'It is a shame that online businesses are taking away from bricks-and-mortar shops. There's no real substitute for coming in and trying things on in a fitting room. Being looked after by knowledgeable staff.'

'Surely there's room for both,' I reply. 'There are some people who can't get to the shops easily, or who don't like shopping. I love going into shops, but sometimes it's more convenient to go online.'

'Hm, well, you'll regret it when the high streets are dead.'

'That's all very interesting, but are you going to be a good hostess and get us a drink, Nina?' For once I'm grateful for Mum's bluntness.

'Of course. Come through to the kitchen and then you can go and have a look at everything. Mum, there are some gorgeous satin clutches that I think you'd love.'

The doorbell rings again and I'm surprised to see Chris from upstairs standing at the door in sweatpants and an old jumper. He doesn't smile or even catch my eye. Instead he peers past me.

'Hi, Chris. Are you joining us?'

'What? No. I just need to speak to Vanessa and she's not answering her phone. Is it okay if I come in for a minute?'

'Yes, sure. There are drinks and nibbles in the kitchen. Help yourself.' Mum and Belinda are standing next to me looking expectant. 'Oh, sorry, Mum, Belinda, this is Chris Jackson from upstairs.'

'Hello.' My mother extends a manicured hand which he shakes distractedly. 'I think we met briefly at the house-warming party. You're the engineer, is that right?'

Chris nods. 'Nice to see you again. Okay, well, I'll just find Vanessa and then I'll leave you ladies to it.'

'I think she might be in the front room,' I offer.

He disappears into the living room as I finally take Mum and Belinda to the kitchen to get them a drink.

'Actually, can I use your loo?' Belinda asks.

'Sure. Down the hall, first door on your right.'

'Is that one of your Mistletoe Lane dresses?' Mum asks, nudging me backwards so she can get a good look at my outfit.

I tense. 'Yes. It's actually one of our bestsellers.'

'Very nice.' She wrinkles her nose. 'It's quite a busy pattern though, isn't it?'

'People are loving patterns and florals at the moment.'

'Are they? Gosh, I must be awfully out of date.' Mum is wearing an impeccably cut navy cashmere dress teamed with a grey scarf and a pair of pearl and lapis statement earrings.

'Mum, the last thing you are is out of date. You look amazing.' Which she very well knows. 'Now, what can I get you to drink?'

'Belinda's driving so I'll have a G and T.' She gazes around the kitchen with a critical eye before turning her gaze to me. 'Where's Zac?'

'He's out with friends this evening.' I reach for the gin bottle and a tumbler.

'*Out?* That's not very supportive. I'd have thought he'd want to be here lending a hand.' She sniffs.

I'm used to her snippy remarks about Zac so I try not to let her words rile me. 'Not at all. It was my idea for him to have a night out with his friends.' As I twist the cap on the gin bottle, the music cuts out and the kitchen is suddenly plunged into total darkness. I freeze and blink, unable to see a thing.

There's a second or two of silence, followed by a door slamming shut, then gasps and squeals of surprise and shock.

What the hell?

CHAPTER EIGHTEEN

'Nina, why have the lights gone out?' Mum's voice cuts through the darkness.

'I don't know.' I glance around but it really is a total blackout in here. I don't even have my phone on me. 'Do you have a phone torch?' I ask in a loud voice.

'Is it a power cut?' Mum asks. 'What bad luck, while you've got a houseful of people. You'd better hope no one falls and hurts themselves.'

I take a breath. 'Mum,' I say more firmly. 'Your phone.'

'Oh, yes, hang on, it's in my bag.'

I hear her fumbling around and then finally see the faint light of her phone screen. I take it off her and find my way to the cupboard under the kitchen sink.

'I think there's a torch down here somewhere.' My stomach is in knots. What if I can't get the electricity back on? My event will be ruined. All that hard work for nothing. No. Think positive. It'll be a temporary power cut, or a blown fuse, that's all. 'Got it!' I grip the red-and-black torch handle and pray it has working batteries. Sliding the button, I'm rewarded with a bright circle of light. I hand my mother back her phone and turn to leave the kitchen.

'Where are you going, Nina? Don't leave me here in the dark.'

'You've got the light from your phone. Just stay put for a minute, Mum, while I go and sort this out.'

'But…'

I don't stay to listen to her protestations. Instead I make my way into the hall where I'm met with blinking, squinting guests as my torch beam sweeps over them. I throw open the front door and gasp as an icy blast of wind hits me. I immediately notice that the street lights are still on. I peer out across the road to see bright windows dotting the properties opposite. So the other side of the street still has electricity. I step out onto the driveway and peer up at the Jacksons' place. There's light up there too. Must be a fuse in our flat then.

A crunch of gravel behind me catches my attention. I turn to see a figure move out of sight just beyond the boundary hedge. Someone walking past, perhaps? Hunching my shoulders against the chill, I stride out onto the pavement to see a small figure with dark hair hurrying away.

'Tricia? Is that you?'

She turns and I see that it is indeed my neighbour. She's wearing dark jeans, a jumper and a black parka. 'Oh. Hello, Nina.' She looks startled.

'Everything okay? Were you in our driveway a second ago?'

She takes a step towards me. 'Yes. I was coming to your thing, but the place was in darkness so I thought I must have got the wrong day. Although I'm sure this was the date on the invitation.' She sounds annoyed.

'I thought you couldn't make it… I got your note.'

'I swapped shifts. Thought I'd pop along.'

'Great, but we've got a power cut. I need to go back in and find the fuse box. You're welcome to come along, but it's pitch-black in there right now!'

'Oh dear. That's unfortunate. Do you need any help?'

'Not sure yet.' My teeth are chattering now. I would've grabbed a coat if I'd known I'd be out here so long. 'I really must get back inside and sort things out.' I start walking away and call back over my shoulder. 'Come back in ten minutes or so, if you like. Hopefully, we should have some light by then.'

'Will do.'

I try to remember where the fuse box is located. It was in the downstairs loo of our last place. But here, I think, if I remember, it's in the hall. Back inside, I close the door behind me with a shiver, thankful to be in the warm again, although the heating will have gone off with the electrics.

'Nina!' I glance down the hall to see Cali's worried expression.

'I think it's a blown fuse,' I call back.

She shines her phone torch around the hall and points to a spot near the front door. 'There!'

I look down to see the clear-plastic covered fuse box. Great. Hopefully, all I'll need to do is flip the switch and lights will come back on. Cali comes over to my side and holds the torch while I lift the hinged cover. All the red switches are down, apart from one which is in the 'up' position but has had most of the lever snapped off, leaving only a jagged ring of red plastic. I try to get it to flick back down, but there's nothing to catch hold of. It's impossible.

'Shit,' Cali says eloquently, summing up the situation.

'Nina, what's happened?' I look up to see Vanessa peering down at us.

Cali explains.

'Can you get the switch to go down?' Vanessa asks. 'What about using a pen, or something else like a knitting needle?'

'I don't think we should go poking about in a fuse box with a knitting needle,' Cali replies.

Vanessa's cheeks flame. 'No, of course not. Sorry.'

'Don't apologise, Ness. You were only trying to help.'

'Is the whole street out?' she asks.

'No. Just our place, of course. On the one night when I really don't need it. Don't worry, Vanessa, I saw that the lights are still on upstairs at your place. Is Chris still here? He was looking for you a minute ago.'

'He found me, but then he went straight back up. This isn't really his type of thing.'

'Maybe we could move everyone up to yours?' Cali asks, looking at Vanessa hopefully.

She flushes again. 'Sorry, I would do, but Chris said he's having an early night. He's got an important meeting tomorrow and I don't think he'd be very happy if I brought a houseful of people up there while he's getting into his pyjamas.'

'No, of course not. Don't worry.' I smile at my neighbour to let her know that I totally understand.

Cali shakes her head, annoyed on my behalf. 'Okay. Well, do you have any candles? More torches? We can—'

'Oh my God!' Belinda's voice cuts through the chaos. 'I was in the loo and everything just went dark! Nina? Nina! What's going on?'

I stand where I am in the hall explaining to everyone that there's a problem with the electrics, but that I'd love them all to stay while I try to get it fixed. It's so embarrassing and frustrating. Everyone's talking in hushed whispers. Nervous giggling, muttering, even grumbling. All that work to prepare for a successful evening, and then this has to go and happen.

I manage to locate the number of an emergency electrician and call him from my bedroom – the only room that isn't crowded with guests. He says he's with another client, but I beg him to please come over. I explain about my event and how it's going to be ruined. I realise my voice is becoming shriller and I apologise, my voice cracking. He relents and says he'll get here as soon as he can, but it could be another couple of hours as he can't leave his current client in the lurch. I thank him, but my heart sinks at the thought of two more hours in the dark.

I have to make the best of it. It'll be fine. With Cali and Amy's help, I rummage around in the kitchen cupboards and drawers for candles while Vanessa runs upstairs to get a couple of spare torches.

'Have you found any yet?' I ask, trying to keep my voice level. 'I'm sure I saw some of those pillar candles in one of the cupboards recently, but maybe that was at our last place.'

'I don't think they're in here,' Amy says. 'We've been through everything. Shall I try the dining room?'

'Okay, yes please. The clothes rails are blocking the sideboard though. You'll have to shift them out of the way.' This is such a disaster.

'Don't worry, me and Cal will sort it.'

'Thanks. You two are amazing.'

'Can I do anything to help, Nina?' Mum is standing in the same spot where I left her, sipping her G and T.

I grit my teeth. 'No, that's okay, Mum. My friends are helping.'

'Well, I would have joined in, only I didn't want to get in the way. You should always keep a good stock of candles, Nina. I keep ours in the boot room at home.'

I take a breath and stop the retort that comes to my lips. Instead, I head for the door to continue the hunt for candles.

'It's very draughty, Nina.' Belinda appears in the kitchen, blocking my exit. She's rubbing her arms theatrically. 'Did you have a proper survey done before you bought the place?'

'Yes, we had a survey. The heating's gone off. It'll be fine once we get the electrics back on.' But I realise she's right. The flat is losing heat fast. I edge past Belinda and make my way back into the hall.

Vanessa's returned with two working torches in her hands. 'I'll take one into the dining room and one into the lounge,' she says. 'I can point them at the clothes racks.'

My shoulders sag with relief. 'You star! Thank you.' Maybe the evening will be saved after all.

In addition to Vanessa's torches, Amy manages to locate two chunky pillar candles. We take a while to find matches, but eventually we're able to light them, placing one in the lounge and one in the dining room – not that they're particularly effective, and

I'm also worried about having naked flames with so many people wandering around.

The lack of decent light means it's hard to see the clothes properly – all the colours appear drab and muted. And without the music on, the atmosphere is cold and quiet. The radiators are cooling fast. It's below zero outside and is starting to feel that way inside too.

I can see that everyone else is chilly. They're shrugging on their coats and blowing on their fingers. No one wants to try on anything else, and I can't blame them. After my initial few sales earlier, the only other purchases are a handbag and a couple of pieces of jewellery. It's too dark for selfies and Instagram-worthy photos. My models are shivering, so I have to admit defeat and tell them to get changed if they like.

The whole evening is a washout. I make the decision to call it a night. I try to inject lightness in my voice as I tell everyone that I'll rearrange it for another time. But I'm gutted.

'Want me to stay and help you tidy up, love?' Sandra puts a hand on my arm.

'Aren't you getting a lift with one of your colleagues?'

'Yes, but I can get a cab home.'

'No, that's okay. It won't take me long.' I'm grateful to Sandra for the offer, but I've suddenly run out of energy and enthusiasm, and I don't think I could take making small talk.

'We'll stay and help, won't we, Belinda?' Mum nods at Sandra. There's no real friendship there, but they're always perfectly civil to one another. I'm not sure Mum would have even offered to stay and help if Sandra hadn't offered first.

'Are you sure, Mum?'

'I wouldn't have offered otherwise.'

'Well, thanks, that would be great.'

Cali emerges from the gloom of the dining room. 'There you are! Are you sure you want to call it a day?' she asks. 'I can gee everyone up, try to make it more fun, tell them to stop acting like wet weekends. Lock the door and keep them hostage…'

I manage a small laugh. 'No, don't worry. I don't want to force people to stay. It's supposed to be a cosy, fun evening. I can't blame them for wanting to leave.'

'Well *we'll* stay,' Amy says, blowing on her hands to warm them up.

'No, honestly, you two head off. We'll do it again another time.' I inject as much brightness into my voice as I can, not wanting my friends to feel bad for me.

'Are you sure?' Cali looks reluctant. 'We're happy to stay and help tidy up.'

'That's okay. Mum and Belinda are staying.'

Cali rolls her eyes over Belinda's head and I try not to laugh. 'Well, if you're sure…'

'Totally sure. You two go. I'll call you soon.'

We hug and they leave. It's probably for the best. Cali and Belinda would probably come to blows if they had to spend too much time in close proximity, and I could do without any more drama.

Belinda rubs her hands over her coat sleeves and turns to my mum. 'Joanna, I'm sorry but I think I'm going to have to get in the car to warm up. I have terrible circulation and I'm absolutely freezing.' She turns to me and tilts her head apologetically. 'Do you mind if we go?'

'Bit of moving around will warm you up,' Sandra says.

Belinda gives her an icy smile and then turns to my mum. 'Are you ready, Joanna?'

Mum nods. She leans in to kiss my cheek. 'Sorry, Nina. It looks like we'll be heading off too.'

Trust Belinda to wait until my friends have left before withdrawing her offer of help. Part of me wonders if she did it on purpose. I wouldn't be surprised. Why did my mother have to bring her along in the first place? If Belinda weren't here, perhaps Mum and I would have had a chance to chat properly. I could have asked her what she thought of my products, of the business. We could have had some mother–daughter bonding. Instead, she's leaving with bloody Belinda.

Mum frowns. 'Will you be all right here in the dark? Zac will be back soon, won't he?'

Her concern warms me for a moment. 'I'll be fine, Mum. I've got Vanessa upstairs and the other neighbours either side if I have any problems.'

Mum gives a brisk nod.

'That settles it, I'm staying to help,' Sandra declares.

'No, Sandra. Honestly, get a lift back with your friends,' I insist.

Sandra opens her mouth to object, but then changes her mind and shrugs, hurt by my rejection of her offer. I realise I'm still smarting from her earlier comments about my products.

'Come on, Sandra,' Mum says. 'Let's leave her to it. You know how independent Nina is. Likes to do everything herself, in her own way.'

I'm a little shocked by Mum's comment. Is that how she sees me? I want to reply, to correct her. But I think she might be right. Anyway, they're bustling away now with hugs, waves and air kisses. Out the door and off into the chilly night.

Before long, the flat is empty. I've blown out the candles, paranoid about the place going up in flames, and now it's just me in the cold, dark kitchen, rinsing the empty glasses by torchlight, feeling sorry for myself. The washing-up water is barely lukewarm, but I don't care about my cold fingers. I'm more concerned with tonight's disaster. The whole event has cost me more in time and money than I've made. And rather than improving Mistletoe Lane's reputation, I think I've probably damaged it. The only thing my guests are going to remember from this evening is the power cut. Not the beautiful clothes and accessories. Not the models or the lovely food and drink. I wonder again how on earth that fuse switch snapped off, and something occurs to me.

I dry my hands and pick up the torch from the windowsill before heading back to the fuse box. I shine the torch around the area looking for the missing red-plastic switch, but I can't see it. It must have already broken off before we moved in.

And then my gaze catches a speck of red on the wooden floor beneath the coat hooks. I crouch and shine the torch directly on it. It's flat, just slightly longer than a grain of rice – a splinter of shiny-red plastic.

CHAPTER NINETEEN

I grasp the sliver of plastic between my thumb and forefinger and hold it next to the broken switch in the fuse box, comparing. Trying to keep calm. Trying not to draw unwanted conclusions. It's the same type of plastic. It's definitely a tiny part of the broken switch. Can it have been lying on the floor since before we moved in without me noticing? I guess it's possible. But I've cleaned the wooden floors several times and I vacuum regularly. I must have missed it. Our vacuum isn't great at picking things up. We could really do with a new one, but that's way down our list of priorities.

I lay the piece of plastic on top of the fuse box. My head spinning with the possibilities of who might have done this. Could it really have been deliberate? Surely not. Who would want to sabotage my evening? My heart pounds as names and faces steal into my mind. Belinda sees me as competition, but would she really stoop so low as to ruin my evening? She's practically family. Perhaps she's jealous, insecure… Even if it was her, it's not as though I can go around flinging accusations.

Sandra's face flashes before me. Her earlier words about my products sting, but they're not a reason for her to do something like this. Unless she wants my business to fail so that I can concentrate on Zac more. On being a more attentive girlfriend. On making him my priority so that my thoughts might turn to starting a family.

No. I'm overthinking things.

I stare accusingly at the sliver of plastic on top of the fuse box. I should throw it in the bin, but I want to show it to Zac. See what he thinks.

What an absolute bust tonight was. I sent the Arts University models home with promises to view their fashion collections after graduation. They were really sweet and said they loved the brand and would tell all their friends, so at least I managed to generate a buzz. But even they admitted that it was a little out of their price range.

All I seem to be doing at the moment is spending money and time on things that aren't yielding any results. Thankfully, the online side is picking up – that's the main thing. Perhaps that will be enough to appease Mr Newbury.

While I'm waiting for the electrician to show up, I busy myself by tidying the flat. For an event that only lasted around half an hour, the place is in quite a mess. At least there's a lot of alcohol left over – that'll keep Zac and I going for a few weeks. Not that we're big drinkers, but we do like a few wind-down drinks at the weekend. I'll take the remaining stock back out to the storeroom tomorrow. I can't face doing it now.

It's so cold in here that I wouldn't be surprised if we don't get ice on the inside of the windows. I've changed out of my dress and bundled myself up in joggers, jumpers, a thick cardigan, a woolly hat and a pair of gloves.

Finally, at ten thirty, the doorbell rings. It's nice and loud after I replaced the battery. I open the door to a guy in his forties.

'Nina?' He rubs his hands together and blows on them. 'I'm Jason from Emergency Electrics. It's nippy out here. Winter's definitely come early.'

'Hi, come in. It's not much warmer inside, I'm afraid. Thanks so much for coming out tonight.'

'No worries. You said something about a broken switch?'

I show him the fuse box. 'Would you like a cup of tea? I can boil a saucepan – the stove is gas.'

'I'd kill for a coffee if you've got one.'

I busy myself making his drink and make myself a herbal tea at the same time.

'Here you go.'

'Lovely.' He cradles the mug in both hands. 'Not sure what happened here.' He nods at the fuse box. 'It's pretty hard to break a switch like that. Did you whack it with a hammer or something?' He smiles.

My earlier suspicions creep up again, but I don't want to verbalise my fears with a stranger. 'We haven't lived here long. The power went off and I found the fuse box already like that. Do you think you can fix it tonight?'

'I should be able to get the power back up and running for you, but that switch is knackered. I'll have to order a new one.'

'Okay, thanks so much. I'm dying to get the heating back on.'

'Not surprised. It's only just above freezing out there, but the wind chill's crazy.'

Within ten minutes, the flat is illuminated. The lights seem almost too harsh and bright after the dim glow of torchlight. The rooms feel stark. Cold. And then I hear the comforting whoosh of the boiler starting up.

'There you go.' Jason puts his tools back in his box and gets to his feet.

'Thanks so much. You're a lifesaver.'

He hands me an invoice and tells me he'll be in touch about the new switch. 'Thanks for the coffee. Nice flat you've got here.' He nods, glancing around before heading out the door, and I feel proud that we live here. That we own such a nice place. Even if it is bloody freezing right now.

Now that the place is tidy and everyone's gone, I don't know what to do with myself. I guess I may as well go to bed. There are messages from Amy, Sandra and a few others texting to see if I'm okay and to say they had a nice time. But I'm not sure that's true, because the evening only lasted half an hour. I fire back quick replies, apologising for the power cut and thanking them for coming. I'm disappointed that Mum didn't message, but maybe she'll call tomorrow. It's also a bit strange that Cali didn't text. But she was super helpful this evening so I shouldn't be too upset about it.

As I sit on the end of the bed to take off my slippers, I hear the key turn in the front door. I'm looking forward to a cuddle and some sympathy from Zac after my disaster of a night. The front door closes and I hear him walking up the hall and into the bathroom. I hear the flush of the toilet and the whoosh of the tap. Finally, he pushes open the bedroom door.

'Neens, you're still up. Wasn't sure if your thing would still be going on or you'd be in bed. How did it go? Why's it so cold in here?' His words are slurred and he's blinking a lot. 'You're wearing a hat and gloves. Have you been out?'

I tell him about the power cut and how it ruined the party. Recounting tonight's events has brought home how much of a disaster it's been. How much I was relying on this evening to boost my business. A rush of disappointment overwhelms me. My voice breaks and I realise I'm on the verge of tears.

'Oh, no. Thass rubbish. Ah, sorry.' Zac frowns. 'Why's it so cold?'

'I told you – there was a power cut.' I frown and blink at Zac's apparent lack of concern at how upset I am.

'Ah, yeah, yeah, yeah. You said that.' He stumbles out of his clothes and falls into bed. 'Come and warm me up.' He turns on his side and closes his eyes.

'My evening was ruined, Zac.' I take off my slippers, my suppressed tears of stress and disappointment turning to annoyance that he's not being more sympathetic. That he's not asking me about the evening at all. I know he's had a few drinks, but surely he could at least pretend to be interested.

'Mm, I know,' he mumbles into his pillow. 'That's really bad.'

'Zac!'

'What?' He opens an eye and looks at me as if I've woken him up from a deep sleep.

'Can I talk to you about it? I've put so much work into tonight and it was all for nothing.'

'Come to bed and tell me.'

I peel off my clothes and pull out a pair of warm pyjamas from the chest of drawers. By the time I get into bed Zac's fallen asleep. I shake his shoulder gently.

'Zac, wake up.'

'Nina, I'm tired,' he mumbles.

'So am I, but I thought my boyfriend might want to offer me a bit of support after my shitty evening. Obviously not!' I fling off the duvet and get up again. It's all too much. I'm cold, tired, pissed off, my whole body feels as if it's buzzing with a swarm of angry bees.

Zac's awake now, sitting up, a look of angry confusion on his face. I know tonight isn't his fault. I know he's tired and drunk. But I need him to care about me right now. And I want to tell him about the weird broken switch.

'Hey, Nina, are you annoyed?' He doesn't sound drunk any more. His eyes are focused on me.

'I'm just upset that you don't seem to care that I've had a terrible night.'

'*What?* Of course I care.'

'The sum total of your concern was "oh no".'

'What do you want me to say? You know I'm sorry your night didn't go well.'

'Are you? Because from where I'm standing it doesn't look like you give a shit.' I walk out of our room to the spare room at the back of the flat. There are a few discarded clothes on the double bed, a sore reminder of its brief use as a changing room. I grab the items and chuck them onto the chair in the corner, almost growling with frustration and disappointment. I know I probably overreacted by shouting at Zac, but it's too late now.

I peel back the bedcover and slip beneath the cold duvet, wondering if Zac will come find me. I make myself a deal that if he does come, I'll apologise and hopefully we can make up. I listen out for footsteps, but the house is quiet and still.

With a lump in my throat, I realise he's either really pissed off with me or he's fallen asleep again. Maybe I should go back in. Apologise. But I don't move.

Zac and I have always been quite different; that's what attracted us to each other in the first place. I loved his easy-going free-spirited nature. Most guys wanted to pin me down. To have me be their girlfriend, their wife or whatever. But Zac has never been like that. He just lets me be and doesn't want to put a label on our relationship. I also like that he isn't a pushover. If he doesn't agree with something, he'll say so.

He told me he was attracted to me by my drive and ambition. He liked that I'm not a high-maintenance woman who wants to be looked after. He appreciated my independence. He used to tease me that I could keep him in the manner to which he'd never been accustomed. But now it seems like the things that first attracted us, are the things that are pushing us apart.

I realise that I forgot to turn the light off, but I can't face getting out of bed to walk over to the switch by the door. I stare up at the unfamiliar ceiling with tears pricking the backs of my eyes. It feels like my goals are spiralling away into mist. I thought the move here was supposed to improve things, to set Zac and I on our way to our perfect life. Instead I'm really out of sorts. Not myself. Like I don't fit in my own skin. Like this house is against us. Doing everything it can to ruin my business and my relationship. Like this place hates me.

CHAPTER TWENTY

THEN

'What are you doing sitting here on your own?'

I look up to see a boy from my maths class. Adam. I don't know him that well. He's medium height with brown hair and nice eyes. He's not one of the popular football boys, but he's not a geek either. I realise I haven't answered his question, but I can't think of a reply.

He sits on the wall next to me. Not too close, which I appreciate, but not too far either. He smells nice. Clean. Not drowning in aftershave like some of the boys in my year.

'Sorry about your dad,' he says after a while.

'Thanks.'

'My dad died last year so I know how you feel. It's shit.'

I nod, not trusting myself to reply.

He takes something out of his backpack – a bright packet – and holds it out to me. 'Jelly babies. Want some?'

I take a couple – one green, one yellow – and we sit chewing sweets, staring out across the school field.

This feels okay. Better than before, anyway. I glance sideways at Adam and feel a little lighter.

CHAPTER TWENTY-ONE

I wake up in the spare room with a groan of remembrance. Did last night really happen? The power cut, the chaos, my failed event and, worst of all, my argument with Zac. It wasn't his fault but, in my grinding disappointment, I took it out on him.

I fell asleep with the light on, and now it's far too bright. I burrow under the covers for a moment, not wanting to face the day. All the tasks ahead of me feel like too much – sorting out the clothes in the dining room, assessing how much money I lost last night, apologising to Zac, hoping he isn't mad at me. My stomach is heavy with anxiety. This isn't like me at all.

I open my eyes properly and look for my phone to check the time. But I must have left it in our bedroom. I get out of bed. Okay, first things first, go and make things up with Zac. I inhale deeply and square my shoulders. Once I've apologised and he's forgiven me I know I'll feel better. That's another great thing about Zac – he's not one to hold grudges.

I remember we'd only been going out a few months when we had our first argument. I'd arranged to cook lunch for him at one o'clock and he didn't show up until after two. He breezed in and said sorry he was a bit late but he'd been helping a friend. I'd spent that hour thinking he wasn't going to show. That he was going off me. So when he turned up and casually apologised, I'd been furious. I told him that lunch was ruined and asked him to leave.

It transpired that his friend had had an asthma attack during their football training that morning. Zac had driven him to hospital and sat with him in A & E while he was waiting to be seen. Zac's phone had run out of battery so he couldn't call to let me know what was going on. When he finally showed up late, I hadn't given him a chance to explain.

I wouldn't have blamed Zac if he'd given me the cold shoulder after that – he'd done something good for a friend, and I'd jumped to conclusions. But instead, the next day, he made a picnic and brought it over to my flat by way of an apology, when it was me who should have been apologising. We made up very quickly, and ended up having the picnic in bed.

I head straight for our bedroom. At least the house has warmed up now. I think the heating must have been left on all night. I dread to think what the bill will come to this month. *Don't think about that now.*

Our room is empty, the bed unmade. I check the time on my alarm clock. Six twenty. I check the kitchen. There's a coffee mug and a cereal bowl in the sink. I do a quick tour of the rest of the flat, but Zac's not here. Peering out the lounge window into the frosty driveway, I see his van has gone. He's already left for work. He didn't wake me, or leave a note. Shit. He must be really annoyed.

I retrieve my phone from the bedside table in our room and sit on the bed to text him an apology. I wait for a moment, hoping he'll message back or call, but there's nothing. Trying to push out the anxiety in my belly, I take a couple of deep breaths and resolve to get on with my day.

I unlock the office at eight thirty not expecting Vanessa to come down until nine, but a few minutes later, she pops her head around the door.

'Morning. I saw you're in early and thought I may as well come down now.'

'Hi, Ness. Come in.'

'I'm so sorry the event was ruined. What a nightmare. Did you get the electrics fixed?'

'Eventually. Such a pain though. Of all the nights for that to happen.'

'Hopefully you can plan it for another evening?'

'I will. But I'll probably leave it a month or so. I'm not sure people will bother to come back if I do it too soon.'

'Makes sense.' Vanessa nods.

While Vanessa clears all the emails and packages up today's deliveries, I sort out the items from last night's event, bringing them back out to the stockroom and cataloguing all the sales on a spreadsheet. Things aren't quite as bad as I'd imagined – there was an early sales rush as people wanted to bag items before everyone else, and I've covered my costs plus a bit more. Added to that, my social-media feeds have been pinging away with likes, follows, posts and shares from my friends' networks. There are some really great images of the products, and the art-college models have also been sharing like crazy as well as tagging fashion bloggers who I'm hoping might share to their feeds.

By eleven thirty, I've finished bringing all of last night's stock back in and I'm feeling much more upbeat about things. The only niggle is that I haven't heard back from Zac yet. I know he gets busy at work, but surely he'd have a few seconds to send me a quick reply. Unless he's really mad at me. I did storm off and go to sleep in the other room. Shit. I'm going to have to do some serious grovelling later.

He usually breaks for his lunch at midday, so I'll try calling him then. I'm still kind of annoyed that he wasn't sympathetic about my disastrous night, but I also know what he's like when he's had a few drinks. He's a friendly drunk, but he does tend to get tired and fall asleep.

After a busy morning of clearing up, I've just sat at my desk when Vanessa turns to look at me with a worried expression.

'Erm, Nina…'

'What is it?'

'Have you got your emails open?'

'No, hang on.' I bring them up on my screen.

'Look at the one at the top with the subject header "Itchy". It's just come in.'

'Well that doesn't sound good,' I mutter, opening up the email and skim-reading it. 'She's saying one of our Carl Fallon tops is itchy and she's broken out in a rash. That can't be right, can it? Hang on, she's attached a photo.' I click on the attachment to see an image of a nasty red rash on her neck and stomach. 'Oh no, that looks awful! She said she wore it to her birthday dinner and it ruined her night. They're one of our most expensive tops, but I think we've already sold quite a few. Hang on, let me check.' I bring up my sales sheet and see that we've sold thirty-two of them to date. 'She said she's put it in the returns envelope today, but wanted to email us to let us know about the itching so we don't sell any more of them. She also wants a refund ASAP.' I realise I'm scratching my neck in sympathy.

'Have you had any other complaints about that top?' Vanessa asks.

I shake my head. 'No, nothing, and we've sold a few. What if all the tops cause the same issue? People don't necessarily wear things straight after they receive them. They might be hanging in someone's wardrobe waiting to be worn.'

'Maybe she's just allergic to the material,' Vanessa suggests.

'I suppose she might be. It's a stretch V-neck top, made from elastane. She bought it in black. Ugh, this is all I need. I'll have to apologise and refund her. I think I'll also give her a gift voucher, just in case. I don't want her to post anything negative online.'

'Good idea.'

'It might not even be the top,' I muse. 'Maybe it was a shower gel or body lotion and she just *thinks* it was the top.'

'Maybe,' Vanessa agrees.

'Anyway, you've been hard at it for three hours already, you get off. Thanks for all your hard work this morning.'

'No problem. Like I said, I enjoy it.' Vanessa picks up her phone and bag, gives me a little wave and heads back down the garden path.

I sit back in my chair and take a few deep breaths. Zac warned me it would be a lot of work to set up my own business, but I never realised it would be this challenging. It seems like every day there's a new disaster. I guess that's just the way of things, but maybe I was naive, thinking I'd smash it straightaway.

I inhale again, deeper and longer, blowing out my breath in one long steady stream. Come on, Nina, it's just an itchy top. Nothing to get too stressed about. This is minor-league stuff. It just feels worse because of last night, and because of Zac, that's all. I'll reply to the woman's email, speak to Zac, and then I'll feel much better. Even though what I really want to do right now is go back into the house, crawl into bed and sleep until today is over.

CHAPTER TWENTY-TWO

It's Monday morning and the office is looking a little messy, so I run a vacuum over the rug and tidy my desk. After last week's fall out with Zac, I managed to get hold of him at work on Friday and I apologised for getting angry at him. At first, he was resistant to my apology, giving me one-word responses and generally being moody. But then he too said he was sorry for not being more sympathetic. So we made up, but we're still not quite back on even ground. Over the weekend, things have been a bit shaky between us. Not moody as such, just… awkward.

It's one of Vanessa's days off so I'm on my own. I realise I miss having her here. She's quiet but capable. She knows how to be helpful without being intrusive. That's quite a skill. Although it's probably a good job I have the office to myself today because I've got another dreaded meeting with James Kipling. He called this morning to say he's in the area and could he pop in. I could hardly say no. Maybe he's just stopping by to say hello. Somehow I doubt it.

Goodness knows why he's coming round again so soon. It's only been a month since our last meeting. I guess I shouldn't be too surprised, as since then things with the business have been going from bad to worse. I should have asked him why he was coming. At least then I'd be able to prepare better. Instead, I'm panicking and imagining all sorts of worst-case-scenario situations.

After the itchy-top complaint last week, I've now had two more similar issues with the same item. One customer posted a horrible review online, and I also received a return first thing this morning asking for a refund. I contacted the designer, Carl Fallon, who said he's never had a complaint like that for any of his clothes, but he wondered if I might have contaminated them in some way. The tops are stored individually in recyclable plastic packaging so I don't see how that could be possible.

Most of my designers send Mistletoe Lane orders direct to the customer using my branded delivery boxes, which I supply to them. But, in some cases – such as bestsellers like Carl Fallon – the designers send me a batch of products on a sale-or-return basis, and I send them out to the customer from here.

I immediately sent the returned items back to him and he's sending them off to a lab for testing. I already tried on one of the new tops to see if there was a problem. I wore it for a few hours and it was fine – no allergic reaction whatsoever. In the meantime, I've delisted them from the website. It's so frustrating as they're my bestseller.

My stomach swoops as the doorbell rings. That must be James. I bought an extra receiver for the office so that I can hear the bell and don't miss visitors while I'm working. I'm also going to get a secure storage bin for the driveway so that my deliveries can be left when I'm out or working. That should please Tricia. I took her some flowers by way of an apology, but she's still quite cold towards me despite wanting to attend my Mistletoe Lane party. Hopefully, she'll thaw out over time.

With clammy hands and a thumping heart, I head down the garden and through the side gate to let James in. I decide to be upbeat and friendly. No point in jumping the gun and assuming the worst.

'Hi, James. Nice to see you. What brings you down this way?'

'Hello, Nina. Shall we go into your office?' He's friendly enough but he doesn't actually smile, which is a bit off-putting.

I offer him a drink this time, but he declines. Once we're seated at my desk, he jumps right in.

'So, how do you feel things have been going?'

'Good, I think. Sales are steady.'

'Any thoughts on how to move from "steady" to "increasing"?'

'I'm planning exclusive events where I invite influencers and bloggers.' This sounds better than telling him it's a party at home for friends and family.

James nods thoughtfully. 'Is that going to be expensive to organise?'

'Not at all. I've already made a great contact at the fashion department of the Arts University. They're all really enthusiastic about it and have offered to model the clothes and help spread the word.' There's no point telling him about my failed event at home. The power cut was completely outside my control.

'What about this assistant of yours? Mr Newbury and I don't think you should be employing anybody just yet. We need the money to be flowing in, not out. We were initially impressed by your proactive attitude and your willingness to get this off the ground yourself with hard work and long hours. Mr Newbury's capital was invested specifically for stock and business premises. Not to foot a wage bill.'

I swallow. 'That's why she's not on a permanent contract. It's a casual freelance basis. Vanessa concentrates on the day-to-day admin, which frees me up to sort out the bigger things that will help spread the word and bring in the sales.'

'Look, Nina. I know admin isn't fun or glamorous, but it's all part of running a business. Especially a start-up. It also gives you a feel for your customers. It's a way of connecting you to the business.'

I bristle at his implication that I'm not down-to-earth enough to do the basics. 'I still do most of it.' It's a struggle to keep my tone light. To not become emotional. 'Vanessa's only doing three hours a day, three days a week. But I guess I can ask her to do fewer hours.'

James purses his lips and shakes his head. 'No. I think we'd like to see a higher turnover before taking on any staff.'

'So, what are you saying?' I clench my fists under the desk.

'I'm saying that we're not happy with your decision to employ someone, freelance or not.'

'So, what? I have to let her go?'

'I think that would be best. There's also something else we need to discuss.'

I take a breath, still reeling from the realisation that I'm going to have to tell Vanessa that I don't need her any more. She's only been with me a few weeks. She's going to be so disappointed. And I'm really going to miss her. I've already come to rely on her so much. 'What's the other thing?' I ask, hoping it's not more bad news.

'Have you looked at your Trustpilot reviews recently?'

'Uh, yes, I think so. Last time I looked they were great. I think the average was around 4.8 out of 5.'

'When was that?' James slides a tablet from his black messenger bag.

'Last week, I think.' I normally check it every evening, but things have been hectic and I promised Zac I'd make more time for him since our row after my failed event.

'If you'd checked more recently, you'd see that your average has dipped to 3.7.'

'*What?* No, that can't be right.' My stomach knots.

James hands me his tablet. It's open on the Mistletoe Lane Trustpilot page. The knot in my belly tightens as I scan down the page. All the most recent reviews, except for a couple, are one and two stars.

Terrible customer service. Zero stars.

Would I use ML again? No.
Would I recommend them? No.
Will I shop elsewhere and find a business who appreciate the custom? Yes.

Loved the top, but it was quite expensive and brought me out in a rash. Steer clear!

Late delivery. Rude staff. Avoid.

My face heats up and I feel as though I've entered another universe. 'These are…' My voice tails off.

'It's not great, is it?' James presses his lips together in a thin line.

'I don't understand, though. The only complaints we've had are for one particular top that caused a bit of itchiness. I've refunded those customers and apologised profusely. I'm always super polite, and so is Vanessa. I can show you some of the emails sent by satisfied customers, if you like. And the comments on our Facebook ads are really glowing.'

'That's all very well, but what are we going to do about these negative ones? You need to get that average back up. It might be what's contributing to your stalling sales.'

'What if it's just trolls or someone trying to sabotage the business? A competitor or something like that? You hear about that happening, don't you? Rival companies with no scruples.'

'I thought the same,' James replies, with a hint of sympathy creeping into his voice. 'But I checked the reviewers and they all seem to have legitimate names and reviewing histories.'

'They could have been faked though, couldn't they?' I wonder who would do such a thing. I don't have any enemies as such. And I'm surely not big enough to be a threat to other similar style companies. There's enough room for all of us. For a second, Belinda flits across my mind. She was going on about how online businesses are ruining the high street. Surely she wouldn't be so vindictive…

'Whatever the reason, you're going to have to up the customer service. Get your image back on track. The last thing we want is for your business to fail before it even gets going. Reputation is everything. *We* want you to succeed as much as *you* do.'

I nod and chew my lip, desperate to maintain a calm exterior. I'm a businesswoman, not an emotional wreck. Even though I'm wobbling inside.

After James has gone, I make myself a strong coffee and steel myself to scroll through the bad reviews. I examine each reviewer and attempt to match them up with my customer orders. I'm only able to link one of them to a genuine customer, and that's the one about the itchy top. Which leads me to believe that the others might not be genuine. But why would someone try to sabotage my business in this way and, more importantly, *who*?

Zac's home early for a change so I decide to cook something decent rather than grabbing a ready meal or having something on toast. We need to get our relationship back to a good place. He comes into the kitchen after changing out of his work clothes.

'What shall we eat tonight?'

I peer in the fridge. There's not a lot in there. 'Want me to make risotto?' It's Zac's favourite.

'Risotto would be great.' He pours himself a glass of water. 'Good day?'

With everything still quite fragile between us, I don't want to add bad news into the mix. 'It was fine.'

'Just fine?'

'Yeah. How about you?'

'The part for my customer's sink arrived broken, so she's really pissed off. That's why I'm home early. I've got to rearrange this week's work now. It's such a pain.'

'Customers, right?' I shake my head.

'Yeah but yours are all good though, aren't they?'

I shrug, not trusting myself to speak.

'Neens?'

I let out a half-growl half-sigh. 'I had a few shitty reviews recently and it's got me down.'

'Oh.' He gives me a sympathetic look.

My shoulders sag.

'Hey.' Zac comes and stands next to me by the fridge. He pulls me in for a cuddle.

I squeeze him back and it feels nice to just be held. We stay like that for a moment and I breathe in his warm scent. Finally, I pull away.

'Don't worry, Nina. Everyone gets bad reviews. What's your favourite fashion brand?'

'I don't know. I don't have one. That's why I created my own.'

'Okay, then give me the name of some really popular successful brands.'

I name the first two that come to mind.

Zac reaches for his phone on the counter and starts tapping and scrolling. 'So listen to this. These are some of their latest bad reviews: *Cheap and nasty dress that looks like a bag.* And another: *This company sucks. They don't care about their customers.* What about this one… *bought my daughter these cute puppy slippers and both noses fell off. Not happy.* See…' Zac nudges me in the ribs. 'At least your noses didn't fall off.'

I roll my eyes. 'What are you talking about?'

'Nina? Did your nose fall off?'

'No.'

'Well then. It's not all bad, is it?'

'You're such an idiot, Zac.' I smile despite myself.

'Yeah, but at least my nose didn't fall off.'

He makes a stupid face and I can't help laughing.

'I hate that things have been weird between us recently,' I say, opening the fridge and pulling out some veggies.

'I know,' he agrees. 'It's because everything's too hectic in our lives.'

'Well that's not about to change any time soon.'

'That's what worries me.' Zac points to the chopping board. 'Want me to do anything? Chop anything up?'

'Aside from bad reviewers?' I start rinsing some green beans under the tap.

Zac shakes his head. 'Put those reviews out of your mind. Let's just have a nice evening.'

'Okay.' I nod, wishing it were as simple as *putting it out of my mind*. On top of the bad reviews, I've also got James and Mr Newbury on my back as well as the added worry of speaking to Vanessa tomorrow. I don't want to unload all that onto Zac, but the alternative is that it fizzes around in my brain. I want to have a nice, relaxed evening, but it all feels so impossible right now.

CHAPTER TWENTY-THREE

I walk across the frosty drive towards the pavement to bring the recycling bin back in. They always collect the rubbish really early so we have to put the bin out the night before. After yesterday's bombshell from James Kipling, I'm not looking forward to today. To telling Vanessa she can't stay on. To trying to get my company's reputation back on track.

I pause when I hear voices from out on the pavement beyond the hedge. I'm pretty sure it's Chris talking.

'Sorry, who?' he asks.

'The man in the suit. Very smart. I've seen him here before. He only comes round when her boyfriend's out.'

I tense with outrage. Tricia from next door is gossiping to Chris about me and James Kipling, I'm sure of it. I stay where I am, straining my ears to hear more.

'I don't know him, Tricia. Sorry.'

Well that's a lie. Chris had an argument with James last month in this very driveway. Although, I guess he might not have known who he was. He may have thought he was a snooping stranger, like Zac suggested when he was sticking up for Chris.

'I just thought it was odd, that's all,' Tricia adds. 'We all need to keep an eye out for strangers in the neighbourhood.'

'Sure,' Chris adds. 'Anyway, I better put this bin back and get off to work.'

'Of course. You go. Is Vanessa okay?'

'Fine thanks.'

I hear a bin being wheeled across the tarmac and wonder whether I should dart back inside. But then they might see me and realise I've been eavesdropping. Instead, I continue walking out onto the pavement and give Chris a friendly smile.

'Morning.'

He nods and keeps wheeling his bin without changing his blank expression.

Charming. As I go to fetch our bin, I see Tricia's receding shape wheeling her bin into her driveway. I scowl at her back, annoyed with her for gossiping about me. For insinuating that something might be going on with me and James. I shouldn't let it bother me. She's obviously bored with her life if she has to invent stories about the neighbours.

I turn back towards the drive with a sigh as I remember the task that lies ahead of me today. I need to regain my enthusiasm and drive. Everything I do lately seems to end in disaster. I had this pure vision of a fresh, ethical, sustainable fashion brand that's all about being body positive and making my customers feel good. I knew it would be hard work and that there would be obstacles to overcome, but now I'm in the thick of it with all this negativity flying at me from every angle, I'm not sure if I'm tough enough to do it. I just need one thing to go right. One spark to keep me going.

Ten minutes later, with my heart in my mouth, I sit at my desk and open up the Trustpilot site. It's worse than I imagined. Overnight, Mistletoe Lane's average has plummeted from 3.7 to 3.2, with seventeen new reviews, twelve of which are negative. The comments sear themselves onto my brain: *rude… terrible customer service… wouldn't touch with a bargepole… cheap and nasty.* The green one-stars burn my retinas. I slam my laptop closed. This can't be happening. I pride myself on my customer service and politeness, and I've heard Vanessa on the phone – she's lovely.

These reviews must be a rival company, or a disgruntled customer who's made multiple fake accounts. They can't be real, can they?

For the second time, I wonder if it might be Belinda. She obviously doesn't like me for some reason and has no problem being passive-aggressive to my face. But to wilfully sabotage my business? Is she really that bad? I rack my brains to think who else might do such a thing. Do I have any actual enemies? Could it be the same person who broke the switch? If indeed anyone did break it on purpose…

If this morning is anything to go by, then Tricia is still pretty frosty towards me. I know my business has already caused her some inconvenience. Perhaps she doesn't like the idea of me working from home, having a business next door to her. I don't really know her that well, but I can't imagine she would do something like this. Surely she wouldn't be that petty after I apologised. Maybe I should add a bottle of wine or some chocolates to the flowers just to make sure she's appeased. It can't hurt. Although, she doesn't deserve them after shamelessly gossiping to Chris about me.

I should also try to get on better with Belinda, even if she can be a cow. But, no, I can't think about her like that. I need to shift my attitude. Give our relationship a chance to improve.

If Vanessa weren't working here, I'd almost suspect Chris, because his attitude towards me is pretty rude and dismissive. But I can't imagine he would want to sabotage the place where his wife works. Not when it was him who asked Zac about it in the first place. That makes no sense.

Out of all my theories, I really hope it is a rival company behind the bad reviews, and not dissatisfied customers or someone I know personally. I can take professional espionage far easier than my brand failing or personal hatred. I reopen my laptop and bang out a quick email to Trustpilot's customer service department asking them to investigate. Maybe they'll be able to tell me if the reviews are genuine or not.

The door to my office opens, and Vanessa walks in, rubbing her hands to warm them up. She almost always arrives early.

'Morning, Nina.'

'Hi, Vanessa.'

I'm not looking forward to having this conversation. My throat is tight and I can barely get my words out.

'You okay? You look worried.'

I don't want to launch straight into telling her she doesn't have a job any longer. I clear my throat. 'I had a meeting with my investor's representative yesterday. It was a bit of a wake-up call.'

She shrugs off her coat, hangs it over the back of her chair and sits down. 'Oh?'

I won't go into detail about the whole worrying situation with the reviews and the sales figures, but I guess I have to let her know that her new part-time job is over for now. 'They're not happy about a few things.'

'Really?' She frowns. 'I'd have thought they'd be pleased with your success. You're getting lots of orders.'

'Not enough, apparently. There've been a few bad reviews too.'

'Bad reviews? Where? Not on your social-media ads, I check them daily and customers are loving the brand.'

'Trustpilot, mainly.' All those horrible comments from the one-star reviews march through my brain like vicious little soldiers.

'*Trustpilot?* What's that?'

'It's a review website.'

She wrinkles her nose. 'I can't imagine too many people would bother with that.'

'You'd be surprised.'

'Well, I'm sure it's just a blip,' she offers, opening her laptop.

'Thanks, I hope so.'

'Shall I just get on with the emails? Or have you got anything specific for this morning?'

I take a breath. 'The thing is, Vanessa, my investor has told me that because things are taking a while to get going, I can't employ anyone at the moment. It's nothing to do with you. It's just with orders being slow and money being tight, and the bad reviews…'

Her face pales for a moment before she pulls herself together. 'You mean *me*, right? You can't employ me any more?'

'Unfortunately not. I'm so sorry. You've been nothing but brilliant, and once things pick up I'll be more than happy to offer you more work. I feel terrible about this. Especially as you've only been here such a short time.'

'It's not because… I mean… Was it something I did?'

'Gosh, no! Not at all. It's purely because of my investor. Because they don't think the business can afford to hire people right now. That's all. And, like I said, I'd love to have you come back at a later date, if you want to, of course.'

She gets to her feet and picks up her coat. Her eyes are bright, as if she might be about to cry. 'Okay, I understand.'

'I hope so. I hope you also know that you've been brilliant.'

'Thanks,' she replies. But she doesn't look as though she believes me.

After she's gone, I sit at my desk for a few minutes staring into space. I feel like a right cow. I guess I should never have taken her on in the first place, not without running it past James. I hate the fact that Newbury Ltd are so involved. That I can't simply do what I think is best.

After a few minutes of feeling sorry for myself, I decide that today I'm going to try to cut off any possible negativity towards me and my company. I spend the next hour replying to the negative reviews, apologising and asking each reviewer to get in touch so we can resolve their issues. I wonder if any of them will take me up on the offer. Or whether they are indeed all written by the same person.

Once that's done, I grab a nice bottle of red wine from the dining room and head next door. Tricia doesn't seem pleased to see me but I smile and hand her the bottle, hoping she feels guilty for bad-mouthing me this morning.

'Just another little apology for all the parcels you ended up with.'

'Oh.' She looks at the wine and sniffs. 'You didn't need to do that. You already brought me flowers.'

'I know, but I felt terrible about it. We haven't been here long and the last thing we wanted to do was upset our neighbours.'

'Well, thank you.'

'No problem.' I turn to go.

'How's Vanessa?' she asks.

I turn back.

'I haven't seen her in a while,' Tricia says. 'What is she now… eight months?'

'Seven, I think.'

Tricia nods. 'I always worry about that girl.'

'Worry in what way?' I ask, wondering if she feels the same unease about Chris as I do.

'She looks like she's got the weight of the world on her shoulders.'

I nod, but I don't want to be a gossip.

Tricia reaches out to touch my shoulder. 'Just… keep an eye on her, will you? I don't think she has any friends or family looking out for her. Apart from her husband.' She gives a disapproving sniff.

Hearing this makes me feel doubly bad about earlier. What if working with me was more than just a little job for Vanessa? What if it was giving her purpose, keeping her sane? What if it was her only respite from Chris?

CHAPTER TWENTY-FOUR

The bus lurches away from the pavement while I'm still swaying along the aisle to find a seat. There are plenty available, but most kids have blocked them with their bags, saving them for their friends who'll get on at stops further along the route to school. No one has ever saved a seat for me. Of course, my brother disowns me the second he steps on the bus. But I don't care any more because everything has flipped around.

Home life is miserable. Mum barely speaks to me and on the rare occasions my brother comes out of his room, he's either moody or sarcastic. So I also find myself hiding away in my room. It's the only place where I can relax. Where I can close my eyes and picture sunny days where the four of us used to be connected and happy. Where I felt secure and cherished. Instead of the reality of now – three people living alongside one another without sharing anything. Each locked in our own private misery. The one person who held us together, now gone.

I wonder what it would be like if Mum was warm towards me. If she was a hugger, a kisser, a talker. Rather than saying nothing, and then snapping. I know she's lost her husband, but I can't forgive her coldness. I see her cast loving glances towards my brother. When did she stop sending them to me?

In contrast, school has become the place I can't wait to be. Each morning, even as I navigate the social minefield of the school bus, there's a flutter of anticipation in my stomach. Even my family has noticed that I'm making more effort over my appearance. Not that they ever compliment me on it. No. Instead I get comments like: 'Who are you making such an effort for?' and 'I don't know why you're bothering.'

The reason for this anticipation is Adam. We hang out every day now. At break and at lunch. Annoyingly he lives in Highcliffe, which is just a short walk away from school, whereas I have to get the bus all the way back to Friars Cliff. I would love it if we got to travel to and from school together, rather than having to endure the daily torture of the bus. I'd prefer to sit on my own, but I'm usually forced to sit next to the other social outcasts, who I don't get along with either.

Today, the only seat available to me is next to Matthew Granger, who has terrible dandruff and stinks of BO. Of course I feel a bit sorry for him, but the smell is terrible. I worry that it will permeate my hair and clothes so I angle myself away and perch right on the edge of the seat, daydreaming about Adam.

CHAPTER TWENTY-FIVE

It takes us almost an hour to battle through the Saturday-afternoon traffic to Westbourne. Zac's driving my VW Golf as it's comfier than the van. He wasn't keen on coming here, as we'd promised to spend the day together doing something nice. But I made a bargain, suggesting we could also get a coffee and have a beach walk at Alum Chine.

This afternoon is all part of my plan to bond more with Belinda. She's important to my brother, so I should at least give her another chance and show that I'm interested in her life. Who am I kidding? This is more about winning her over in case she's the one behind the awful reviews. Not having her dislike me as much will be an added benefit.

Westbourne is a pretty suburb close to the beach with an upmarket shopping centre full of bougie boutiques, quirky coffee shops, cool bars and classy restaurants. Belinda's clothing boutique sits in a prime location on the main street just outside a characterful arcade. I've only been in a couple of times, as it's quite a snooty shop and the clothes are way outside my price range.

It's always busy in Westbourne, and previously we've had to drive several times around the one-way system before finding a parking space. But today, as Zac cruises down the main drag, I spot a parked car waiting to pull out. Zac slows and flashes his headlights at the driver, who pulls out, letting Zac expertly nip into the space which just happens to be opposite Belinda's.

We exit the car and pull our coats tighter around us against the cold wind, waiting for a gap in traffic so we can cross the road. I've toned down my look today, wearing black jeans, brown boots, a luxurious white sweater and a brown faux fur coat. My hair falls over my shoulders in gleaming brown waves. Zac looks handsome in jeans, trainers, a navy cable-knit jumper and a black wool coat and scarf.

'We won't be long here will we, Neens?' Zac looks up at the sky. 'It looks like it might rain and I'm desperate for a walk, I need fresh air. Maybe we should go to the beach first? Come here on our way back.'

I shiver and glance up too. 'I don't know where those clouds have come from. It was clear blue sky when we left home.'

'It's so annoying,' Zac replies. 'So… beach now, Belinda's later?'

'We're here now. Let's just go in and get it over with.' I take his arm as we cross, but he's grumpy and unwilling. I pause outside the shopfront. 'You'll be nice though, right? I'm trying to make her like me. She's marrying Henry next year. I need to show I'm interested in her life.'

'Yes, I'll be nice,' Zac grumbles.

I kiss him and push open the door.

Inside, I spy Belinda at the back of the shop. It looks like she's explaining something to one of her staff. There are a few customers browsing the minimalist chrome racks of clothes – thirty- and forty-something slim polished women who look as if they spend a lot of time in the gym. I dressed specifically for this visit, but I already feel hugely out of place.

We head towards Belinda, who still hasn't spotted us. As we draw closer she looks up and scans our outfits, frowning, before settling her gaze on our faces. Recognition dawns. 'Nina! And Zac!' She turns to her colleague. 'Sam, this is Henry's sister, Nina, and her boyfriend, Zac.'

We all say hello and then Sam moves off to serve a customer. So far, Belinda has seemed quite pleased to see us. Almost gushy. It feels strange.

'What are you two doing in Westbourne?'

'Well, after you made the effort to come to visit us a couple of times, I thought we'd come over to see you and pop into the shop. I haven't been here in a while. It's looking lovely, by the way.'

'Yeah, really nice,' Zac adds, sounding bored stiff. If we were at a table, I'd kick him under it.

'Oh, well, that's lovely of you,' Belinda replies. 'We've recently had a refit. I like to keep things fresh. Are you looking for anything in particular?' She looks me up and down with a worried expression. I can tell she's thinking that nothing here will fit me.

'No, not really. Like I said, we're here to see you. Although I did notice a gorgeous zebra-print scarf in the window that I might try on.'

She relaxes a touch. 'Yes, I know the one. It would definitely suit you. It's quite expensive though. But I can give you the friends-and-family discount.'

'Thanks, that's kind.'

Suddenly she stiffens and her eyes narrow. 'I don't think any of our labels would be right for your brand, though, if that's why you're here.'

'Sorry?'

'You know, for Mistletoe Lane. Our labels are high-end designers. They wouldn't be suitable for your company.'

'No, of course not. We're appealing to different customers.'

'Oh, good. It's just… we don't normally see you over this way. I wondered if you might be scoping out the competition.' She raises an eyebrow and tries to smile, but it's obvious she believes she might be on to something.

'Nina just wanted to be friendly,' Zac says gruffly. 'She said that since you're marrying her brother, she'd like to get to know you better. This visit is nothing to do with her business.'

I could kiss Zac right now.

'Oh.' Belinda starts fiddling with a jewellery display on the wall. 'Well, yes, I suppose we probably should get to know one another better. It's not like we were friends at school or anything.'

I think this is a veiled dig at me. I was quite popular at school and didn't pay her too much attention. I was never mean. I just didn't really know her. She was a hard worker, but didn't exactly have many friends. We didn't move in the same social circles.

'Maybe the four of us should go out for a meal some time?' I suggest.

Belinda purses her pouty lips. 'If I can get Henry to commit to a date – you know how busy he is – then yes, that would be great.'

I still haven't gauged whether or not she might be the one responsible for trying to sabotage my company, but it's not exactly something I can come right out and ask. Then again, I can't stand here and say nothing.

'What do you think of Trustpilot?' I ask.

'Sorry, of *what*?' She reddens and frowns, which makes me instantly alert.

'You, know, the review site, Trustpilot?'

'Oh, yes, sorry, I misheard you. Thought you said *trespassing*!' She gives a short laugh. 'Yes, it's a blessing and a curse, isn't it? Of course the majority of our reviews online are glowing, but you always get the odd mean one, don't you?'

I nod, unwilling to share Mistletoe Lane's dismal ratings. Whether she's behind the bad reviews or not, I don't want to give her the satisfaction of knowing it has me worried.

We stay and make small talk for a couple more minutes. Before long, she's needed by a customer. Zac and I say our goodbyes and leave the store. I forgot to try on the zebra scarf, but it's probably just as well as it would have been far too expensive, even with a discount. All the price labels in the window are facing down, hidden from the customer. If you have to ask the price, you know you can't afford it.

The sky outside has darkened further. Zac and I dart across the road and get into the car.

'Thanks for sticking up for me in there.' I pull my seat belt across.

'I can't believe she thought you were going there to snoop. Talk about paranoid.' Zac noses the Golf out into the stream of traffic and turns left down Alumhurst Road, towards the sea.

'She's a strange one. But Henry obviously loves her, or he wouldn't have proposed.'

'I reckon she bullied him into it.' Zac shakes his head. 'Tell me we don't have to go for dinner with them.'

'Well, we will at some point. But I'll try to put it off until next year.' I'm still no nearer to finding out if she's the one behind the horrible reviews, but she's not exactly going to come out and admit it. My senses say it's probably not her, but it's impossible to know for sure, especially after her initial reaction when she claimed she misheard me.

As we pull into the beach car park, heavy spots of rain begin to fall and Zac's expression darkens.

'I told you we should've gone for a walk first.'

'Come on, it's not too heavy. We can get a takeaway coffee and if we get wet it doesn't matter. It'll be fine.'

But as we head from the car park towards the promenade, people are streaming off the beach. We're the only people heading that way. We hurry to the café kiosk but the shutters are already closing as the heavy black clouds open. The rain comes down in torrents.

'You were saying?' Zac has to raise his voice over the gushing rain and crashing waves.

We turn and race back towards the car.

'Sorry, I didn't think it would be so heavy,' I pant. 'It wasn't forecast. Why don't we head back into Westbourne to grab a coffee? There's a lovely little place right down near the church that does fresh pastries.'

But Zac is annoyed with me. I'd promised we'd spend today doing something nice together and it's all gone astray. I should have listened to him and gone for a walk first.

'We'll never get parked again,' he says as we slide into the car, soaking wet. 'Let's just go home.'

'Okay.' I glance across at him, hoping to win him over with an apologetic smile, but he's staring straight ahead, his jaw rigid, his eyes hard.

CHAPTER TWENTY-SIX

After a tense car journey, we're finally back home. From initially feeling remorseful, I'm now becoming annoyed with Zac for being so moody. After all, it's not my fault that the weather turned bad and we couldn't have a walk. When did things between us start to become so tense? There was a time, not so long ago, when we would have laughed about getting caught in the rain. When we would have revelled in getting soaking wet, been exhilarated by it. We would have made it into a fun afternoon and gone for a cosy coffee afterwards.

A bit of bad weather wouldn't normally make Zac so angry. He loves the outdoors. He likes being in the fresh air – rain or shine. I don't know how he's going to cope when we start doing the renovations and he's at home all day. Today has made me wonder whether we might need to rethink that idea.

We change out of our wet clothes in awkward silence. I can't bear the thought of us ignoring one another all weekend. Of Zac sulking and me treading on eggshells again. This isn't like us. We're not that kind of couple.

I can't decide what to wear, so I decide to go straight for pyjamas. We're not going out tonight, so I may as well be comfy. The doorbell chimes. Zac goes to answer it without even looking at me. I sigh and wonder how we're going to get out of this cloud of bad feeling. Maybe I'll just apologise again, even though it's not all my fault. But it's better than the status quo.

I hear Zac talking to someone on the doorstep. I tug on my slippers and head out into the hall as Zac closes the front door. He turns to me with an enormous bouquet of flowers.

'Who are they for?' I ask.

'You, apparently.' He hands them to me. It's an ostentatious arrangement of red roses, carnations, and other red, white and pink flowers.

'Who are they from?'

'Don't know.' Zac peels a card off the cellophane. 'Shall I read it?'

'Okay.'

He opens it and reads aloud. '*Thanks for this week Nina, love J xx.*' Zac scowls. 'Who the hell's "J"?'

'I've got no idea,' I reply, baffled. 'The only "J" I can think of is James Kipling. But he certainly wouldn't be thanking me or sending me flowers.'

'*James?* You mean that investor's lackey?'

'He's not a lackey! I suppose it could be him. Maybe it's like a corporate gift or something. Bit weird though.' I'm puzzled. I'm almost certain they're not from James. But who else could it be?

'Why are there two kisses at the end of it?' Zac has never been the jealous type, so I'm not sure why he's getting funny about this. Maybe because he's already in a bad mood. If we'd had a nice day out together, perhaps we'd be laughing about this instead of arguing.

'Look, let's just forget the flowers. I think they must have been sent by mistake.'

'How is it a mistake? Your name's on the card, Nina.' He waves it at me then tosses it onto the coffee table.

'I'm going to have a glass of wine.' I head to the kitchen. 'You want a beer?'

'Yeah.' He goes into the living room and I hear him switch on the TV.

I place the bouquet on the draining board, although there's no way I'll be putting the flowers into a vase, so maybe I should just throw them out.

I shouldn't really be drinking wine as I have work to do later. But I'm stressed, and one glass won't hurt. I pour Zac's beer, and then pour myself a generous glass of Sauvignon Blanc, taking both glasses into the lounge. Zac's pacing the room on his phone, speaking loudly over the sound of a panel show on the TV. I set down our drinks and pick up the remote to mute the TV.

Zac ends the call, picks up his beer and downs half the glass.

'Who was that?' I ask, taking a sip of my wine.

'I called the florist.'

'The *florist*?'

'The name and number was on the card. It's a place in Bournemouth. The woman on the phone said the order was paid for in cash and they don't have the name of the person who ordered it.'

'That's a bit over the top, isn't it? Calling the florist?'

'It's not over the top to worry about who's sending my girlfriend flowers.' He sits on the couch, his face dark as thunder.

'Zac?'

'What?' he snaps.

'You're not seriously jealous, are you? I already told you I don't know who the flowers are from.'

'Are you sure?'

'I swear, Zac. The only people I can think of with names beginning with J are James, and my mum, Joanna. But my mum has never sent me flowers and if she did, she'd never send such a garish bouquet! She also wouldn't sign it "J". James is giving me some grief about the business right now, so it's definitely not him, and I can't imagine him shortening his name or adding two kisses.'

Zac shakes his head. 'Well, it's weird.'

'I know.' I go to take another sip of wine and am surprised to see my glass is empty. 'Just going to top up my drink. Do you want another?'

'Please.' He drains his glass and hands it to me.

As I return to the kitchen, I realise I'm already a little drunk. I top up our glasses and head back to the lounge where Zac is again on his feet, pacing.

'Are you okay?' I ask, handing him his beer.

He shrugs. 'The card said *thank you for this week*. What did you do this week?'

'I don't know. I already told you about having to let Vanessa go.'

Zac stops pacing for a moment and turns to stare at me. 'Yeah, you said James told you she had to go. Did he call you?'

I don't answer immediately.

'Nina?'

'He came round on Monday for a meeting. That's when he told me about the bad reviews and said I couldn't employ anyone yet.'

'He came round?'

'Yes. He was in the area.'

'So why didn't you tell me he was here?'

'I thought I had.'

He raises his eyebrows. 'You thought you had? Well that's a lie. You know you didn't tell me.'

I puff out a breath of air and take another gulp of my drink. 'Only because I didn't want to worry you. He came bearing bad news. You're already stressed about work; I didn't want to overburden you.'

Zac shakes his head. 'No.'

'What do you mean, "no"?'

'I mean, no. That's a cop out. I always tell you when my work sucks, and you do the same. What's the real reason you didn't tell me about him coming round?'

'I told you the reason!' My heart is beating double time. I can't believe the turn our conversation has taken.

Zac downs his beer and marches out of the living room.

I can barely hear anything over the rapid tap of my heart. This conversation is spiralling out of control.

'Zac!' I try to steady my breathing and follow him out of the room. I hear clattering from the kitchen. He reappears with his drink topped up and we go back into the living room. His eyes are glassy and he looks like he's already halfway to drunk.

I think I'd be better getting out of his way for a while. Leave him to calm down.

'Look, Zac. James is a colleague, end of story, and I have no idea who sent those flowers. Why don't I go and catch up on work for an hour or so and you can relax and watch a movie or something.' As soon as the words tumble from my lips, I know I've said the wrong thing.

Zac shakes his head and sits down heavily on the sofa. 'It's Saturday night, Nina, and you're telling me you have to go and work. Ever since you started this business, you've been stressed, and we've been arguing.'

'That's not true,' I reply. Although a part of me acknowledges that things haven't exactly been great lately. 'Look, I'd got used to Vanessa's help and I'm struggling getting it all done right now, that's all. Plus, I'm locked out of my accounting software and need to update my password. There are just a few small things I have to get sorted before Monday and then I'll come back in and we'll get a takeaway or something.' I'm struggling to hold myself together right now. Is Zac really blaming all our recent troubles on my business?

'Why did you let Vanessa go if it was working so well with her?' Zac frowns across at where I'm standing by the door, poised to make my escape from this confrontation.

'I already told you. It's because James said—'

'Yeah, James said *this*, James said *that*,' Zac snaps. 'Newbury invested in the business, but it's still *yours*. You should be able to run it how you want, otherwise what's the point? You may as well go and work for someone else!'

I realise that Zac's put into words exactly what I've been thinking. Recently I've been feeling trapped by Newbury's involvement. By his scrutiny and demands.

Zac keeps going. 'Is working all the hours really worth it? You know I support you and your ambitions, but this isn't fun, is it?'

I shrug.

'You know what?' he says, waggling his finger at me. 'We should both jack it all in and go travelling.'

'Oh, for goodness' sake, Zac. It always comes back to that, doesn't it? To you feeling trapped and wanting to go off travelling where you can live a life with no responsibility.'

'What's wrong with that? In my opinion, that would be a great way to live.'

'Because at some point we have to put down roots and start building a life. We have to have something to aim for. We're in our thirties, do you want to be a wanderer forever? Do you want to wake up at sixty with *nothing* but a few memories of some nice beaches?'

'Wanting to take a couple of years to go travelling is hardly being a wanderer forever. Wouldn't you like to leave all this shit behind, and have some fun for a change?'

'Of course, that sounds amazing. But is that actually reality, or is it just… I don't know, some childish fantasy?'

'Oh, well, thanks a lot. Nice to know you think I'm childish and a fantasist.'

'That's not what I meant.'

'So why did you say it?' He slams his empty glass on the coffee table. 'Know what, Nina? Go to your office and do your work. It obviously means more to you than anything else. I'd hate to keep you from achieving your goals.' He gets up, walks past me and goes into the bedroom, slamming the door behind him.

'Nice.' I exhale. My whole body is trembling with shock and rage. How can our evening have descended into such a disaster over a bunch of bloody flowers?

I stand in the hallway, unsure what to do. Should I go into the bedroom and try to talk to Zac? I honestly don't know who sent those flowers, and what's wrong with my dream of owning my own business? Did I force Zac into settling down before he was ready? I don't think so. But, then again, I can't read his mind. Maybe he's holding on to all these hopes and dreams that he's not talking about. Maybe he blames me for this stressful period in our lives.

How did today turn into such a disaster?

CHAPTER TWENTY-SEVEN

I take a step towards the bedroom, but my guts clench at the thought of another argument with Zac. We were supposed to have spent a nice day together. How did it all go so wrong? Why did I insist on going to see Belinda? I don't even like her. And those flowers. Who sent them? There has to be a logical explanation.

I think back to earlier in the week when Tricia was jumping to conclusions about me and James, confiding her nasty suspicions to Chris. It makes no sense for her to have sent the flowers. She's just a busybody neighbour.

I'm ninety-nine per cent certain they're not from my mother, but I need to rule her out. Reluctantly I go into the living room to call her.

She answers after two rings. 'Nina?'

'Hi, Mum.'

'Is this important?' she says impatiently. 'We've got friends over.'

'Um, no. Well, yes, kind of.' I perch on the arm of the sofa and try to think how I'm going to phrase this.

She tuts. 'Well?'

'Did you send me flowers?'

'Is this a trick question? It's not your birthday until May.'

'No, it's just someone sent me flowers and it was signed with a "J" so I thought—'

'You thought I'd sign my name as "J"? Do you know me at all, Nina?'

'I know. I didn't think they were from you, but…' I lower my voice. 'Zac thinks I have a secret admirer and I think he might be jealous.' I realise I'm babbling, and my mother hates it when I babble. But I always seem to turn into a flustered idiot when I'm speaking to her. I think it's because she's so calm and cool.

'A secret admirer?' Mum sounds interested. 'Is it your investor? How exciting.'

'No, it's not exciting. It's creepy and Zac's not happy about it.'

'I should think he isn't. Do him good to have a bit of competition. Might get him to up his game.'

'His game doesn't need upping, Mum. Don't worry. I just needed to check the flowers weren't from you.'

'Well, let me know when you find out who your admirer is. You should be flattered. Happy. You don't sound happy.'

'I'm fine, Mum. I'll let you go, you're obviously busy.'

'Yes. Monica and Richard Halpin are here. You remember them? Their son's going through a divorce at the moment – Tobias. Handsome boy. He's a surgeon at Poole Hospital, you know.'

I ignore her unsubtle attempt at matchmaking. 'Okay, well I'll let you get back to your guests.'

'Fine. Speak soon.'

I end the call feeling worse than I did before I made it.

After dilly-dallying about what to do next, I decide to leave Zac alone for an hour or so to cool his temper. I'll go into the office and get on with my work – that's if I can even concentrate. Then, when I come out, hopefully we'll have both calmed down and can talk to each other civilly.

I realise that I'm in my pyjamas. I can't go into the bedroom to get changed because it will set off another confrontation. Instead, I grab my office keys, go to the kitchen, and peer out the window into the dark evening. The rain has eased up at last. It'll be okay. I'll just go to the office like this. No one will see me.

Soon, I'm sitting at my desk, trying to lose myself in spreadsheets and graphs. I'm feeling quite satisfied with the upward trajectory of sales this week despite the crappy reviews. I try not to think about Zac, but his angry face keeps popping into my head. My stomach lurches at the thought of us being at odds with one another. I'm sure he'll have cooled down by now, but I'll give it another half hour, just in case.

We've had more arguments in the two months we've lived here than in the whole of our previous time together. It's not like us – these emotional blowups and shouting matches. We need to fix our differences, get everything out in the open. Maybe it's a good thing we argued today, maybe this will clear the air and we'll be able to get on with our lives together.

A flash of light startles me from my thoughts. I look up from my desk but I don't see anything. A few moments later there's a deep boom from outside – thunder. A storm is coming. Maybe I should head back to the flat before it starts pouring with rain.

Another flash of lightning stirs me. I stand. I need to face my boyfriend and make up with him. I lock up the office and pick my way back down the garden path as a low rumble of thunder vibrates through me. The flat is dark, the kitchen light off. Zac must still be in one of the front rooms. Cold drops of rain are beginning to fall again. I can't wait to get inside and sort things out.

I push the metal handle down and push the door but it doesn't move. Is it stuck? The rain is falling faster now, drops becoming a steady stream of water. Thunder and lightning roar and flash at the same time. I push at the door handle once more but the door isn't budging. It's locked. I don't remember locking it, but I was in quite a state when I left the flat. I probably did it automatically. But no, I only have my office keys with me, so I couldn't have locked it. That means…

Did Zac lock me out? *No.* I can't believe he would have done that. Would he? I bang on the wooden door with my fist a couple of times.

'Zac!' I cry, but my voice is no match for the drumming rain. 'Zac!' I try again, louder this time. I bang the door half a dozen times in quick succession. 'Let me in!'

I step across to the window, having to stand in my slippers on a muddy weed-filled flowerbed. I bang on the glass. There's no way he won't be able to hear that. I peer through the window, but it's dark inside. No light from even the hall. A crack of thunder sets my teeth on edge. Another jag of lightning illuminates the garden.

I don't even know if Zac's still in there. I can't work out which is worse – the thought that he's inside listening to my pleas, yet choosing to ignore them, or that he's left without telling me.

I move from the window to the back door, alternating between the two. Yelling and battering the wood and glass with my fists. Why didn't I bring my phone out with me? Instead it's lying uselessly in the flat. Of course it is. Because that's exactly the way my luck's running at the moment.

I suddenly have an idea. Heading around to the side gate, I slide back the rusty bolt and pull the gate open. I hurry along the side of the house and into the driveway. Zac's van is still here. He wouldn't drive after drinking anyway. The bedroom and hall lights are off, but light spills through the living-room curtains. I run up to the front door and ring the doorbell, my teeth chattering. I wait ten seconds before ringing it again. And again. Why isn't he answering?

I walk across the gravel to the living-room window and squint through a chink in the curtains. The TV is on, but I can't see any sign of Zac. It doesn't look like he's in the living room. Could he be asleep in the bedroom? I bang on the bedroom window, call his name over and over. Ring the doorbell again. Nothing.

This is bloody ridiculous. Should I knock on Chris and Vanessa's door? The thought of Chris's judgemental face when he sees me in my pyjamas, soaked through and hysterical, is enough to put me off that course of action. I'm also reluctant to call round to Tricia and Rob's, or to Marion's. I have to live alongside these people. I can't expose them to this kind of drama. It's too humiliating. It's not how Zac and I *are*.

Suddenly scared of attracting the attention of the neighbours or of passers-by, I scoot back around to the rear of the house and take up banging on the door and window once again. Icy rain streaks down my face. My pyjamas are soaked through, clinging to my frozen skin. My throat is raw from screaming, fists bruised from battering the back door and window repeatedly and to no avail.

'Let me in!' I cry for the hundredth time. 'Open the door! Zac, please.' My voice is carried away on the moaning wind, drowned by the creak and swish of the trees. I curl my fingers into a fist once more and pound the wooden door.

A sharp crack of thunder judders through my bones as a flash of lightning as bright as daylight illuminates my reflection in the kitchen window. I look like a ghost. A spectre of misery. Hair plastered to my head. Face pale as death. Eyes wide. What a mess!

What should I do? What *can* I do? I step away from the back door and gaze up at the flat above. It too lies in darkness. But as I squint through the driving rain, I'm startled to make out a shape through one of the windows. A silhouette.

The curtains are open and someone is staring down at me.

Is it Chris or Vanessa? And why are they just staring like that? It's bloody creepy. I shudder and move closer to the house, out of sight. I can't stay out here forever. I'll freeze or fall ill, get pneumonia. Whether Zac is inside the flat or whether he's gone out, it's clear he's not coming to let me in.

I pummel the door one more time and give a hoarse, useless cry before slinking back to my office. Once inside, I stand panting in the middle of the room, my pyjamas dripping, making a dark stain on the rug.

What do I do now? How did my day end up like this?

CHAPTER TWENTY-EIGHT

THEN

There's nothing romantic going on between me and Adam, but as the days pass, I'm finding that I want there to be. I wish I knew if he felt the same. A few of the girls have asked me, but I tell them we're just friends. Not that they believe me.

'You two are totally doing it,' Abigail Parks crows later while we're getting changed for PE. 'No question.'

'Slag,' someone comments, just loud enough for everyone to hear.

Laughter fills the changing room until Miss Thomas strides in and tells us to pipe down and get a move on.

My cheeks are flaming. But alongside the embarrassment I also feel something else…

The faintest sliver of hope.

CHAPTER TWENTY-NINE

Another weekend rolls around. Things have gone from bad to worse between me and Zac. We're barely speaking. Just two strangers sharing the same space. Polite yet distant. It turns out that the night I was locked out of the flat, Zac had stormed off down to the beach to clear his head and calm his anger. He locked up the house before leaving, assuming I had keys to get back in. When he got back, he came out to the office to see me. I yelled at him for locking me out, and we had another horrible argument.

During the week, things didn't seem quite so bad because at least I could concentrate on my work. But he went over to his mum's for dinner twice. He said it was to check out her boiler, which has been playing up lately, but I'm sure it was so he could avoid spending another awkward evening with me. I wonder if he confided in her about our strained relationship. If so, would she have advised him to try to patch things up? Or would she have sowed further doubts in his mind about us? I can't be sure either way. And I can't exactly call her to give my side of the story.

Now that Saturday's here again, Zac and I are faced with actually having to talk to each other. I can't go and hide in the office, because then he'll say that all I care about is my work. But the truth is, I feel like whenever we speak to one another recently, it always ends in a row.

'Do you want a cup of tea?' Zac pops his head around the door of the living room where I'm curled up on the sofa, updating

Mistletoe Lane's Pinterest board. His request seems kind enough, but there's no smile, no lightness. Just a dead-eyed question.

I look up. 'Yes please, that would be great.' Our words are polite, stilted.

Five minutes later he comes back into the room and puts the mugs down on the coffee table. He sits on the other sofa. My heart thumps uncomfortably. Does this mean he wants to talk?

'Thanks for the tea.'

'No problem.'

I put my phone down and try to give Zac a smile, but it comes out more like a weird grimace.

'How's work?' he asks.

I swallow the lump in my throat. 'Yeah, it's okay. Harder without Vanessa. I'm actually quite worried about her. I've knocked on her door a couple of times, but she either doesn't answer, or says she's busy.'

'Well, maybe she really is busy. I guess she'll have a lot to organise with the baby coming.'

'Maybe. It's just… I get the feeling she's unhappy, or scared of something. I can't quite put my finger on it. Have you spoken to Chris at all?'

'Yeah, a few times. He's seems fine. Excited about becoming a dad.'

'I still think there's something weird about him.' I think back to the night I was locked out of the flat when he was staring down at me. 'And they're still having really loud arguments. Well, I say arguments, but it's more like Chris yelling at her.'

'Look, Nina, I'm not being funny, but why are we talking about the neighbours again? You seem more worried about another couple's relationship than ours.'

My stomach rocks with uneasy anger. 'I'm just making conversation! I'm concerned about her, that's all. Doesn't mean I'm not feeling sick about the fact we've stopped talking. You do realise those flowers are still a total mystery to me. I have no idea who sent them!'

'Fine. And let's not talk about those flowers any more.'

'I thought you *wanted* to talk. We can't just sweep everything aside like it never happened.'

'God, Nina. I can't win. If I say, "let's forget the flowers", then I'm sweeping things under the carpet, but if I want to talk about them, then I'm being jealous and unreasonable!'

I shake my head and take a breath. 'Okay, you're right. Let's not talk about neighbours or flowers or work. We'll start again. Rewind the past week and get back to where we were before.' I pick up my mug and blow on my tea before taking a sip. 'How about we go for a walk. We moved here to be close to the beach, but we never seem to go there.'

'Who's fault is that?' Zac mutters.

I try to rein in my temper. 'Look, I'm suggesting we go and have a nice walk. But if you're going to make sly comments... if you don't want to go...'

Zac's shoulders slump. 'No, you're right. I'm sorry. Let's go out. It's stopped raining, at least.'

We wrap up against the cold breeze and leave the flat. Around the side of the house, Vanessa and Chris are unloading grocery bags from their car. We wave and say hi. Zac tells them we're going down to the beach for a walk. Vanessa doesn't speak and barely catches my eye. I hope she's not upset with me about the job.

Zac and I head down to the seafront. The air is fresh and salty, the sky all shades of blue, grey and white. Seagulls dive and wheel, squawking and screeching over the sand and water. Families, friends and couples march along in their little units, most of them with dogs on and off their leads. I catch Zac's eye and we properly smile at one another for the first time in days. I breathe deeply, hoping the fresh air will loosen the tightness in my chest and the unease in my heart, drinking in the open space above my head.

'This is nice,' he says. 'Good idea to come down here, Neens.'

'It's lovely, isn't it? We should make a pact to come down here every weekend. Even if it's just for an hour.'

'Definitely.' Zac points to a golden retriever that's lolloping about in the shallows. 'Be nice to get a dog one day.'

I look at him sideways, and stop myself from making a quip that it would be too much responsibility for him. 'That would be nice,' I say instead.

We end up walking for over an hour, neither of us wanting to return home just yet. The sun even makes an appearance for a brief while. We don't talk too much, but when we do, the conversation is light, neither of us willing to talk about anything heavy in case we trigger another fight. I have so much on the tip of my tongue that I want to say. That I want to ask. I want to know if he's still annoyed with me. If he still thinks I know who sent the flowers. If he's happy. If he loves me. But I'm scared to hear the answers, so I stay quiet, enjoying the truce we've called.

'I'm starving,' Zac announces. 'Shall we head back? Have we got anything good in the fridge?'

'Not a lot. We need to go shopping at some point. Why don't we go to the café? I went there with Vanessa last month. It's called something Bistro… Tides Bistro. They don't do lunchtime reservations so we can just show up.'

'That sounds good. I wonder if they're still serving breakfast.'

'It's almost twelve, so maybe not. But you never know.' I feel suddenly buoyant at the thought of us sitting down to treat our-selves to a nice leisurely lunch together. We can put the past week behind us and concentrate on the good stuff. This is just what I imagined living here would be like – walks on the beach, relaxing lunches. 'Have you got any money on you? I left my bag at home.'

'I've got my wallet.' Zac taps his coat pocket.

We stride back towards the café and by the time we get there I'm light-headed with happiness and hunger. Thankfully, the line moves quickly and soon we're being ushered inside. The warmth is wonderful, and the smells coming from the kitchen are making my stomach gurgle and my mouth water.

'This is so perfect.' Zac kisses my cheek and I'm suffused with contentedness.

'Zac! Nina!'

We both turn at the sound of a man's voice.

My mood plummets when I see Chris sitting at a table near the back with two other men. He waves us over. Zac smiles and leads the way as my heart drops further and further. The waitress accompanies us and it appears she knows Chris as they greet one another by name and ask after each other.

'You here for lunch?' Chris asks us.

'Yeah.' Zac nods. 'Hoping for a full English actually.'

'We normally stop serving breakfast at twelve,' the waitress says. 'But if you're a friend of Chris, I'm sure we can sort something out.'

'Amazing.' Zac's eyes light up.

'We haven't ordered yet. You should join us,' Chris suggests. He looks at his friends and at Zac for confirmation.

No one's looking at me. Everyone else nods and smiles.

Finally, Zac looks at me with a raised eyebrow. What am I going to say in front of everyone? *No?*

'Sure,' I reply, hearing the lack of energy in my voice, but I can't fake enthusiasm for this.

Chris and his friends stand and we help push two tables together and rearrange the chairs. Inside I feel sick with disappointment. Maybe I'm being irrational, but I wanted Zac and I to spend some time alone, just the two of us without the stresses of work, or the flat, or the neighbours. Normally, I'm a social person. I love to sit down and eat with friends. But this is *Chris*, and the timing couldn't be worse. Zac and I were just starting to fix things between us today, but I can already feel this morning's closeness crumbling away. Right now, there's a simmering fury building in my gut. How can Zac not see that I don't want to spend my precious free time with Chris and his friends. That this is the last situation I want to find myself in.

Even so, I'm reluctant to say that I don't want to have lunch with them. I don't want to come across as a miserable, unsociable cow. The truth is, I want Zac to say, 'Actually, that's really nice of you to offer, but Nina and I are just going to have a quiet lunch.' I want him to want to have lunch with *me*. Not with a group of lads we don't even know. But that's not what's happening. I try to stay calm. If I can just get through this lunch, then hopefully Zac and I can spend the afternoon together. Maybe go to town and look round the shops, or even go for another walk if it stays dry.

Zac and I sit side by side, opposite Chris and with one of his friends opposite me, and the other next to Zac. Chris introduces us, but I don't register their names. They're all dressed in sports gear and apparently are having a quick lunch followed by a bike ride.

'Don't suppose you want to join us on the ride?' Chris asks Zac. My heart sinks.

'Uh…' Zac's gaze travels from Chris to me. 'I guess you'll be working this afternoon?'

'Well, I wasn't going to, but…'

'So this lets you off the hook,' he teases.

'If you want to go, that's cool.' I manage a smile, but it's taking a huge effort to curl my lips upwards. I catch Chris staring at me. I swallow. 'How's Vanessa? I haven't seen her in a while.'

'Yeah, she's fine. Putting her feet up at home.'

Zac gets his full English breakfast, and I order a toasted sandwich, even though my appetite has now completely deserted me. It puts me in mind of another English breakfast and another toasted sandwich ordered five years ago. I couldn't eat that sandwich either, only for a completely different reason. It was the week after I'd returned from our girls' holiday in Crete, where I first met Zac. He'd invited me out for brunch at a beachside restaurant, and I'd spent ages getting ready. I had so many butterflies that I barely managed to eat a thing. I wasn't used to feeling that way, I'd always been so confident around boys. Despite my nerves, I had the best time. Zac's attention had been focused solely on me, and mine on him. We'd talked and talked, and laughed so hard. There was no stilted conversation, no awkward silences. It was late afternoon by the time he picked up the bill and we left. Months afterwards, he told me that that was the day he really, truly fell for me.

Today couldn't be further away from that moment in time if it tried. As I listen to Zac, Chris, and his friends talk about work, mountain biking and other topics of conversation, I can't help wishing I could rewind the clock and go back to that day. To that Zac. Instead, I'm here with these virtual strangers, unable to engage in any of their chatter because my thoughts are all over the place. I realise that this is no one's fault exactly, but it doesn't stop me feeling disappointed in Zac. Hurt. Can't we please just have one day together without being interrupted or something going awry – the weather, the electrics, work, the neighbours?

Ordinarily, a situation like this might make me mildly irritated. But, right now, it feels like a tipping point. If Zac and I had just been able to sit and have a lovely lunch together, everything could have got back on an even keel. Instead, my whole body is seething with annoyance. With disappointment, and a kind of longing.

And I don't know how I'm supposed to get over it. I'm not sure where we can go from here…

CHAPTER THIRTY

I pull up outside Cali's cute little terraced house in Lower Parkstone. It's near where Zac and I used to rent and it makes me feel nostalgic being here. She and Ryan scrimped and saved to buy the place a couple of years ago just before they got married. It used to be a total wreck but they poured their hearts and souls into fixing it up. They still have a way to go, but the downstairs is almost finished now.

Cali's an early years assistant and works in a nursery just up the road from where she lives. Luckily, she finishes work early on Mondays, so I WhatsApped her and Amy – who works shifts as a nurse – and asked if I could meet up for a chat. We agreed on Cali's place because it's easier to park.

I was going crazy at home after the weekend descended into another utter disaster. When that interminably long and hideous lunch at Tides Bistro was finally over, and Zac and I left, I could barely talk to him. He either didn't pick up on my mood or he was choosing to ignore it. He just went on about what a great morning we'd had and how the food was so nice, and how he was looking forward to getting out on his bike that afternoon.

When we got back home, I went straight out to the office, not trusting myself to speak to Zac. Not wanting to have another argument. Twenty minutes later he came out to tell me he was going. He asked if I was okay. I gritted my teeth and nodded my head, and said I was fine. He could see I wasn't happy, but he chose to ignore me and left anyway. Our communication completely broke down after that and we were back to being frosty. My stomach has been in knots and I've felt nauseous ever since.

After working all day yesterday and again this morning, I needed to get away from the flat. I needed to see my friends and ask them what they think I should do. The roads were blessedly empty on the drive over here, unlike my brain, which is full to bursting. I don't even know how I'm actually feeling, there are so many conflicting emotions. I'm hoping that opening up to my friends might help me to sort through everything.

Cali opens the door before I'm even out of the car. She's standing on the doorstep in a cosy, pale-pink tracksuit and fluffy slippers, her straight black hair tied up in a messy ponytail. Cali refuses to follow the latest fashions and instead charts her own course. I'd describe her style as WAG meets eighties punk.

'Hey, Nini Banini.' She always calls me stupid names.

'Hey, Cals.' I lock the Golf and squeeze past her faithful Renault Clio in the small driveway.

'Come in, my little honeybun. Amy's in the kitchen. Apparently, she's making some kind of life-changing drink.'

'Sounds good.' I want to sound more enthusiastic, but it's hard to get worked up about a drink when my life feels as though it's falling apart. Everything good seems to be sliding away and I can't seem to haul it back. The more helpless I feel, the worse I react. It's like I'm helping to sink my relationship, even though I don't want that at all. I don't know what's wrong with me. Am I going mad? Or is it simply that I'm taking on too much – the house, the business, the investment? It's all putting pressure on Zac and me. Or perhaps everything's fine and I really am self-sabotaging… I just don't know any more.

Cali gives me a hug and we go through to the large kitchen/dining/living room at the back of the house. It's a stunning and unusual room with dark-stained wooden floors, an exposed brick wall, dark wood units, green velvet sofas with Japanese silk cushions and lots of plants and wicker accessories. Amy blows me kisses while she stands at the counter frothing coconut milk with a handheld whisk, her dark curls held back off her face by an oversize wooden hair clip.

'Nina!' she cries. 'How are you doing, my little chicken?'

My friends are treating me like they know something's up. I haven't told them anything about my troubles with Zac, so why are they being all sympathetic?

'Come and sit down.' Cali leads me over to the sofa as if I'm an invalid and sits next to me cross-legged.

'Okay…' I shrug off my coat. 'What's going on?'

Amy brings a tray of drinks over to the seating area and sits opposite us.

'Nothing's going on,' Cali says. 'We just thought you might need cheering up.'

'Why?'

Cali shifts in her seat. 'Well, Ryan mentioned you and Zac might be going through some stuff at the moment.'

'*Ryan* said that?'

'I think he's been talking to Zac.'

'Great. So everyone knows we're not getting on.' I sink back into the sofa and close my eyes briefly.

'Ryan's not everyone,' Cali soothes. 'He's Zac's best friend.'

I'm definitely feeling pissed off that Zac has confided in Ryan, even though I know I'm going to be doing the same thing with Cali and Amy. As well as being upset that Zac and I are going through a rocky patch, it's also humiliating to have to admit it. To know that Zac is also admitting it. I always thought Zac and I were the perfect, unbreakable couple. Not like Cali and Ryan who are always bickering and falling out, then making up again. Maybe it serves me right for being so smug.

'Here.' Amy leans forward and passes me a mug that's smothered in whipped cream, mini marshmallows and chocolate flakes.

I stare down at it and then look back at Amy. 'It looks amazing. What is it?'

'It's my special cheer-you-up hot chocolate.'

'Aw, thank you.'

Cali leans her head on my shoulder for a moment. I take the spoon and scoop up a bit of cream and marshmallow. I don't have the heart to tell Amy that I'm off chocolate since my bout of food poisoning.

I spend the next hour filling them in on my troubles. I tell them about how Zac has bonded with Chris from upstairs, while I think the guy is a dick. I tell them about running into Chris and his friends on Saturday and how I was so mad that our lunch was hijacked.

My friends don't comment for a moment and I give them each a look. 'What?'

'Well,' Cali starts. 'It's not really Zac's fault that Chris invited you to sit with them. You could've said "no".'

I start to feel hot.

'But I totally get why you were pissed off,' she adds.

I take a breath and try not to get angry that she's taking his side. After all, this is why I came here – to get my friends' perspectives.

'I was just annoyed that Zac didn't seem to get it. We'd been in a bad place all week, we were finally getting along, and then it felt like he ditched me for a group of strangers. I was looking forward to having lunch, just the two of us.'

'I get that, honey.' Amy gives me a squeeze. 'He was being oblivious. It's annoying.'

'But you can't let that one lunch ruin your relationship,' Cali adds sternly.

'I know. Ugh, I hate that we're arguing so much. And when we're not arguing, we're not speaking. I just feel sick all the time.'

'You do sometimes overthink things, Neens.' Cali shakes her head. 'When Ry and I argue it's like a big thunderstorm – boom! It's explosive, but then afterwards the air's all fresh and clean.'

'Yeah, we're not like that,' I reply with a bitter laugh and a heavy feeling in my heart.

I go on to tell them about the Jacksons' scary arguments. Amy says their negative energy is probably affecting my relationship with Zac. I also tell them about the flowers, and how Zac didn't believe that I don't know who they're from.

'That's creepy,' Cali says, spooning out the last of her hot-chocolate froth. 'Do you think it's a stalker?'

'Well I do *now*!'

'Oh, sorry.' She covers her mouth briefly. 'Who do we know beginning with J? Apart from your investor and your mum?'

I shrug. 'I don't even care about the flowers. I just want me and Zac to get back to how we used to be. It's all so weird between us.'

'Everyone has their weird times, Nina.' Amy gets up and comes to sit on the other side of me. 'You two will be fine. Zac loves you.'

'He doesn't act like it at the moment.'

'Yeah, but are you acting like you love *him*?' Cali asks.

My shoulders slump. 'Probably not. What did Zac say to Ry?'

'Just that he's worried about you. That you're working really hard and you don't seem very happy. He said he's nervous to say anything in case you snap his head off, and…' Cali breaks off before adding, 'Yeah, that's it really.'

I turn to look at her. Her face is red but she's trying to act nonchalant.

'And *what*? You were about to say something else, Cal. What is it?'

'Look, don't get mad, but Zac told Ryan he thought you might be seeing someone else.'

'*What?*'

'He's worried there's something between you and your inves-tor – James. That's why Zac's been acting strangely. He said that one minute he thinks it's all in his head, and the next minute something happens to make him think it's true. He's tried bringing it up with you but you've been distant and keep shutting yourself in your office.'

'But that's mad. There's absolutely no reason to think that. Okay, the flowers are… unfortunate, but they're nothing to do with me.' As I'm saying all this, I can't help wondering if maybe Zac's right. Could I be pushing him away somehow? Zac's accusations are way off base, but maybe I'm doing something to give him the wrong idea.

'Are you sure, Neens?' Cali looks at me. 'You know you can tell us anything.' She draws a little square with her fingers. 'Safe space, and all that.'

'Cali! I am not having an affair. I'd never do that to Zac. I love him!'

'Okay, okay, calm down. I believe you. I just had to ask.'

Another horrifying thought hits me. 'What if he's told his mum that he thinks I'm having an affair? I'm sure she already thinks I'm not right for him.'

'All mothers think their son's girlfriends aren't good enough.' Amy rubs my arm soothingly. 'I wouldn't worry about Sandra.'

I take a deep breath. 'You're right. Thanks for being here for me. Sorry for shouting just now.'

Cali throws her arms around me and gives me a squeeze. 'No need to apologise. We're your mates, innit?' She grins.

Amy nods. 'And you were there for me while I was going through my divorce, so of course we're here for you while you're having a tricky time. But that's all it is – a tricky time. You two will be fine.'

'I love you guys. I'm so glad I came over.' I'm finally feeling more optimistic. 'Okay, so hopefully now that I know why Zac's been going hot and cold on me, I can have a proper conversation with him and sort things out.'

'Definitely,' Cali says. 'Anyone else need a glass of water after all that hot chocolate? It was amazing, by the way, Ames.'

Cali goes over to the kitchen area to fetch us some water while I tell them about my trip to Belinda's and my quest to discover whether she's behind the bad reviews.

'That girl's so annoying,' Cali calls over.

'Sorry you're having to put up with someone sabotaging your business on top of all the Zac stuff,' Amy adds.

'I don't know where Belinda got her confidence from,' I muse. 'She was quiet as a mouse at school. Yet now you'd think she was the queen of Dorset. Not that I'm criticising her confidence, just that I wish she'd use her powers for good instead of being…'

'A cow?' Amy suggests.

Cali comes back with three waters. I gulp mine down even though I barely touched my hot chocolate.

'I was pretty quiet at school too,' Cali says.

'You?' I look at her in disbelief. 'I can't ever imagine you being quiet.'

'It's true.' She shrugs as she sits back down, this time opposite me and Amy. 'I didn't really have any friends. I was a bit of an outsider. You two are my besties.'

'Aww,' Amy and I look at one another with soppy expressions.

'I was gobby at school,' Amy declares.

'No change there then.' Cali smirks and we all laugh.

'How about you, Nina?' Cali asks.

'I wasn't really quiet or gobby. I guess I was just in between, and lucky to have nice friends. Not that I really kept in touch with many of them. I moved around. Grew up in London, then came to Dorset.'

'How come we've never talked about school before?' Cali asks.

'I don't know. Too busy having a good time to bother about the past.' Amy laughs and we cheers our water glasses. 'Talking of good times…' Amy gives an embarrassed smile and Cali and I glance at one another.

'What's happened?' Cali demands, her eyes widening. 'You've met someone, haven't you!'

Amy gives me a sideways look.

'*What?*' I ask.

'George texted me to go out for a drink,' she confesses.

'George, as in my *brother?*' I grin at my friend, silently congratulating George for making the effort.

Amy rolls her eyes affectionately. 'Calm down, Miss Matchmaker, it's just a drink.'

'But you are going, right?' I ask.

'You *better* be going,' Cali adds.

'Yes.' Amy grins. 'This weekend.'

Cali and I squeal with excitement. It's nice to think about something else for a while other than my seemingly endless problems. I stay for another hour where we all get carried away with Amy and George's future relationship, and also talk about Cali's plans for the rest of her house. I'm itching to get home though, and sort things out with Zac once and for all. Things have become so strained between us that I don't even know how late he's working tonight. Normally, he'd tell me in the morning, or drop me a text. But I'm determined to get back to how we were. *No.* I'm determined to make things *even better* than they were.

Back home, I immerse myself in work. I sit in the living room with my laptop instead of in the office, because I want to be there when Zac gets home. I'm ready to have this frank conversation, to reassure him that there's nothing going on between me and James. Even the thought of that is laughable. James is so not my type. I'm feeling re-energised now that I know there's a reason why Zac and I have been so off track. I can still hardly believe that Zac would think I'd cheat on him.

With a leap of nervous anticipation, I realise Zac's van is turning into the drive, the twin beams of his headlights travelling across the room. It's dark out and I realise I've been working without the lights on. I close my laptop and breathe deeply a few times, trying to quell the butterflies in my stomach. I need to stay positive and calm. I hear the van door slam and I wait to hear Zac's key in the door. I'm so nervous it's ridiculous. I just hate confrontation.

After thirty seconds or so, Zac still hasn't come in. I listen and hear voices outside. Zac's talking to someone. I get up to look out the window and see that it's Chris, the exterior lights illuminating them. My hackles rise at the sight of that man, but I can't allow Chris to throw me off course. When Zac comes in, I'm not going to mention Chris, I'm going to talk to Zac about our relationship. The neighbours have nothing to do with it.

Outside, Chris is speaking intently and Zac's face is reddening, his eyes hard, his jaw clenched. What on earth is going on out there? Is Zac angry with Chris for some reason?

Chris places a hand on Zac's arm and Zac looks down at the ground, shaking his head slowly. There's a flicker of movement and a dull thud. I gasp. Zac has punched the side of his van! *Why has he done that?* I need to get out there and see what can have happened to make him so angry.

I rush to the hall, slip on my shoes and open the front door just in time to see Zac reversing the van out of the driveway with a crunch of gears. The headlights blind me for an instant. As the van swerves backwards and then forwards again, I see that Chris is in the passenger seat.

I run out after them, but the van disappears in a blaze of red tail lights, leaving me breathless in the middle of the road. I realise I'm shaking. *What just happened?*

CHAPTER THIRTY-ONE

I stand on the pavement outside the flat watching Zac's van screech away. Where can those two have gone together in such a hurry, with Zac in such an awful rage? I race back inside to get my phone and call Zac's mobile. It rings but he's not picking up. It goes to voicemail so I end the call and ring again. Voicemail again. I leave a message:

'Zac, I just saw you drive off. What's going on?' I end the call and bang out a text message.

Where are you going with Chris? Call me.

There's no reply to either message, but I guess he's driving. I wish I had Chris's number. I stand in the living room at a loss, a feeling of unknown panic setting my pulse racing. But I can't just stand around doing nothing. I leave the flat and hurry to the side of the building to the front door of 15B.

I ring the doorbell and wait. Frustratingly, there's no reply, but Vanessa's not big on answering the door so I guess I shouldn't have expected anything else. I ring it again and rap on the opaque double glazing. This is important; I need her to come down and tell me what's going on.

I stand, shivering under the security light outside her door for several minutes, knocking and ringing, but she either doesn't want to answer, or she's out – which I doubt. I feel bad for disturbing her, but I'm really worried about Zac. I've never seen him that angry. He punched his van, for goodness sake! He loves that van.

After five minutes of standing outside Vanessa's door like a lemon, I make my way reluctantly back to the flat. Inside, I try calling Zac again, but again it goes to voicemail. Next, I call Cali, but she's not answering either, so I leave a message for her to ask Ryan if he might know where Zac's going. I don't have Ryan's number, but we're Facebook friends so I plonk myself down on the sofa, open up the Facebook app and type in Ryan's name. I click on his profile pic – it's one of him and Cali on their wedding day. His page opens, but my heart sinks when I see that he hasn't posted anything in over two years. I message him anyway, just in case he still gets notifications.

Next, I call Kit. He answers straight away.

'Hey, Nina. Haven't spoken to you in ages. I'm still waiting for you to come and be interviewed on our YouTube channel. How about next week?'

'Sorry, Kit, I've just been so busy.'

'No worries. Let me know when you're free. How's it going?'

'Long story,' I reply, anxiety lacing my voice.

'Oh. That doesn't sound good.'

'Don't suppose you've spoken to Zac recently?'

'No, and he hasn't been returning my calls either.' Kit pauses. 'Is he okay? Did I do something to annoy him?'

'No, but I can't talk about it now. He and I are going through some stuff and he's just driven off in a temper. I don't know where he's gone and he's not answering his phone!' My voice catches and I realise I'm sounding hysterical.

'Hey, hey, are you all right, Neens? Want me to come over?'

I wipe a tear from my cheek. 'No, I'll be fine. I'm just worried in case he has an accident or something.'

'Oh, I wish I could give you a hug down the phone.'

'Thanks, Kit. Just hearing your lovely voice has helped. Say hi to Ben from me.'

'I will. And call me to let me know when he's back home safe. Otherwise I'll worry.'

'Okay.'

'Love you, sweets, and if you change your mind and want me to come round, just say the word.'

'Thanks.' Once the call ends, I feel lonelier than ever. Where's my boyfriend? Where *is* he? And what could Chris have possibly said to make him so angry?

The next hour drags. I periodically call Zac's phone and go out to knock on Vanessa's door. Neither action yields anything. I wrack my brains to think what could have got Zac so angry. Is it something to do with me? Or with his work? But then why would Chris be involved? It makes no sense.

All my plans to reconcile with Zac have gone out the window. I'd had visions of us having a good talk and then going out for a celebratory meal, or maybe cosying up on the sofa with a takeaway and a movie. Instead, I'm home alone with no idea what's going on.

The flat feels large and empty. I can't find an ounce of comfort in any room. I won't be able to concentrate on work so there's no point in trying. I hear the TV being switched on upstairs. Loud at first, and then the volume being lowered. Vanessa *is* up there! I should have taken her phone number when she started working for me. Why didn't I do that? I grab my coat and march back around to her front door. This is ridiculous. She must know that Chris has gone off with Zac. Surely they need to keep in touch now she's only a couple of months away from giving birth. Chris wouldn't have gone off without telling her, would he?

I ring the bell again, holding it down with my finger. I hear the chime, but it only sounds once, so I lift my finger and press it again. And again. And again. I rap on the glass and call through the letterbox.

'Vanessa! *Vanessa!* Can you come down for a minute? *Please?*'

The space beyond the glass pane in the door remains dark. Silent.

I give a grunt of exasperation and slope back to the flat. My stomach is hollow with hunger. My throat dry. My head swimming with anxiety. What should I do? I sit on the sofa in the dark lounge with the curtains open so I can see out. I feel like a ghost. Someone out of time. Out of place.

I look at my phone. There's a short text from Kit asking if Zac is home yet. I text back saying no. I check Facebook. Ryan still hasn't seen my message. But then I see that Cali's left a voicemail. With shaking fingers I tap the play button, hoping she might have some news for me. She says that Ryan hasn't spoken to Zac for a couple of days so he doesn't know where Zac might have gone. She says she and Ryan will try to track him down and she'll call me if they have any luck. She tells me not to worry. Might as well tell a fish not to swim.

My mind drifts over my relationship with Zac. How everything was good until we moved in here. How I'm coming to realise that I'm not happy in this place. Not settled. I wonder at how quickly everything has deteriorated. My company, my relationship, my happiness. At least I still have my friends.

My stomach lurches as a vehicle pulls into the drive. Light floods the living room for a few seconds as the vehicle turns into its usual spot. *Zac's van.* He's home.

My heart batters my ribcage. I don't know whether to be angry or relieved. I get to my feet feeling shaky. I still don't know if Zac is angry at me or at something or someone else. My belly tightens at the sound of a key in the lock. I snap on the living-room light. Zac tramps into the hall, his face shadowed with rage.

'Zac! Where have you been? Why were you with Chris?'

His eyes sweep over me with hurt and what looks like... *loathing.*

I step back, my heart in my throat. 'Zac? What's happened?'

He opens his mouth as though about to speak, but then clamps it shut again. He turns away, goes into the bedroom and closes the door firmly in my face.

Shit. What's going on? I wrack my brains to think what could have caused Zac to look at me that way. With such undisguised contempt. What have I done? I try to think… I confided in Cali and Amy today, but that's not a hanging offence. And anyway, he talked to Ryan about our relationship. No. There's something more. Is this to do with his misguided suspicions that I'm having an affair? Yes! I bet that's what it is. He's got it into his head that I'm seeing someone else. But what's that got to do with Chris? What did Chris say to make Zac punch his van?

I knock timidly on the bedroom door. 'Zac, can you let me in?' He doesn't reply, so I tentatively push open the door. I'm dismayed to see him stuffing clothes into a gym bag. 'What are you *doing*?'

'I don't want to talk to you right now,' he says gruffly.

'Zac, this is crazy. You need to tell me what's going on.'

'I should be asking you that,' he mutters. He casts his eyes wildly around the room and then walks past me out into the hall, still holding the open gym bag.

I follow him. 'What did Chris say to you? Out there in the drive, he said something and you punched your van.' I notice his knuckles are red and swollen. 'You need to put some ice on that.'

He ignores me, goes into the bathroom and grabs his toothbrush and shaving kit.

'So, you're walking out, is that it? You're just leaving without telling me why?'

'I'll come back when I'm calm. Just get away from me, Nina. I'm too angry to talk right now.'

'Angry about *what*?' I cry.

'I'm crashing at a friend's tonight.' He zips up his bag and slings it over his shoulder, walks out of the bathroom and heads towards the front door.

'What friend? Where? Where did you go this evening?'

He doesn't reply.

'*Zac!*' This can't be happening. Is he actually leaving? 'Tell me what I'm supposed to have done!'

He stops and turns without actually looking at me. 'We can talk tomorrow,' he says, walking out the front door.

'Why can't we talk now? Zac, wait.'

'Bye, Nina.' He dumps his bag on the passenger seat and climbs into the van. Closes the door and starts the engine. He doesn't even look at me as he drives away, his hard gaze focused straight ahead.

I stand out on the drive gazing at the empty space where Zac's van should be. Thinking about the nice evening we were supposed to have had.

This is something to do with Chris! He's told Zac some lie about me. But *why*? I gaze up at the flat above. The lights are off, but I know they're up there. Are they talking about me right now? Do they know why Zac's so angry?

How is it that my neighbours know more about what's going on in my life than I do?

CHAPTER THIRTY-TWO

THEN

'Are you sure your mum won't mind me coming back to yours?' I ask.

'No, not at all.' Adam swings his backpack over one shoulder as we walk out of the school gates and onto the dusty pavement. With a lightness in my heart, I glance back at the crowd of kids waiting for the hated school bus, so glad I'm not getting on it this afternoon.

I think about how my mother would react if I said I wanted to invite Adam back home after school. She'd either say no, or she'd give me the third degree. If she did somehow agree to it, she'd never let us go up to my room, and the atmosphere would be so awkward and uncomfortable that there'd be no point in him coming round in the first place. She doesn't know I'm going to Adam's today. I told her I was staying late to help with costumes for a school play.

I'm both proud and embarrassed to be seen leaving school with him. He's not my boyfriend, but I'm hoping that maybe after today he might be. At school, I've been elevated from invisible loser to someone with potential. I glance across at Adam, his face tanned, his shoulders relaxed. 'So, it's just you and your mum at home, right? No siblings?'

'Yeah. I always wanted a brother or sister, but…' He shrugs.

'You're better off, trust me. You can have my brother if you like.'

'Ed, right? Two years above us?'

I nod. 'He's even worse at home, if you can believe that.'

Adam laughs. 'Poor you.'

'*I know. You think he'd at least be nice to his sister.*' Ed is a bit of a bully at school. Nothing physical – that I know of – but he does enjoy intimidating the younger kids. I tried calling him out on it once. It didn't end well.

The sun warms our faces as we walk along wide leafy roads towards Adam's house. My belly flutters and my heart leaps with each step. Our banter is natural and I feel smart and funny, something I've never felt before in the company of friends. I'm usually the quiet one. The drab girl who has nothing interesting to say. But with Adam, I'm a different person. A somehow brighter version of myself.

I've never felt this way before.

CHAPTER THIRTY-THREE

I sit in my office answering my emails on autopilot, going through the motions, polite and businesslike. No trace of the fun, light tone I usually prefer. There's already a backlog of work from yesterday that feels too huge to get through. It's all slipping away from me. I don't know how I ever thought I could run this type of business on my own. I'm just one person. I can't keep up with it all. I'm a fraud. I'm not capable of any of it.

I haven't heard from Zac since he left last night. He won't return my calls or texts. Both Kit and Cali tried calling me a few times, but I can't bear to call them back and talk about what happened. It's all too upsetting. I don't think I could find the words to explain something I don't even understand. Is Zac going to leave me? What will I do without him? He's my best friend in the world. He's the one I talk to about everything. At least, he used to be. Until we moved here and everything got screwed up.

An email from Carl Fallon lands in my inbox with the subject line: *Itchy Top Results*. Oh good, more shit news.

I take a breath and open the email, praying that it's nothing too bad. I skim the email to get to the meat of it. I read it and re-read it.

What? This can't be right, can it?

The results are back from the lab. It would appear that the returned tops have all been coated with a fine powder of something called *Mucuna pruriens*, a type of legume that produces seedpods.

These pods are coated with thousands of detachable needle-like hairs, called spicules, which contain the enzyme *mucunain*. Which causes severe itching. It's an ingredient that's been sold commercially as itching powder.

Carl is going to send more batches of his stock to the lab to see if any other tops have been contaminated. He's asking me to do the same with my stock. But he ends the email by saying that he doesn't think *his* stock is the problem. He thinks the contamination has occurred at my end. If that is indeed the case, he says I'll no longer be able to stock his brand on my website until I can reassure him that it won't be contaminated.

I close my laptop, push it away, rest my head on my arms and weep. I can't do this any more. I can't keep going while all this crap keeps piling up on top of me. I don't understand any of it. Not the contaminated tops, not Zac's departure, not the neighbours' weirdness. I don't even feel like myself any more. My face is hot and sticky, my throat raw. I take huge gulping sobs, crying and crying until I feel as though I'm made of tears.

Finally, I close my eyes and just stay like this, hiccupping and sniffing. My arms and neck are stiff, but I can't move, because if I move then I'll have to face the mess that is my life. Maybe I should simply crawl into bed and stay there. I didn't sleep at all last night, so the thought of pulling the duvet over my head and falling asleep sounds like a good course of action. A way to block everything out.

My phone pulls me from my misery. I sniff and sit up. It could be Zac. I look at the screen. It's not Zac. It's James Kipling.

I don't have the stamina or presence for a conversation with my investor so I let it go to voicemail. Thirty seconds later, my phone rings again. It's James. Again. The ringing and buzzing triggers wave after wave of anxiety. No. They're waves of *fear*. I don't have to answer my phone. I should just turn it off. But I can't do that because what if Zac tries to call? My phone pings – one new voicemail. James must have left a message. Good. Hopefully now he'll leave me alone. My phone starts ringing and buzzing again. It's James. *Again.*

Sod it. I take a swig of cold tea, sniff back my tears, pat my face and answer the phone.

'Hi, James!' My voice doesn't sound like me, but I'm going to act like I'm fine. I'm going to give this phone call all I've got, and then I'm going to go to bed for at least the rest of today. Possibly also tonight and tomorrow.

'Nina? I just left you a message.'

'Did you? Sorry, I was on another call. It's all really busy at this end. The orders are flying in! How are you?' I almost laugh at the brightness I'm exuding. Maybe I should have been an actress.

'Not good, actually.' His voice is stern.

'Oh. Sorry to hear that.' The lightness in my voice belies the intense sinking sensation in my stomach. Something else is about to go very wrong. I can feel it.

'I thought you might have contacted me,' he says.

'Sorry? You thought I—'

'Yes.' He cuts me off. 'After your boyfriend came to my office yesterday and threatened me with violence.'

My skin turns icy. 'After my boyfriend *what?*'

'Your boyfriend, Zac Ainsworth, showed up at my office with another man. They intimidated and threatened me. Or to be more accurate, Zac threatened to "beat the living shit out of me". He accused me of having an affair with you.'

'He did *what?* He…' I gasp. 'I mean, Zac came to your…? He… *I'm so sorry.*'

'Quite aside from him being way off base, this is just not the sort of behaviour I can put up with. Mr Newbury is a professional. I'm a professional. And we don't take kindly to heavy-handed threatening tactics. If this is your idea of trying to intimidate me into cutting you some slack with the business, well, you're way out of line.'

'What? *No!* Not at all. I had no idea Zac came to see you. I'm absolutely mortified. Look, can we meet up?' I think about my swollen, tear-stained face and how long it will take me to make myself presentable. 'Maybe later this afternoon?'

'I think that would be a bad idea under the circumstances. I don't want your boyfriend getting the wrong idea.'

'I just can't believe he did that.'

'Well, I can assure you it happened. You're both very lucky I decided not to call the police. But if he comes near me again, that's exactly what I'll be doing.'

'How can I fix this?' I pause for a second, weighing my words, trying to think of something that might make amends for such an awful thing. 'I'll speak to Zac. I'll straighten it out and I know he'll want to apologise.' But as I offer my solution, I wonder how likely that is to happen. Zac won't even speak to *me* right now. I know what he's like when he takes against someone. Zac is mellow… until he's not any more. It's one of the other reasons I was so keen to move out of our last place. Zac got into a bit of an altercation with one of our old neighbours who had a small crush on me and would openly flirt. It wound Zac up and caused a lot of tension between us. I feel sick at the thought that something similar might be happening again. Only this time, Zac is way off base – James has done nothing wrong.

'Look, Nina, I'm very sorry to say this, but with the business not doing as well as it should, all the negative reviews, and the threat of violence from your boyfriend, I'm afraid I'm going to recommend that Mr Newbury stops the next stage of your funding. I think we've gone as far as we can go with this project.'

'*What?* No, please. I'm sure there's something I can do to make things right. Sales are really picking up at the moment and we're getting some great testimonials.'

'I'm sorry, Nina, but my mind's made up. I'll formalise things with a letter, laying out the reasons.'

I don't hear the rest of his words, because I know that it's over. Without the next phase of funding, I won't be able to pay for stock or advertising, I won't be able to keep up the mortgage payments. The whole business is imploding anyway. The reviews are shocking, my best designer thinks I've contaminated his clothes, and right now I'm too sad and too exhausted to even try to fix it. I end James's call.

How could Zac have got this so wrong? He's not usually the jealous type. Last night and this morning I was devastated by Zac's willingness to believe I'd cheat on him. But right now I'm beyond devastated. I'm furious. Quite apart from our relationship, his unfounded suspicions have helped to ruin my dream. Leaning back in my chair, I stare out the window at the tangled garden, at the weed-filled flower beds and the overhanging trees. My gaze travels across the wet, unkempt lawn to our flat beyond. I catch my breath at the sight of a face at the kitchen window.

Someone's inside the flat.

My heart pounds.

It's Zac. He's home.

CHAPTER THIRTY-FOUR

I get to my feet and take a breath, my eyes raw, my head throbbing. Before speaking to James, I felt miserable about my life. Like I'd ruined everything. But Zac's behaviour has ensured that there's no coming back from this. Mistletoe Lane is dead and my relationship with Zac might be following in its wake. The thought makes me sick.

I place my hands on my desk and push myself up out of my seat. Zac might be angry at me, but it's not a one-way street. I'm shaking with fury. Bloody Zac. Bloody Chris. What gave them the right to ruin my business like that? Zac didn't even do me the courtesy of talking to me first. He just waded in with his fists like some kind of Neanderthal.

Exhaustion threatens, but anger is fuelling me right now. I leave the office on a wave of adrenaline. The cold November air stings my eyes and burns my lungs. Zac is looking at me through the kitchen window, a blurred face behind the condensation-covered glass.

I open the back door and walk into the kitchen. I know I look like hell but I don't care. Let him see how his actions have affected me.

'You're back then.' I close the door, leaving the cold, fresh air behind. The kitchen is warm, yet the air feels stale. Neglected.

'We need to talk.' Zac's voice is hoarse. He drags his fingers through his hair.

'No shit.'

He flinches at my tone. 'Do you have anything you want to tell me?' His fingers flex and clench at his sides.

'I could ask you the same thing.'

'God, Nina, why can't we just have a straightforward conversation? I'm sick of this.'

'Sick of *what*?' I cry. 'Sick of being jealous over something that's happening in your imagination?' I'm no longer treading on eggshells. No longer pleading and apologising, because I have nothing to be sorry about.

Zac shakes his head. 'Chris saw you both.' He looks directly at me and I stare right back.

'Saw who? Ah, I take it you're talking about James?'

Zac's face tightens at the mention of his name. His whole body is rigid.

'Of course Chris saw us! I work with James. He comes here for business meetings sometimes. You know that!' *Although that's all in the past now.*

'And do your "business" meetings include fucking him in your office?'

I screw up my face in disbelief at what I'm hearing. '*Excuse me!?* Zac, what are you talking about?'

'Chris saw you two out there. He wasn't sure whether or not to tell me, but he thought I deserved to know the truth.'

I can't believe I'm hearing right. 'Chris from upstairs told you that he saw me and James Kipling… together? Is he on crack?'

'So you're denying it?' Zac inhales, storms out of the kitchen and then marches straight back in, his face white with stress and anger. 'Why would Chris lie about something like that?'

'I have no clue, Zac. It's messed up. I have not, nor would I ever sleep with James Kipling. Not least because I already have a boyfriend, even if he is currently behaving like a jealous twat. And why would you believe the word of a neighbour – a virtual stranger – over me, your actual girlfriend, who you've been with for five years?'

'He's not a stranger, he's our neighbour and a friend. And what would be his reason for making something like that up? There's no motivation for him to lie. And it would explain why he doesn't like you very much – because he knows your dirty little secret.'

Zac's words, his tone, hurt worse than if he was physically wounding me. He's filled with such contempt. As if he hates me. He actually hates me.

'Well!' I choke back. 'You'll be pleased to hear that James called me this morning and thanks to your bullshit macho display yesterday – going over there, threatening to beat him up or whatever – he's pulling the plug on my business. So thank you very fucking much for that!' My whole body is trembling and I can barely think straight. I cannot believe that Zac actually thinks I slept with someone else. And as for *Chris*? The man's insane. What's he playing at?

Zac's face reddens. 'I'm sorry about your company, Nina, but right now I'm more upset about your cheating and your priorities. The problem is, you care more about the business than you do about us. And that's the truth. Did you—' He stops talking mid flow, expels air. 'Never mind.'

'No!' I snap. 'Tell me what you were about to say. You haven't held back so far. Why stop now?'

His chin juts. 'I was just wondering, if you might have felt pressured to sleep with him because of the business.'

I choke out a bitter laugh of disbelief. 'You think I'm sleeping with him to get ahead? If you truly believe I'm capable of that, then it looks like we really do have a problem.'

'So you admit you slept with him?'

'*What?* No!' Through this haze of pain and anger, something occurs to me. 'What about Vanessa? Did she witness my imaginary affair too?'

'I don't know. Does it matter?' Zac stares up at the ceiling for a moment. 'Look, until you can admit what you've done, I don't think we've got anything to talk about.' He grits his teeth. 'I've got to go to work. I'm already late as it is. I think I'm going to stay round Kit and Ben's tonight. Call me if you want to have a truthful conversation.'

I throw my hands up in the air. 'Zac.'

He turns to go.

'Zac! Look at me. I *am* telling you the truth. For some reason, Chris is lying to you. Why won't you believe me?'

'Because I don't know why he would lie. It makes no sense.'

'Maybe he's deranged. Maybe he's a psychopath. Maybe he needs an eye test. Who knows? Who cares? Because it's. Not. True.'

'To be honest, Nina, my head is so screwed up right now I don't know what to believe. I have to go.'

'Fine! Go!'

Zac sighs, turns on his heel and leaves the kitchen. A moment later the front door closes and I hear the faint sound of his van starting up. Tears drip down my cheeks unchecked. How can Zac believe that I would sleep with someone else? I know his previous girlfriend cheated on him, but I'm not like that. I thought he *knew* that.

I leave the kitchen and go into the bedroom. Sit on the edge of the bed, my body numb, my mind in turmoil. I don't even feel like I'm here. What is going on? Why is everything falling apart?

CHAPTER THIRTY-FIVE

THEN

The two of us turn into a wide road with deep front lawns and large single-storey dwellings that are all variations of the same style.

'This is my street,' Adam says, swinging his backpack off his shoulder.

'It's nice.'

'It's good for skateboarding anyway.'

'I didn't know you skated.'

'Yeah. Do you?'

I shake my head.

'I'll teach you, if you like.'

'Thanks, but I don't think I'd be any good.' My mouth goes dry at the thought of how embarrassing it would be. I picture myself wobbling and falling. Not a good look. I change the subject. 'Have you always lived here?'

'Yep. Born and raised.'

'Me too. At my house I mean.'

He turns into one of the drives and takes a key out of a zip-up pocket in his backpack. The front door is white UPVC. I follow him inside. He takes off his shoes so I do the same. I tense up in anticipation of meeting his mum.

We go into a clean square kitchen that overlooks the back garden. My gaze sweeps across a collection of photos that sit on one of the countertops. Most are of Adam at various ages, but there are also a couple of who I assume are his mum and dad. They look nice. Happy.

'God, don't look at those.' Adam grins. 'Embarrassing.'

'They're not as bad as mine. At least you don't have a wonky fringe in yours.'

Adam opens the fridge and scans the shelves for a moment. 'Want some orange juice?'

My mouth is dry, but I'm too nervous to drink juice. I need something plain. 'Could I just have some water?'

'Sure.'

'Where's your mum?'

'Oh, she's at work. She doesn't get home until after six.'

The time on the oven says 15.40. That means Adam and I will be in the house alone for hours. My heart beats a rapid tattoo. Will this be the day we kiss? Does Adam even feel that way about me? I think he does, but I can't be sure.

I decide right now that I'm not going to be the one to make the first move. No way. It would be mortifying if he rejected me. And I'm not prepared to ruin our friendship. Much as I want it to turn into something more, I'd rather have what we have now than nothing at all.

CHAPTER THIRTY-SIX

The temptation to climb into bed and forget about my worries vanished with Zac's visit and his crazy accusations of sleeping with my investor. The thought of Zac believing those things about me makes it hard to breathe. Like having broken glass in my lungs. I pace the flat, trying to make sense of what's happening.

The one constant in all this is Chris bloody Jackson. He's the one who told Zac that James had called round that first time. He also speaks over me to Zac, as if I'm not even there. But, then again, I don't think he speaks nicely to Vanessa either. So maybe he's just a misogynist. He lied to Zac about seeing me and James sleeping together. I'm also willing to bet he's behind those flowers arriving for me, signed 'J'.

The question is *why*? Why does he want Zac to think I'm having an affair with James Kipling? I need to confront Chris. I need him to look me in the eye and explain why he's been stirring the pot and lying to my boyfriend. What's the point of it? The thought of confronting him is scary, but I don't think I have much of a choice.

It's late morning. I need to have it out with Chris but I still have hours until he gets back from work. What am I supposed to do between now and then? I need to keep busy or I'll work myself up into even more of a state. But how can I concentrate on anything meaningful? I stride into the kitchen and pour myself a glass of water. It gushes out of the tap too fast, splashing and making dark stains on my top. I gulp the liquid down, feeling its cold descent through my gullet. I should eat something too, but the thought makes my stomach roil.

Instead, I go to the lounge and pull open the curtains. Weak light creeps into the room, highlighting its neglected state. Tea stains grime the coffee table, a layer of dust covers the TV stand and the floor needs a good vacuum. I drop onto the sofa, glaring out at the driveway, my outrage still bubbling away while misery and devastation fight for second place. I can't let myself sink. I need to keep my anger sharp for when I confront Chris.

I stay seated as everything churns through my mind. As the injustice of it all hits me over and over. I keep checking my phone in case Zac has decided to call or message, but there's nothing from him or anyone else. I haven't opened any of my work emails since James's call. It's all such a mess, I can't face it right now. The thought of sorting out the business makes me want to curl up into a ball and hide.

I realise that I won't be able to concentrate on any work stuff until I've fixed things properly with Zac. And as he won't even speak to me, it seems talking to Chris is my only option. Maybe once Zac and I have straightened things out, then I'll be able to decide what to do about the company. Until then, I don't even want to think about it.

Turns out, I don't have to wait hours for Chris to return after all. At midday, his navy Audi turns into the drive. I lurch to my feet, grab my coat and keys and leave the flat, striding around the side to where Chris is getting out of his car. He glances up and swears under his breath when he sees me coming towards him.

I narrow my eyes. 'I need a word with you.' Annoyingly, my voice is shaky, like I'm nervous. But it's not nerves. It's furious emotion.

'Sorry, Nina, I'm having lunch with Ness and then I have to get back to work. Some other time, okay?'

'No. It's not okay. And don't act like you don't know why I'm here.'

Chris locks his car and walks towards his front door, key ready to insert into the lock.

I dart around his car and stand with my back pressed against the door, blocking his way. My heart pounds and sweat prickles under my armpits despite the chill wind.

'Can you get out of my way, please, Nina. I don't have time for this.' Chris's face is white, his lips pressed tight, his whole body rigid, but his voice is calm and measured.

'Why have you been lying to Zac about me?'

Two spots of colour appear on his cheeks. 'I don't know what you're talking about. Please move away from my front door.'

'Bullshit. You know exactly what I'm talking about. I can see it in your face. Why did you tell Zac I had an affair with James Kipling? You've been dripping lies in his ear for weeks. Was it you who sent those flowers?'

'Nina, I don't know anything about any flowers. I'm sorry if you and your boyfriend are going through a rough time, but that's not my fault. Right now I need to go and check up on my pregnant wife.'

'Is Vanessa okay?' I frown, realising that I haven't seen her in a while.

'She's fine. Now please move.' He tries to reach around me to fit his key in the lock, but he won't be able to do that unless he manhandles me out of the way.

'I'm not budging until you tell me why you lied to Zac.' I stand firm, even though I'm half scared he might get violent.

Chris sighs and takes a step back, folding his arms across his chest. 'I didn't lie. I told him what I saw.'

'And what was that exactly?'

'I told him that I looked out the kitchen window and saw you and your business colleague having sex in your office.' His face is serious, he looks almost regretful, like he wishes he didn't have to tell me.

'Liar!' I'm incredulous.

'I'm sorry, I'm only telling you what I saw. And I know it's none of my business, but I like Zac and I thought he deserved to know what you've been doing.'

'This is unbelievable,' I mutter.

'I didn't ask to see you doing that. If you didn't want people to know you were sleeping together, then maybe you should have picked a more private venue, or closed the blinds.'

'I don't know what you think you saw out there, but it wasn't me sleeping with anybody! And even if you really do believe you saw that, why did you then encourage Zac to intimidate my investor? To go to his office and threaten him? That kind of behaviour is nothing like him. It's completely out of character.'

Chris exhales. 'When I told Zac what I'd seen, he was so angry he said he was going to kill the guy. I thought I'd better go with him to make sure he didn't do just that. I simply went along to try to keep him out of trouble. That's it. I wish I'd never got involved.'

I shake my head. 'You're lying, I know you are. You're really good at it, I'll give you that.'

'Believe what you want, Nina, but I'm telling you the truth.'

'Did Vanessa see what you claim you saw?'

'She was taking a nap at the time.'

'Well, that's convenient.' I roll my eyes. 'Can I talk to her? I'll move out of the way if you let me come up to your flat and hear what she has to say about it.'

'No!' Chris's expression clouds over. 'I don't want you upsetting my wife. Ever since you've moved in, we've put up with your parties, your endless deliveries, the arguments, the slamming doors, but I will not put up with you harassing my wife. She told me you've been constantly ringing our doorbell and knocking on the glass. It has to stop, do you hear?'

My jaw drops at his blatant twisting of the facts. '*Us* arguing?' I cry. 'What about *you*? What about the scraping of furniture across the floor at night, the screaming matches?'

'You're delusional, Nina. Now, I'm going to ask you one more time to step away from my front door, or I'll have no choice but to call the police. This is absolutely unacceptable behaviour.'

I'm shaking with rage. There's a pounding in my ears and a fog in front of my eyes. 'How can you stand there and act like *we're* the ones being antisocial? The only reason I was knocking on your door is because I saw you speaking to Zac yesterday. I saw you lie to him about me, get him all riled up and then drive off together. I wanted to speak to Vanessa to find out what was going on. Thanks to you, my boyfriend hates me and I'm losing my business. So you tell me who's the antisocial one!'

'Who's the one blocking me from getting into my house?' Chris asks, shrugging his shoulders and throwing his hands wide. The man is just short of being smug. He thinks he's got one over on me, but this isn't the end.

'Whatever your game is, Chris, it's not going to work. You won't split me and Zac up.'

'Sorry to say this,' he says, shaking his head and feigning sadness, 'but you seem to be doing a good enough job of that yourself.'

I'd rather he were rude and obnoxious than maintaining this pretence of feeling sorry for me. Is this all part of his plan? To make me doubt myself? No wonder Zac believed him. He almost has me believing him, and I'm the one he's lying about.

Chris pulls his phone from his coat pocket. 'I was serious about calling the police. You need to move, Nina.'

'Fine.' I raise my hands. 'I'm going.' I step away from the door and watch as he unlocks it, opens it a tiny fraction and squeezes through the gap. It closes behind him with a dull thud and I hear his footsteps clomping up the stairs.

I hug myself as cold raindrops start to fall. Aside from my argument with Zac, that was the most unsettling encounter I've ever had. Despite what I told Chris just now about not believing a word of what he said, I can't tell whether he really did get the wrong end of the stick about me and James, or whether he's lying on purpose.

I have enough to worry about with my relationship right now, but I also can't help fretting about Vanessa. I'm almost convinced that Chris is keeping her isolated against her will. That he's told her not to talk to me. I think I'll wait until Chris goes back to work and then I'll come back to see her. See if I can get her to at least open the door to me.

For now, I turn and head back to my lonely flat. But I can't help hearing Chris's words ringing in my ears – *delusional... antisocial... harassing his wife*. Surely that's not right. That's not *me*. I swallow and push away the unwelcome thought that I might actually be losing my mind.

CHAPTER THIRTY-SEVEN

Through the lounge window, I watch Chris drive away thirty minutes after he first arrived. Now's my chance to try to get Vanessa to open the door and talk to me.

I wait a short while, just to be sure he's gone, and then I leave the flat and return to the Jacksons' front door, the icy wind and spitting rain doing its best to deter me. If I can just get Vanessa to open the door I can ask if she has any idea what might be going on here. Because I sure as hell have no clue.

I ring the bell once and wait, listening for any sound through the glass. It's silent. I try to remember when I last actually saw her. I think it was over the weekend when she and Chris were unloading their shopping bags. Just before Zac and I had our lovely walk on the beach. Before everything went to shit. Has she been holed up in their flat ever since then? Is she okay? Crazy thoughts flicker through my mind, of her being locked in a room up there, or even tied to the bed. Or worse. But I'm probably only thinking these things because I'm stressed. I'm sure she's just resting. Tired. Am I making things worse for her by ringing the bell? Am I causing her anxiety? I hope not.

I'm torn between leaving her be, and ringing the bell once more. I need answers, and I really believe that Vanessa might have them. Reluctantly, I press the bell again. This will be the last time. If she doesn't answer, I'll leave her alone. Try to figure out some other way of getting to the truth.

The hallway beyond the door remains stubbornly dark and quiet. No one is coming.

Reluctantly, I slope back along the wet drive, dreading returning to my empty flat. My business is no longer the safe, enjoyable refuge it once was, so once I'm inside all I'll be able to do is wait for Zac to call or come home.

I've never been good at waiting.

Changing course, I head out onto the pavement. I stop, turn and stare up at the house, hoping to catch a glimpse of Vanessa in the window. But there's no movement up there. No face behind the glass.

Ignoring my tired eyes and growling stomach, I slide into my car and turn on the engine, flick on the wipers and take a breath.

The drive over to Ashley Cross is miserable. Rain and low light levels make for poor visibility. The red tail lights of the cars in front blur and shift, tyres hiss across puddles, and the fact I haven't slept gives everything a surreal quality. But having a car accident on top of all the other crap I'm dealing with is not an option, so I open my window and breathe in deep, keeping myself awake and alert.

Luckily, there's a free car space at the back of the building where Parker-Smith Architects is housed. I didn't forewarn them of my arrival so I hope Kit and Ben aren't out on site somewhere. I'm already damp from earlier, so I don't bother trying to shield myself from the downpour as I head to the back door of their practice and ring the bell. As I wait, I look down at myself. I'm wearing jeans, trainers and an old sweatshirt I use for decorating or gardening. I already know my face is blotchy from crying, and goodness knows what state my hair's in. Normally, I wouldn't be seen dead going out like this. Right now, I don't care.

I look up at the security camera. The glass door, etched with 'Parker-Smith Architects' in gold, swings open. Kit and Ben's assistant Marcel stands in the doorway looking at me through his designer glasses without recognition.

'Can I help you?'

'Hi, Marcel, it's Nina Davenport, Kit and Ben's friend, I—'

'Nina! Sorry, I didn't recognise you. You're soaked. Come in.'

'Thanks.'

'How long have you been standing out there? I only just heard the bell, but I've been on the phone, so maybe you've been ringing for a while.'

'No, it's fine, I just got here, don't worry.'

'Oh. Okay. Well, come in.' He walks along the corridor, past the offices of a firm of accountants on the ground floor. I follow him up a set of light-oak stairs which open out into a vast room with a mix of dark wood and polished concrete floors, and steel floor-to-ceiling windows. All the walls are white except for one, which is made from stacked grey stone of various tones and thicknesses. Most of the ceiling is double-height, apart from a suspended ceiling area made from reclaimed planks of wood, which hang over a massive trestle table that runs almost the length of the room. It usually takes my breath away, but today it's all a blur.

'Kit's out on a visit, but Ben's here.' Marcel points to where Ben is seated at the far end of the trestle, focused on his laptop. There are three other people working at the table too, but I don't recognise any of them.

I suddenly regret coming. What did I hope to achieve? Kit is first and foremost *Zac's* friend. They've been besties since school. And Ben is Kit's husband, so of course their loyalties will lie with him not with me.

Ben looks up and clocks me. He squints and gets to his feet. 'Nina? Is that you?'

'Hi, Ben.' My voice is thin. I walk towards him. 'I'm sorry for dropping in unannounced.'

'Don't apologise, it's fine. Marcel, can you get us both a coffee?'

'Sure.' Marcel turns to me. 'Flat white… or?'

'Flat white would be great, thanks.'

'Come into the rec room with me.' Ben leads me into their little lounge area at the rear of the building. It's full of comfy sofas and chairs – a place for them to take power naps when they have to pull all-nighters. Ben closes the door behind us.

'How was Zac last night?' I ask.

'An absolute mess.' Ben sounds cross with me.

I perch on the edge of a pale-blue armchair. 'Did he tell you why we argued?'

'I'd say it was more than an argument.' Ben sits in the middle of the sectional sofa, resting his elbows on his knees and his chin in his hands. 'How could you do that, Nina? You know Zac worships the ground you walk on.'

'That's just it, Ben. I didn't do anything. And I can't believe you and Kit would think I did! Let alone Zac.' My cheeks heat up and my heart pounds as I realise they all believe I did this.

'Look, hon, I don't want to get in the middle of this. Zac needed a place to stay and that's fine, but please don't ask me to take sides or anything like that. You know Kit and I love you both.'

'But that's just it. There's nothing to get in the middle of!' I give him a quick rundown of Chris's part in all of this, trying and failing to keep my voice even.

'So, you're saying that Chris lied about seeing you and James together?' He pulls at his bottom lip.

'Exactly.'

Ben straightens up and inhales as Marcel comes in with our coffees.

'Thanks.' I nod as he puts mine down on the side table next to me.

Marcel leaves, closing the door behind him. I wonder if *he* knows what's been going on too.

'Don't worry,' Ben says, reading my mind. 'None of the staff knows anything. Kit and I aren't gossipy – unless we're with you guys of course.'

I'm too stressed to smile at his quip. 'Thanks. So how am I supposed to prove to Zac that nothing's going on with James?'

'So, there was really nothing between you two at all?' Ben's eyes narrow, his caramel hair flops over one eye and he pushes it back.

'Nothing whatsoever. He's not even my type. Zac's the love of my life, so why would I jeopardise that? We've just bought a place together.'

Ben nods, but he doesn't reply. He picks up his coffee cup and takes a sip.

'I just don't know what to do. Zac came round earlier this morning and he wouldn't listen to me. He believes Chris's story. I know this is going to sound paranoid, but Chris has had it in for me ever since we moved in. He's been twisting the knife with Zac. Trying to turn him against me.'

Ben opens his mouth and then closes it again. There's a long pause while we both sip our coffees. 'I mean…'

'I know it sounds crazy when I say it out loud, but I don't know how else to put it. My neighbour is… he's weird. And I'm worried he's abusive to his wife. And Zac's been suckered in by him. He doesn't see what I see.' I'm willing Ben to believe me. To not think that I'm the crazy one. But I can tell he's uncomfortable with my revelation. Torn between wanting to stay loyal to Zac, and not offend me.

'Oh, Nina,' he replies eventually. 'I hope you and Zac are able to sort things out. You're our favourite couple.'

'Thanks, Ben.' I swallow, knowing that this is the most I'm going to get out of this conversation. Maybe Kit would have believed me. I wish he'd been here too. 'How's Kit?' I ask.

'Yeah, he's okay. He just had to… go and pick up some stuff.'

'Marcel said he's on a site visit.'

'Yes, he's going on a visit after picking up the stuff.' Ben's face goes red as he realises how bad he is at lying.

'He didn't want to see me, did he?' Hurt and frustration flare as I realise that neither of them believes me.

Ben blows air out of his mouth. 'You know how protective Kit gets about Zac. Especially after Mel broke his heart. Kit was the one who picked up the pieces after she left.'

'I know. But this isn't like that. I'm not Mel!' When I first got together with Zac he was still getting over his ex-girlfriend, who cheated on him. I think this is partly why he's been so quick to believe Chris's lies. But I thought he knew that I'm not like that. I love Zac. I would never hurt him that way.

'I know, sweetie. Like I said, just give Zac some time.'

'So Kit's hiding from me?'

'No, not hiding. Just, not ready to talk to you yet.'

I get to my feet. 'I don't believe this. I haven't even done anything wrong!' I drag my fingers through my hair. 'This was a complete waste of time.' I turn to leave, aware that I'm being unfair to Ben. He's in an awkward position, caught between two friends. But I'm just so angry at the whole impossible situation.

'Just give him some time,' Ben repeats.

I'm not sure whether he's talking about Zac or Kit.

I leave the building and walk to the car in a haze of exhausted grief. Everyone has turned against me. They all think I've done this terrible thing and are closing ranks around Zac, freezing me out. I wonder if Cali and Amy feel the same way. I should call them, but I'm too scared in case they have the same reaction. I think Amy might be sympathetic, but Cali's married to Ryan, who's one of Zac's best friends. How is this happening? *This is a nightmare.*

I wonder if Zac's mum also thinks I cheated on her son. I realise that her opinion means a lot. I've always been paranoid that she doesn't like me, and I think it's because I feel like I'm not good enough for Zac. That he's nicer than I am. More easy-going. Kinder. Whereas I'm this ambitious, desperate-to-prove-herself person who's forced him into buying a flat and into going along with my plans. Although I know this is nonsense. *But is it?*

I can't even think straight any more. I think the only thing I can face doing right now is sliding under my duvet and trying to get some sleep. Blotting out the whole hideous mess.

I sink into the car. Before I can change my mind, I call Sandra. Maybe she'll have some advice for me. I'm half relieved when it goes to voicemail. Opening my mouth to leave a message, I instantly change my mind. Instead, I end the call and fire off a short text.

Hi Sandra. Hope you're okay. Just wondered if you've spoken to Zac lately?

Maybe she'll intervene. If I can get her to believe me, then she can persuade Zac that he's got it all wrong. Would she do that for me? Or is this the moment she's been secretly praying for? My stomach lurches. I really hope not.

Somehow, I make it back to the flat in one piece. It's early evening already. The lights are on upstairs and I curse Chris in my head and under my breath, calling him all the names under the sun.

My flat is cold and dark, unwelcoming, like everything and everybody else right now. I think back to our first month here, when we had that stomach bug and then the power cut and all the weird noises and arguments from upstairs. And on top of all that, there's been all the hassle with Mistletoe Lane – the bad reviews, the returns, the itchy tops, the failed party-plan evening. Rather than the dream come true I thought it would be, moving here has been a disaster. A horror show.

I'm cold and damp and miserable. I should have a hot shower or bath before getting into bed, but I just can't be bothered. I hesitate outside our bedroom. I couldn't sleep last night without him there beside me. I realise I don't want to go in there without him. I miss him so much. He's my soulmate. My best friend. What's happened to us? How did we get to the point where we can't even talk?

My heart skitters as my phone pings.
It's a text.
It's from Sandra.

I'm very disappointed in you, Nina.

That's all it says. I'm shocked but not shocked. Of course he'll have told her and she'll have believed him. Yet, despite my assumption, part of me had thought – had *hoped* – that she might at least have wanted to hear my side of things before passing judgement. That she'd call me and say, *Tell me it's not true!* Give me a chance to explain my side of things. I stare at the message on the screen until it automatically switches off.

Sandra and I have known one another for five years. Surely, even if she doesn't think I'm right for her son, she wouldn't instantly believe that I'd cheat on him. Or perhaps it's not even about that. Maybe, this is just a convenient excuse to turn him off me. To get him to meet a more traditional girl who wants to get married and start a family.

There's no point in replying right now. I angrily wipe away a fresh set of tears. I'm fed up with crying. I just need to sleep. My stomach growls and I realise I haven't eaten anything all day, but the thought of food repulses me. I head to the spare room, yank off my trainers and sweatshirt, and climb under the covers in my sweatpants and T-shirt. I'm cold, gritty and uncomfortable, but I'm also bone-tired so I close my eyes and drift off almost instantly.

A sound wakens me. I have no idea what time it is, but it's dark. My mouth is dry and my face feels raw and swollen. Must be down to all the crying. Everything comes back to me in a horrifying rush. I try to push it away and return to the sweet oblivion of sleep.

But a thud from outside makes my skin prickle, makes the hairs stand up on the back of my neck.

Someone's out there.

I remember I'm in the back bedroom. Maybe it's just a fox or a cat in the garden. But it sounded heavy, like a footfall. There are no security lights at the back of the property, it was one of the more urgent jobs on our to-do list.

My eyes are wide. I sit up, trying to acclimatise to the dark. My body is tense. I should open the curtains and look outside, put my mind at rest, but I'm scared. Properly scared like I haven't been since I was a kid and imagined demons hiding under my bed. Right now, it's just me alone in this unfriendly flat with its unfriendly neighbours.

I remember what Marion from next door said about the name of this road. She told me that mistletoe was a parasite. At the time, I was annoyed with her for ruining the magic and charm of not only the place I live, but the name of my business too. Now I think it might have been a warning.

I hold my breath and peel back the duvet, cool air on my arms causing me to shiver. I place my bare feet on the wooden floor and stand, the creaking boards making me flinch. I stiffen at a crunch from outside. My heart is beating so fast I feel like I might have an actual heart attack.

I take a step towards the window, inch back the curtain and freeze in absolute shock.

There's a figure standing in the garden.

The light on their phone illuminates their face.

Oh shit.

It's Chris, and he's looking directly at me.

He's coming closer!

I open my mouth to scream, but he comes right up to the glass and puts a finger to his lips.

CHAPTER THIRTY-EIGHT

The wall outside the English block has become my regular place to hang out with Adam at break and lunchtimes. It's perfect because it's a little further away from the main school, it also isn't on the main drag where the cool kids walk around, and it has a great view of the field so we can people-watch without it being too obvious. There's also a massive oak tree that's perfect for sheltering when it's too hot or it's raining.

Since visiting Adam's house last week, we've definitely grown closer and I feel really easy and relaxed in his company. We still haven't kissed or anything like that, but I know it's only a matter of time.

I put my sandwich box on the wall and open my packet of crisps.

'What do you think of that new girl in Maths?' Adam asks.

'She seems all right. She was on the bus this morning.' I hold out my crisp packet.

Adam screws up his face 'Cheese and onion, bleurgh.'

'What? They're the best flavour.'

'Not if you don't want onion breath for the rest of the day.' He grins.

My stomach lurches. I have cheese and onion flavour crisps most days. What if that's the reason Adam hasn't kissed me? I finish what's in my mouth and stuff the open packet back in my bag resolving never to eat them again when I'm around Adam.

'She was on your bus?' he asks.

'What?'

'The new girl.'

'Oh, yeah.'

'Did you sit with her?'

'No.' The truth is that even though she was sitting by herself, she looked really cool and confident. Not like the sort of person who would want to hang out with me. So I walked past her and sat next to Matthew Grainger again, BO and all.

'Maybe you should get to know her. It can't be easy being the new girl.'

I glance across at Adam, a queasy feeling settling in my stomach. Why is he so interested? I tell myself he's just being friendly. He's a nice person. But I don't think that's the reason at all. My chest tightens at the thought that he might fancy her, but then I resolve to stop worrying about it. She'll soon be assimilated into the popular kids' clique and be out of the reach of Adam and me. And then it will become irrelevant whether he fancies her or not. At least, I hope so.

CHAPTER THIRTY-NINE

Standing outside, staring through the window, Chris looks genuinely scared.

'Can you let me in?' he mouths.

I shake my head vigorously, and take a step back from the glass. What the hell is this man doing in my garden in the middle of the night?

'Go away,' I mouth, making a shooing motion with my hand. I snatch up my phone from the bedside table and see that it's only eleven thirty. I thought it was the early hours of the morning.

'Please, I need to talk to you.' His voice is muffled by the glass. He glances up quickly and then switches his gaze back to me. He places a hand on the window.

What if he breaks the glass? What if he's really dangerous? 'Go, or I'll call the police. I'm warning you!' I hold my phone out so he can see I mean business. It strikes me that earlier today our roles were reversed: I was desperate to speak to *him* while he threatened to call the police. So what's changed? Why is he here?

'Nina, I can explain everything if you just let me in.'

Where was this offer to explain everything earlier? Why sneak around my garden after dark?

'No way.'

'Please.' He slips his phone in his pocket and places his palms together, pleading. 'I promise I'll tell you everything, but it has to be now. I don't know when I'll get the chance again.'

My body is vibrating with tension. I don't know what to do for the best. He sounds so genuine. Looks so worried. But I also know he's an accomplished liar.

'Go away,' I hiss. 'There's no way I'm letting you in here.' I suddenly worry about whether I've locked the back door. I was all over the place earlier when I left the house. What if it's unlocked? As I have that thought, my panicked gaze turns towards the wall of the spare room that's next to the kitchen.

It looks like Chris might be having the same realisation. He dashes towards the back door. I fumble my way through the dark guest room, flip on the light switch and run towards the kitchen. I'm too late. Chris is already inside, the back door closed behind him. He's panting, eyes glittering with relief or menace, I'm not sure.

'*Fuck.*' I exhale. I still have my phone in my hands. Why didn't I use it earlier? 'Get out! I'm calling the police right now!'

'Vanessa! It's *Vanessa!*' he pants.

'*What*, is she having the baby?' For a second I think I've got it all wrong. Maybe Vanessa is in trouble and Chris really *is* here to ask for my help.

'Shh, keep your voice down,' he hisses. '*No*. She's not… she's not in her right mind. Lately, she's not… It's all her, it's not me. I didn't want to, but she made me, and I can't do it any more. I just can't.' His words are a nonsensical jumble, his eyes wide, darting all over the place.

I don't think he's well. Maybe he's high. Whatever's going on, I think he might be genuinely dangerous. With shaking fingers I try to hold down the buttons on my phone that lead to the emergency SOS screen, but Chris is wise to what I'm trying to do. He lunges towards me and I scream. My phone goes flying out of my hands, slides across the countertop and into the empty sink next to him. He reaches across, picks it up and pockets it.

'What are you doing?' I cry.

'Shh.' He looks up at the ceiling. 'Please be quiet.'

'Give me back my phone!'

'Sorry, but you can't call the police. This is important.'

'What do you want, Chris?' We're both standing here in the dark, both trembling, there's a faint trickle of light coming from the spare room, but I'm too scared to step back and turn on the main light in here. I'm too scared to move in case it triggers him to lunge for me again.

'Listen,' he whispers, glancing up at the ceiling, 'she's having a bath. I don't know how long she'll be. We don't have much time. I shouldn't be here. Today, earlier, when we were talking outside, she was standing on the other side of the door, listening, which is why I had to lie to you. She would have gone mad if I told you the truth.'

I'm trying to follow what he's saying, but it all sounds so improbable. 'You're talking about Vanessa?'

'Yes. I'm sorry, but she made me lie to Zac about you and James.'

'She made you lie?'

'All this stuff that's been going on, it was all her. I went along with it at first because… well, I love my wife and I want to make her happy. But it's gone too far. I'm sorry, Nina. I'm so sorry.'

'You're telling me Vanessa's behind this thing with Zac, and James?'

'Exactly.'

'Why would she do that? Why should I believe you? You already lied to Zac about me and James having an affair. You lied to my face about it too. Made *me* out to be a liar. To be crazy.'

'I told you why.' He hisses in frustration. 'My wife. You don't argue with her.'

I shake my head, trying to wrap my brain around what Chris is telling me, but it just doesn't fit with everything that's been going on. I'm so confused right now, and I don't trust him one bit.

'You're mad. She's the quietest, sweetest—'

'That's what she wants you to think,' he cuts me off, his eyes boring into mine. 'But she's not like that at all.'

'No.' I shake my head, thinking back to earlier when he was so convincing. 'I don't believe you. You're either a fantasist or a liar.'

'I'm sorry, I know I lied before but, like I said, I had no choice.'

I stare at him for a moment, desperately trying to work out if I'm being played again. Manipulated in some way.

'If that's true, will you tell Zac what you just told me?'

Chris nods. 'Of course.'

'You promise?' My heart swells at the thought of all this being straightened out at last. But what if this is simply another of Chris's twisted games?

We both jump at the sound of a bang at the front door.

There's a woman screaming out there. 'Chris! I know you're in there! You'd better not be talking to Nina!'

Could that really be Vanessa?

Chris's eyes are wide, his hands trembling. He stares at me and swallows. His terror really does seem genuine. Has he been telling the truth after all?

CHAPTER FORTY

I make a move towards the front door, but Chris grabs my arm. I flinch and give a little scream.

'Don't let her in,' he hisses. 'Don't let her know I'm here.'

'Chris!' Shrill and insistent, Vanessa's voice calls from out the front of the house. The bell chimes and there's a sharp knocking at the door. 'Nina! Can you open the door?'

I shake off Chris's hold on my arm, and stagger back. 'I'm letting her in. Then you can both explain to me what's going on.'

'Please, don't!' His eyes are wide, his face pale. This isn't the same Chris I know. This isn't the cocky, dismissive man who's been ruining my life. This person in front of me seems fearful and unsure.

'Why?' I snap. 'Why should I do what you tell me?' I turn and march down the hallway, half expecting Chris to try and pull me back again, but he doesn't follow.

I yank open the front door.

Vanessa stands there in navy joggers and a sweatshirt, hair damp, face red. Her eyes shine and her expression has a manic quality. 'Is Chris here?' She peers past me down the dark hall.

'Are you okay?' I ask.

'I was in the bath. I was calling for him and he didn't come. Why is he down here? What's he been saying?'

'Vanessa? What's going on? Has he hurt you?'

She wrinkles her nose. 'Chris wouldn't hurt a fly. He's here, isn't he? Can I come in?'

I move back and gesture to her to come inside.

She takes a step over the threshold and looks at me. 'I heard a scream earlier. Was it you?'

'Um…'

'I heard voices, and I know Zac's not here, so I was wondering if it's my husband…' She takes another step. 'Is he here? You still haven't answered me.'

I move to let her past, and switch on the hall light before closing the front door. 'I was asleep,' I reply, still not sure what to say, who to trust. 'Chris woke me up. He was in the garden! I've been trying to get in touch with you for days, Vanessa. But you wouldn't answer your door. Are you okay?'

'I never answer the door,' she says, walking away from me down the hallway. 'It's always people trying to sell something.' She goes into the kitchen without waiting for me.

I rub my arms, take a breath and follow her. I don't like this at all. I don't like them being in my flat together. Right this moment, I don't trust either of them and I want them to leave. But I also want to find out what's happening here.

Vanessa has turned on the kitchen light and is having a go at Chris. 'Why did you come down here? I was in the bath – what if I'd slipped? You know how hard it is for me to get out while I'm pregnant. If I'd fallen and hurt the baby it would have been completely your fault! You can be such a thoughtless prick!'

I'm shocked by her vicious tone.

She realises I've come in, turns and shakes her head. 'Men, eh? Some of them are so selfish, aren't they? Look at your boyfriend… he's left you, hasn't he? When you didn't even do anything wrong. See, *selfish*. Although I bet that's never happened to you before, has it, Nina? Bet you've never had a man leave you.'

I open my mouth to reply but she carries on talking.

'No. Everybody loves Nina Davenport, am I right, or am I right?' She smiles, but it's not a nice smile. It's not her usual sweet, unconfident smile. It's a sneer. A slash of menace.

'Have I done something to upset you?' I ask, my chest constricting.

Chris shoots me a look of worry. Of warning.

'*Did you do something to upset me?*' She holds her chin as though trying to think. 'Hmm? Did you? Did you?'

'Leave her alone, Ness.'

'Oh, shut up, Chris.'

His eyes are bright as though he might cry, his hands clenching and unclenching at his sides. His voice trembles. 'You need to stop this, Vanessa. It's enough now.'

She throws him a look of contempt. 'Look who's grown some balls at last. I told you what would happen if you spoke to her! You only had to wait a few more weeks and it would have been over. But now you've wrecked everything. Ugh, I'm so mad. I can't believe you've done this. I'm supposed to be your wife, the one you stick up for. But you're more worried about Nina bloody Davenport. Along with everyone else. Poor Nina, let's all flock around Nina and make sure she's okay.'

'Can someone explain what the hell is going on?' I cry.

'She never used to be like this,' Chris tells me quickly without looking at Vanessa. 'But it's been getting worse. She's obsessed!'

'I told you to SHUT UP!' Vanessa stamps her foot.

I inhale sharply at her outburst.

Chris swallows. 'I'm only telling the truth, Ness. I'm worried about you. You're going to stress out the baby.' He hugs himself and rocks back and forth on his heels.

'Yes, because that's all you care about, isn't it?' Vanessa cries. 'The baby, the baby, the baby. No one gives a shit about ME! It's exhausting. I'm exhausted.'

I take a step backwards towards the hall. 'Vanessa, Chris is right. Why don't you come and sit down in the lounge for a while?'

She turns from Chris to focus her attention on me. 'You don't remember me at all, do you?'

'*Remember you?*' I don't know what she's talking about, but the way she's looking at me makes my stomach squirm. What's going on here? Vanessa's acting like I've done something to upset her, but I've only ever been nice, supportive, even. I really want her to leave. I don't want to hear what she's about to tell me. But the way she's looking at me with her eyes glittering, her mouth twisted into a spiteful smile, lets me know that she's not going anywhere soon. Not until she's said what she's come here to say.

CHAPTER FORTY-ONE

THEN

I'm late out of History today because Miss Llewelyn asked me and a couple of the others to help move some tables. I hope Adam doesn't think I've abandoned him.

Finally, after ten minutes (that felt like ten hours), our teacher lets us go. I grab my bag and hurry over to the English block. I scan the wall for Adam, but I can't see him. Perhaps he gave up on me and went somewhere else. I don't think he'll be annoyed that I was a no-show; he's not that kind of person.

Disappointment tugs at my chest. I live for the moments when we can hang out, so the fact that I now have to spend the remaining forty-five minutes of my lunch break without him sends me into a spiral of gloom.

But wait, I think that's him beneath the shade of the oak tree. It is. It's him. My heart flips.

'Hey, Adam!'

He turns with a frown, then smiles when he sees me, beckoning me over. His eyes are sparkling. He's happy I'm here.

As I draw closer, I realise he's not alone. A girl is leaning with her back against the trunk of the oak. She's twirling a lock of her chestnut hair around her finger. She's tall and voluptuous, her skin blemish-free, her face open and confident.

'Where've you been?' Adam asks as I walk over, my previous anticipation replaced by something darker, something unnamed.

'I had to help Miss Llewellyn with some stuff. So annoying. She made us—'

'This is Nina, from our Maths class,' Adam says, interrupting me. 'She was lost coming out of Science so I said she could hang out with us if she wanted. Cool, right?'

'Uh, yeah, sure.' I swallow. 'Or… we could help you find your friends, if you like?'

'This is Vanessa.' Adam introduces me, ignoring my suggestion.

'Hi, Vanessa.' Nina gives me a warm smile. 'I recognise you. We're on the same bus.'

I frown. 'Are we?' I don't know why I'm pretending not to know that.

She laughs. 'Yes! You get on a couple of stops after mine. We should totally sit together.'

'Yeah, that would be good,' I reply. I'm trying to be nice, but inside I'm wondering what's happening here. Is she interested in Adam? Is he interested in her? Or is he simply being friendly? This whole exchange has wrong-footed me. I was sure I would be too boring and plain for someone like Nina to associate with. But maybe that's because it's not me she wants to hang out with at all. I glance over at Adam and feel sick at the way he's looking at her. Nina is everything I'm not. I don't know why I ever thought I stood a chance with him.

In the days that follow, Adam confides in me that he is indeed smitten with Nina. I pretend to be excited for him. I pretend that I'm not dying inside. That the loss of our intimate circle of two doesn't feel like the end of the world.

I'd thought that Adam and I were bonded together by the loss of our fathers. That it made our friendship special. Deeper. That it was *meant to be. But it was nothing of the sort. I'm simply another friend. A person to sit on a wall with and pass the time.*

So I pull my friendship away. Making excuses that I'm busy, or catching up with homework, or I have chess club, or some other lie that doesn't involve me watching Adam drool over Nina.

I don't sit with her on the bus. I don't even give her any eye contact. Nina's puzzled by my coldness, but I'm sure she doesn't lose any sleep over it. I'm simply that weird quiet girl who used to hang out with Adam.

I revert to being a loner. It's safer that way. No chance of misconstruing things and making a fool of myself. I can see in his eyes that Adam's hurt by my rejection of his friendship, but he'll get over it. He doesn't make a big deal of it anyway. He's not heartbroken.

Once again, school becomes a lonely place and home reverts to being my sanctuary. The place that connects me to Dad. The only place I feel I belong… despite my family.

As I predicted, Adam and Nina eventually get together. I hear about it from Abigail Parks in PE. Apparently they snogged at Jane Marciano's party over the weekend.

It didn't last long. Nina ended things after a few weeks apparently. Left Adam broken-hearted. She moved into cooler circles and left him behind.

Serves him right.

I still don't speak to Adam, even after Nina broke up with him. He treated me badly. He doesn't deserve my friendship.

CHAPTER FORTY-TWO

'I can't believe you don't remember.' Vanessa's gaze skewers me. 'We went to school together at Highcliffe.'

'Wait!' Chris looks from Vanessa to me and back again. 'You went to *school* together?'

'*Vanessa…?*' I try to think back to my circle of friends there, but none of them were called Vanessa… Maybe she's got it wrong. Mistaken me for someone else.

And then I get a faint but sudden flashback of my first few weeks, just after we'd moved down from London. There was a boy in my Maths class who had a crush on me. What was his name? *Adam.* But he got too intense too quickly so I backed off. Yes! He had this odd little friend called Vanessa who was actually quite rude towards me, if I remember correctly. I turn to Vanessa with recognition, it's all coming back to me now.

'Oh, my goodness, yes, you were on my bus! Was that *you*? It was, wasn't it?'

'So you do remember.' She cradles her bump.

Now that I really look at her, I can still see the girl she was back then. She hasn't actually changed that much. She was always so quiet and unassuming. But it looks like she's found her voice now. When I first started at the school, I'd thought she was nice, sweet. But for some reason she didn't welcome my overtures of friendship, so I gave up.

'You were Adam's friend.'

Vanessa's face tightens.

'Why didn't you tell me you knew each other?' Chris is speaking to his wife, but she's only focused on me.

'Did you recognise me when Zac and I moved in?' I ask.

Vanessa shrugs and nods.

'Why didn't you say anything?'

'I wanted to see if you'd remember on your own. But, of course, you didn't.'

'Sorry, but it was almost twenty years ago. If you'd jogged my memory, of course I would have remembered. So are you going to tell me what all this is about?' I wonder if she's pissed off because I didn't recognise her.

'It's just something that got out of hand,' Chris says.

'*Chris!* Can you just keep your mouth shut.' Vanessa's fists clench and she takes a deep breath.

I'm not accustomed to seeing her act so rudely. It's unsettling.

She turns to me. 'Ignore him,' she says, trying to keep her voice steady. 'He's had a few drinks and he doesn't know what he's talking about.'

'I haven't had *any* drinks,' he mutters.

'Chris and I are going to go back upstairs, and you can just forget whatever it is he's told you tonight.' I catch the threatening look she throws him.

I shake my head. 'I don't think so.' I turn to her husband. 'You've already started coming clean, just tell me the rest.'

He runs a hand through his hair. 'Sorry, Ness, she needs to know. This has all gone far enough.'

'Chris, I swear if you open your mouth—'

But Chris ignores her and starts speaking.

CHAPTER FORTY-THREE

Cinnamon and ochre leaves cover the driveway. The air is crisp and sharp with the smoky scent of bonfires and rain. It's the scent of my heart breaking.

'You know I can't afford that amount, Ed.' I look up at my brother's hard face. His lack of warmth. His eyes not even focused on me and my grief. 'Why do you have to sell it? You'll want a family one day. You know it was Dad's dream for one of us to raise a family here like he did. Like Grandpa did before him. I don't know how you can bear to let it go.'

Ed looks at me for the first time since he got here. But it's a look of irritation, of resentment. 'He wanted YOU to start a family, Ness. Dad didn't care about me.'

'Of course he did. How can you even say that?'

He gives a harsh laugh. 'You're joking, aren't you? You were always Dad's favourite. He treated me like shit.' Ed jams his hands into his jeans pockets and kicks at the leaves and gravel with the toe of his boot.

'Don't exaggerate. I know it wasn't fair the way he was harder on you and softer on me, but he was stuck in that traditional idea, thought boys had to be toughened up. He only did it because he loved you. He wanted you to be strong. Take care of the family.'

'Easy for you to say. You weren't the one bearing the brunt of it.'

'No, I had Mum breathing down my neck being critical instead.'
I wrap my coat tighter around me as the wind sweeps in from the sea.
'And who did we spend more time with? It was Mum, wasn't it? So
don't tell me you had it worse, because you didn't.'

'Yeah, well, Dad's been gone for years. And now Mum's not here
either. So it's all irrelevant. There's no point holding on to the past. I'm
sick of thinking about it. This place needs to go. Mum was right about
you, Ness – you need to stop being such a crybaby about everything.'

I almost choke at his words. He always knows just how to aim his
blows so they sting the most. 'And Dad was right about you! You don't
know how to look after your family. You'll never be the man he was!'

Edward laughs. 'You're so pathetic, Vanessa. And so was he.'

At the age of twenty-four, Ed's already doing well for himself, while
at twenty-two, I'm struggling financially and emotionally. Which is
why it was a real kick in the guts when Mum died and left almost
everything, including the house, to my brother.

It's been a rough year. At the age of fifty-nine, Mum was diagnosed
with stage four breast cancer and passed away within five months of
the diagnosis. I nursed her at home while she criticised everything
I did. Meanwhile, Ed visited once every couple of weeks, and she
showered him with grateful thanks for taking the time out of his busy
life to show up.

And now, after the funeral and the grieving and the bittersweet
memories, I'm left with no home and a few pieces of her jewellery that
I'll never wear. That's it.

I'm not a materialistic person, but it hurt that, even in death, she
chose to favour Ed over me. I guess I should have expected it. And now
Ed wants to sell the house to strangers. I asked him to sell it to me. I
begged him. I offered to pay him in instalments over a few years – it
would be a nice top-up to his income. But he said that he wants to
get rid of it. That he needs the lump sum to invest in his business.

I try not to think about my brother pocketing all that money. Try
not to think about how little Mum truly must have thought of me to

leave everything to Ed. I'm hurt by her disregard for me, and by my brother's betrayal of our father's legacy. I'd hoped to change his mind today. To spark a little sympathy or nostalgia. But he's as impenetrable as he ever was. I tell myself to stay calm. Not to rise to his smug, horrible comments. But I can't help my disappointment turning to hostility.

Before leaving the house, I tell Ed that I never want to have anything to do with him again. I let him know that he was never a good brother to me. That he was mean and shallow and always made me feel like I was worthless.

Rather than being upset by my honesty, he shrugs and tells me that he feels the same about me. That I'm a pathetic daddy's girl who never grew up. Bitterness lodges in my throat as I leave our childhood home, probably for the last time.

I need to put the past from my mind and move on with my life. I now have a lovely boyfriend who worships the ground I walk on. We're even talking about moving in together. That's what I need to focus on.

The years pass. My boyfriend becomes my husband. Chris is a hard worker with a good job and between us we've saved up a decent deposit for our own place. He wants us to buy a nice new house, so we spend our weekends with estate agents looking at properties. But none of them feel right. None of them measure up. I feel a pang at the thought of my beautiful family home, but it's gone. Out of reach. Way out of our price range anyway. Useless to even think about it.

All this focus on buying a place has stirred up those bitter memories. I give into nostalgia for once, and go for a drive-by of our old family house. My heartbeats gather pace as I cruise down my old road. It looks just the same. I wonder if any of our old neighbours still live here.

And suddenly there it is — my childhood home. It's funny, but when I see it, I don't think about those unhappy years after Dad died. I'm reminded instead of when Ed and I were young and we used to tear around the garden, or help Dad fix stuff in his garden shed, or when we'd all sit round the dining table for Sunday lunch. Golden recollections of a time long gone.

It's been over seven years since I was last here, arguing with my brother on the driveway. More memories assault me. Cycling up and down the pavement as a child. Walking to the shops with Dad to get the Saturday papers, my hand in his. He'd buy me sweets and tell me to 'eat them quickly before your mother sees'. The four of us walking down to the beach laden with towels, picnics, body boards and fold-up chairs. Complaining because our arms were aching, but looking forward to dumping everything on the sand and running into the freezing sea.

I'm so busy reminiscing, that I almost don't notice the blue-and-white board outside our old house.

My heart almost comes to a complete stop.

It looks like our old house on Mistletoe Lane is for sale again.

CHAPTER FORTY-FOUR

As Chris tells me about Vanessa's history with this house, I steal glances at her. She's furious with him for sharing her personal history, but I don't know why she's upset about it. I think it's nice that she's ended up back in her childhood home again.

'I was shocked when I realised it had been converted into two apartments,' Vanessa mutters. 'Devastated, in fact.'

'But at least it meant we could afford to buy it,' Chris says. 'The whole house would have been way over our budget.'

'I suppose so.' She shrugs. 'I'd rather have had the downstairs flat with the garden though. *This* flat.' She gestures around her. 'But it had already been sold to the family you bought it from.'

Chris continues. 'We spent years saving for the day when we could buy the ground-floor flat too. So when the previous owners eventually put it on the market earlier this year, we couldn't believe our luck. Ness was pregnant so the timing couldn't have been more perfect. The mortgage company agreed to increase our loan so we had just about enough to put in a decent offer. Ness was ecstatic when the family who lived here accepted it. It was like it was meant to be.'

'You were going to buy this flat?' I ask, as realisation dawns.

'Until you and Zac gazumped us,' Chris says flatly.

I look from Chris to Vanessa. 'I can't believe you were the other party trying to buy the flat.'

'We were so close to getting it,' Chris says.

'And then we came along with the full asking price. Oh, that's… That must've been disappointing.' I let the information sink in for a moment, realising how gutted they must have been. 'But I still don't understand what that's got to do with you telling Zac I had an affair.'

'You really are stupid,' Vanessa mutters.

I bristle at her tone. 'Well maybe you should explain it to me then!'

'We didn't want you here!' she cries, her eyes narrowed. 'That clear enough for you? We were trying to drive you out. Get rid of you.'

'Drive us out?' I try to wrap my head around what she's telling me.

'It wasn't personal,' she snaps. 'Although… when I saw that it was *you* who was moving in, that just added insult to injury.'

'What? *Why?* We barely knew each other at school. If I remember rightly, I tried to be friendly but you just blanked me.'

'You were too self-absorbed to realise why I hated you.'

'*Hated* me?' I leave the school connection aside for the moment, focusing on the present. 'When you say you've been "trying to drive us out", what exactly are we talking about here?'

Vanessa clamps her lips together.

I raise my eyebrows as I gradually connect the dots. 'Right. So you made those weird banging noises in the middle of the night on purpose, that kind of thing?'

Chris reddens.

Realisation dawns more fully. 'Oh my God, you totally did that. And the arguments? Dragging furniture across the floor at three a.m.? All done on purpose to make us want to leave!'

Vanessa smirks while Chris looks at the floor.

My chest tightens uncomfortably. 'You came to work for me… Did you… Were you also responsible for the bad reviews and the itchy tops?'

'That's not even the half of it,' Vanessa replies with a nasty smile. 'You were so gullible.'

'You bitch!' I breathe. 'You tried to destroy my business. You *did* destroy my business!' I feel sick thinking about the access she had to my customers, to my email account, my social media. With a lurch of dread, I remember being locked out of my accounting software. 'Did you go into my accounts?'

She smirks. 'I tried. Couldn't crack your password.'

'How dare you!'

'This is *my* house. Not yours,' she says through gritted teeth. 'You've got my garden, my driveway, my beautiful front door. You've been swanning around in Dad's workshop, calling it your office. You've been hosting tacky parties. You're planning to knock down walls to destroy the heart of the place. You've got no right! Why are you even here? This isn't your home! Go and live somewhere else!'

'How the hell was I supposed to know you used to live here? That you were hoping to buy it back? I'm not a mind reader! You sabotaged my business because of something that isn't even my fault.' And then it hits me. 'I know why you lied to Zac about me and James! It's because… because you wanted to split us up! So we'd be forced to sell the flat… and you could buy it back!'

She blinks slowly in agreement. 'Well done.'

I turn to Chris. 'And you let her manipulate you into all this?'

'I'm so sorry,' he says, massaging his chest with the palm of his hand.

'So you should be!' I cry. 'What about the flowers? Was that you? Did you send them to make Zac think I had someone else?'

'Duh.' Vanessa rolls her eyes.

'That's such a vile thing to do!' I cry.

'I'm sorry,' Chris repeats. 'It was Tricia who inadvertently gave us the idea. She insinuated that you and James were having an affair.'

'I know. I heard you both talking out on the street.'

'You did?' His eyes widen and then his shoulders droop. 'Well, I'm sorry… for all of it.'

'Don't apologise to her.' Vanessa gives Chris a filthy look.

Something else occurs to me. 'The power cut…'

Chris inhales and gives a nod.

'You broke the switch? You ruined my event?'

He mumbles his confirmation.

'Why did you go along with it?' I demand of Chris. 'With *her*?' I jerk my hand at Vanessa. 'Can you not see how messed up this all is?'

'I know, but she's my wife. She wanted our child to have the same idyllic upbringing as she did.'

'It doesn't sound idyllic to me. She was a misery at school. And look at how she's turned out!'

'Look who's talking,' Vanessa mutters.

Chris's face reddens. 'We never planned to take things this far. It all just escalated.'

'That's no excuse. Even the small stuff you did is outrageous. I should report you to the police! Surely you can't get away with this type of thing. You need to come clean to Zac. Tell him what you've been doing. You can't screw with people's lives like this!'

'We don't need you to tell us what we can and can't do,' Vanessa says haughtily. 'You and Zac aren't welcome here. And if he's only now just realised that you're an uncaring, spoiled little brat, then good for him. You both need to move out.'

'What, and sell to you. I suppose?' I lean in close to her face, my heart pounding with fury, my blood running hot in my veins. 'There's no way in hell we would ever sell our flat to you, Vanessa. Not after what you've done. I'd rather *give* it away.'

Her face blanches, realising she's lost whatever chance she might have had.

'Now get out of *my* flat,' I hiss through gritted teeth. I'm desperate to call Zac. To tell him everything that's gone on here.

To get our relationship back on track. I'm already thinking about putting this place on the market. I can't stand the thought of living below the Jacksons any longer. And with the funding from my business withdrawn, we won't be able to afford to stay here anyway. I'm already having uncharitable thoughts about selling to the most obnoxious buyer I can find.

'I guess it's always easy for people like you, isn't it?' Vanessa mutters as Chris tries to usher her out of the kitchen.

'What's that's supposed to mean?' I fold my arms, sick of her snide tone.

'Rich parents,' she scoffs, shrugging Chris's hand off her arm.

'My parents have nothing to do with any of this.'

'That's such crap. How could you have afforded this place without Mummy and Daddy's help?' she sneers. 'Your business makes no money and your boyfriend's a self-employed plumber. It's almost impossible to get a mortgage when you're self-employed.'

'Not that it's any of your business, but I've never taken money from my parents. I work hard like everyone else.'

'I don't believe you.'

'Come on, Ness, let's go.' Chris puts his arms around her to lead her away.

She shrugs him off again, more vehemently this time. 'If you hadn't come along with your smug asking-price offer, we'd have our family home by now. It's all I ever wanted. And you ruined it for us.'

I shake my head. 'You're the one who sounds like a spoiled child, Vanessa. We can't always get what we want. And you can't blame everyone else for not putting their dreams aside so you can have yours.'

'Unless you're Nina Davenport with your perfect life and doting parents who love you.' Vanessa gives me a last malicious glance before marching away down the hall towards the front door.

I can't wait for her to be gone. I'm sick of her thinking that I've had things easier than her. I think of all the passive-aggression I get from my mother – Vanessa has no idea. Nobody's life is perfect, whatever it might look like from the outside.

'If you must know, Vanessa, we were able to buy this place because I managed to get an investor for my company. So it was nothing to do with my parents.'

She stops and turns. 'Was your investor a friend of the family by any chance? Because you know that's pretty much the same thing as getting a handout from Mummy and Daddy.'

'And if it were, would that be so wrong? But, actually, no it wasn't. I was contacted by a local investment company, Newbury Limited. They liked the sound of my business and wanted to invest. We wouldn't even have known about this place if Newbury hadn't tipped us off that it was on the market. The fact that it had a large outbuilding for my stock was one of the reasons we moved here. So, you see, no family connections or handouts.'

The colour leeches from Vanessa's face. She clutches her stomach and exhales.

'Ness, are you okay?' Chris peers down at her. 'Is it the baby?'

'What did you say?' Ness whispers to me. 'Did you say *Newbury*?'

'Yes. Edward Newbury is my investor.'

Chris frowns and looks at his wife. 'Edward Newbury? Isn't that your brother's name?'

'Yes.' She swallows. 'Yes, it is.' And then she clenches her fists, screws up her face and screams with rage.

CHAPTER FORTY-FIVE

What the hell? I stare at Vanessa. Trying to wrap my head around this new piece of information.

'Ness… *Vanessa!*' Chris is standing helplessly in front of his wife trying to calm her down while she has what looks and sounds like a full-on screaming tantrum.

'I can't believe it!' She clenches her teeth and her fists, and pushes past Chris towards the front door. She yanks it open and steps out onto the icy driveway, gulping down the freezing night air. 'I just can't believe he's done this to me again!' she cries.

'You really need to calm down, Vanessa. This isn't good for you or the baby. I'm seriously worried you're going to do yourself some damage.' Chris throws me a worried look and shakes his head at his wife, stepping outside to join her.

I slip my feet into a pair of trainers and follow them both outside. 'Your brother is my investor?'

'He did it out of spite!' Vanessa cries. 'Edward knew I hated you at school. He taunted me back then because I liked Adam and you took him away from me.'

'You fancied *Adam*?' I stare at Vanessa, at the pain and anger contorting her face. She truly is an unhappy person. I almost feel sorry for her. 'I thought you two were just friends.'

'That's because you were self-obsessed. You never saw any further than your own needs!'

'That's not true, Vanessa. I tried to be your friend, but you wouldn't let me. So I moved on. Maybe if you'd been nicer we might've got to know each other and you could have told me you liked Adam. He wasn't even my type. Too much of an introvert. Too intense.'

'It was always so easy for you, wasn't it?' She's crying now. 'You just breezed in and took him. He was my only real friend back then.'

'Who's Adam?' Chris asks, his face a picture of confusion.

Vanessa ignores him, still talking to me. 'My brother was always so jealous because I was Dad's favourite. Then after Dad died, our relationship went from bad to terrible. But Ed had the last laugh because Mum loved him the most and left him the house in her will.' Vanessa stares up at the building, her face illuminated by the security lights. 'My brother knew how much I loved this place, but he sold it to strangers anyway. He must have been so mad when I eventually bought the upstairs flat.' She's shivering now, her teeth chattering. 'But then, for him to manoeuvre you into buying the other flat just to spite me… to help out the one other person I couldn't stand…'

I realise she's talking about me. It's disconcerting and upsetting to realise that I've been the focus of someone else's hatred for so many years. Hated for things that I was oblivious to. I feel blindsided. As if my life has been lived on the sunny side of the street while there were dark shadows stalking me. Shadows I never knew were there, but are now blocking out my light.

'Who's Adam?' Chris repeats.

'Just a boy from school,' I reply. 'Ancient history.'

'What's Ed's address?' Vanessa demands, glowering at me.

I stare back stupidly.

'Ed's home address,' she snaps with a fevered glare. 'We're not in touch any more and I need to speak to him. I'm going over there now.'

'I don't have it,' I reply. 'I only have the office address.'

Chris shakes his head. 'There'll be no one there now, Vanessa. You can't go getting worked up over this. It doesn't matter any more. Just let it go.'

'You're such a waste of space, Chris. You realise you've wrecked everything by coming down here and speaking to Nina behind my back? Acting like I'm the bad guy when all I want to do is create a wonderful home for our family. What part of that don't you get?' She pokes him in the chest with her forefinger, sharp little jabs to emphasise her point.

Chris's eyes blaze. 'Don't do that, Vanessa! I've been bending over backwards to do everything you wanted, putting up with your demands and your rages. You've been fixated on this house for years and I've gone along with all your dreams, your ambitions, your… *obsessions*. But I've had enough of it.' He inhales. 'I'm sorry, but I'm not going to be bullied by you any more. I'm done.'

She shoots him an incredulous look before wrinkling her nose. 'You'd better do what I say, Chris, or I'll make sure you *never* see our child.'

His burst of anger deflates and his face pales.

I've been in two minds about Chris's version of events up until now. But this exchange between him and Vanessa has removed any doubt. I'm certain he's been telling the truth this evening. I can't believe I was so taken in by Vanessa.

'Chris…' I put a hand on his arm. 'Despite what you've done, I'll be a witness for you if it comes to it. I'm sure she can't keep you from your child.' I try not to catch Vanessa's eye, but I can feel the heat from her stare.

'You're such a sanctimonious bitch!' she cries. 'Chris, let's go.' She turns to leave.

He doesn't move.

Vanessa stops and turns back. 'Come on, Chris.'

'No.'

'What do you mean, *no*?'

'I just told you, I can't do this any more. These twisted schemes of yours, they aren't going to work. It's gone too far. Nina's already said she's not selling the flat to us.'

'What about Zac?' I interrupt. 'You have to call him, Chris. Tell him you lied about me. You have to fix this.'

He nods in agreement. 'I will.'

'No!' Vanessa cries. 'You don't tell Zac anything.'

Chris rubs his forehead. 'Look, Ness, I'm sorry but I'm going to put this right. What we did… it was a terrible thing. I think I'm going to crash at Dave's place tonight.'

'*What?*' Her forehead creases. 'Why would you do that?'

'I'll come back tomorrow and we'll talk.'

'*No.* If you've got anything to say to me, Chris, you need to say it now.'

'Stop ordering me around!' he yells, making me jump. Vanessa takes a shocked step backwards. Chris's face is bright red, his whole body shaking. 'You want to talk *now*? Okay, we'll talk! I'll tell you what's happening, Vanessa – I'm leaving you and we're selling this bloody flat! If you must know, I never want to set foot in it again!'

She pauses for a moment, shocked by Chris's outburst, but she quickly recovers and squares her shoulders. 'Go on then, piss off!' she cries. 'Leave, like everyone else! And for your information, we are NOT selling the flat!' Vanessa throws him a vicious scowl before turning to me, her lip curling. 'And don't think you've won, *Nina*. This is so far from over you have no idea.'

I'm too shocked to reply. My whole body trembles as she turns and disappears off around the side of the house towards her front door, her feet crunching over the icy gravel.

Chris and I stand in silence for a moment.

He winces as their front door slams. 'I'm so sorry, Nina. About *everything*. I really am. I… I don't even know what got into me over the last few months. I'm not that person. I know it's no excuse, but my wife can be very persuasive. I let myself be bullied and blackmailed. I don't know when our relationship became so toxic. It wasn't always this bad, but her obsession's been building ever since we moved into the flat. I should never have let it get this bad.' He shakes his head and stares at the ground. 'It got worse after she fell pregnant. And then the disappointment at losing the flat to you guys… it tipped her over the edge.' He twists his fingers and glances up at me.

'If we're being blunt, Chris, I hated you. I knew there was something going on but I couldn't work out what.' I shiver in my sweatshirt, wrapping my arms around my body.

'I feel ashamed,' he admits. 'I purposely tried to break up you and Zac. I tried to make him paranoid about you. I hate to say it, but I was pretty believable. I really made him doubt you. I'm so incredibly sorry.'

I give a short nod of acceptance. 'I'm just relieved it's all out in the open now. That you've admitted it. That it wasn't me losing my mind.'

'I'll call Zac and own up to what Vanessa and I did. I'll tell him the truth – that Vanessa wanted to split you guys up so you'd sell the flat and we could buy it.'

'Okay, good. Just promise me you won't give in to Vanessa's blackmail any more. I meant what I said – I'll speak up as a witness for you to get access to your child, if you need me to. But you have to fix things between me and Zac first.'

'I don't deserve that. But thank you.' Chris's face is taut, the muscles jumping beneath his skin. 'I still can't believe I let things get this far. The way Vanessa is right now makes me worried for our baby. She needs help. I can't even…' His voice trails off and he swipes at his eyes with his fingertips. 'This is all just…'

A sudden empathy washes over me. 'What will you do now?'

He takes a breath. 'I don't know. Text my mate. See if I can kip in his spare room for a while.' He gives a short bitter laugh.

'Oh…' he reaches into his pocket and pulls out my phone. 'Here. Sorry about earlier in the garden – scaring you, then coming in and taking your phone.'

That encounter with Chris already feels like days ago. My head is spinning after everything that's happened this evening. The shock of it all. The discovery that Vanessa isn't the person I thought she was. That she's actually unhinged. She *threatened* me. Did she mean it? My knees buckle suddenly. Chris reaches out to grab my arm and steady me.

'Whoa,' he cries. 'You okay, Nina? Stupid question. You should go back inside. Sit down. Want me to come in, make sure you're okay?'

I realise I need to get inside ASAP. My legs are like jelly. But, much as I believe Chris is almost as much a victim as I've been, I still don't feel comfortable enough to let him back into my flat. I need to get some distance from the Jacksons. From both of them.

'Thanks, but I'll be fine. I just need to sit down.'

'Of course. You sure you don't want me to come in with you?'

I shake my head, suddenly desperate to get back inside and lock the door.

'Okay.' Chris lets go of my arm and shoves both hands in his pockets. He hovers awkwardly for a moment.

My whole body is now numb with cold. I hope my legs will carry me back inside.

'Lock your doors,' he advises before he leaves. 'And don't let Vanessa in. You've already seen how good she is at putting on an act to get what she wants.'

I nod and stagger back into the flat feeling shocked, alone and still very, very vulnerable.

CHAPTER FORTY-SIX

'Zac, please can you call me back! *Please*.'

I'm sitting on the sofa in the living room. I've tried calling Zac half a dozen times but he's just not picking up. I left a garbled, hysterical message about everything I've learned this evening. I told Zac that Chris admitted to lying. I just wish Zac were here so I could explain everything properly.

This evening has all been too much. I'm reeling from everything that Chris and Vanessa have unloaded on me. And the fact that Mr Newbury is Vanessa's *brother*. That's just crazy. It sounds like the two of them have a really screwed-up relationship.

I put my phone down next to me and blow on my icy fingers, trying to warm them up. If what Vanessa says is true, then the only reason Edward Newbury invested in my company was to mess with her. He knew she nursed some misplaced grudge against me and he wanted to use that against her. He obviously wanted Zac and I to buy the ground-floor flat to stop Chris and Vanessa from creating their dream home. Newbury was the one who encouraged me to buy it in the first place. He made me believe it would be a great idea. I thought he'd spotted something unique and investment-worthy in my business. Turns out I was being used. And now he's ditched me. My self-esteem is through the floor right now.

The flat feels so horrible without Zac here. I'm still mad at him for believing that I would cheat on him, but at least I sort of understand why he might have thought such a thing. Chris admitted that he'd been whispering in his ear for weeks, planting seeds of doubt, before telling him the lie that he'd actually seen me and James together. I wonder if I'd have believed Vanessa if she'd told me that she'd seen Zac with another woman. Possibly.

It makes me shudder to think that Vanessa and Edward grew up in this place. That this was their living room. That my office was her dad's garden shed. If I hadn't wanted to sell the place before hearing that piece of information, I definitely do now. I'm also freaking out at the thought of Vanessa being upstairs while I'm down here alone. She's walking around up there. I can hear the floorboards creaking above my head. What crazy thoughts are going through her mind right now?

How did I get things so wrong with the Jacksons? I'd thought that Chris was brash and abusive while Vanessa was meek and downtrodden. When in fact she was the manipulator and he was the one being bullied. Although, they were both putting on an act in front of me so I shouldn't beat myself up too much about being fooled.

I flinch at a crash from upstairs. It sounds like crockery being smashed. I picture Vanessa throwing things in a temper up there. Chris was right – she needs to calm down and think about the health of her baby. I hope her anger doesn't bring her downstairs again.

How will I ever sleep tonight with thoughts of Vanessa and her unpredictable behaviour ricocheting around my brain?

Perhaps I should just get in the car and go to Mum and Dad's place. At least I could relax there. On second thoughts, could I? I'd have to explain what's been happening here, and Mum would ask if Zac and I were still getting on. Even if I made something up, Mum would be curious. She'd suspect that Zac and I had fought and then she'd never forgive Zac. She'd use it as an excuse to have a go at him, to criticise our relationship.

Dad would get all protective. Henry and George would then find out. So would Belinda, which would be a fate almost worse than tonight's revelations. She'd be all fake concern while being thrilled that my relationship was in trouble. *No.* I can't go to my parents.

I realise I can't call Cali or Amy either. They would want to know all the details and would then criticise Zac for taking Chris's side over mine and he would never be the same again in their eyes. It would taint all of our friendships. I can't put them in the middle of this. What I really want is for Zac to come home. To be with me and have my back.

With a sinking heart, I realise the best thing is for me to stay here tonight and then sort out everything tomorrow. I tell myself I've nothing to be scared about. Vanessa is simply an unhappy, deeply disturbed woman who wants something she can't have.

For my peace of mind, I go around the flat re-checking all the windows and doors once more. I did make sure they were all locked when I first came in, but it doesn't hurt to double-check. Common sense tells me that Vanessa can't get in, but Chris was scared of her and I realise that so am I. I'm not sure why, because I'm far taller and stronger than she is. Plus she's pregnant so she's not exactly going to physically attack me. Is she capable of breaking a window to get in? I've always loved these traditional sash windows, but now I'm wishing we had unbreakable double glazing.

Back in the living room, I sink down onto the sofa. My eyelids are suddenly so heavy, I feel like I could fall asleep right here. I close my eyes and lean my head against a cushion. The main light is too bright, and I'm still chilly, but exhaustion takes over.

As I drift off, my mind is still fixated on Vanessa. How can such a small person create such an aura of fear?

Perhaps because she's so unhinged.

Volatile.

Unpredictable.

CHAPTER FORTY-SEVEN

I'm suddenly awake and the air is thick and heavy. I'm choking. Gasping. My throat is raw. The room is somehow bright and dark at the same time. Everything's blurred. I don't know if I'm really awake or in the middle of some terrible nightmare.

Panic bites. I sit up and blink, but that only makes things worse. There's a roaring in my ears and I can't stop coughing. I reach out and grab a cushion, pressing it gently over my face to block out the smoke. *Smoke!* Oh shit, I think the flat's on fire! I hear the distant splintering of glass but I still can't see anything. The smell is acrid, like burnt chemicals. I need to get out of here. Which way is the door?

My heart pounds, sweat drips down my back and my eyes are watering, stinging. I can't see any flames, but I can feel their heat, hear their crackle and whoosh. Feel the place burning around me. I drop to the ground where it's a little easier to breathe, but not by much.

I have to get out.

I crawl towards what I think is the lounge door, scrabbling with my fingers, but all I find is a wall. I'm completely disoriented.

Am I about to die?

A distant crash makes me fear that the whole house is about to collapse.

Please let me find a way to get out of here.

There's a fizz and a pop, and the room suddenly becomes darker. I'm crawling, edging my way along the wall, praying that I reach a door or a window or some way of getting out of here before it's too late.

A nearby smashing sound makes me rear back in terror. Another splintering sound. And yet another. A cool sweep of air finds my face, my nose, my lungs. I inhale. Fresher air finds its way down my scorched airways.

'*Nina!*' A man's voice, gruff and panicked. 'Nina, are you in here?'

'Zac?' I croak. 'Is that you?' But my voice is weak. Too small to be heard above the inferno. I still can't see a thing.

'Nina? Please be in here! Oh shit!' He's coughing now. 'Nina, *please.*'

I swallow and cough again. 'Zac!' I cry as loud as I can manage.

'*Nina?* Oh, thank God. I thought you were…'

I feel hands pat my hair and my back.

'Stay low and turn around,' he instructs.

I don't know how Zac can see where he's going. I feel as though I'm blind. I try to do as he says, but I'm feeling faint, like the roaring in my ears might not be the sound of flames.

'Stay low and follow me,' Zac barks. But his voice is fading. *I'm* fading.

Strong hands grip me and I feel myself being lifted. The air is suddenly thicker. We're moving and there's a rush of freezing air. Something sharp grazes my face. I think Zac's climbing out through the window with me in his arms. I catch glints of jagged glass.

On the edge of my hearing I make out the whine of sirens. Red and blue lights flash through the thick dark night. Zac staggers with me, carries me out into the road where there's a jumble of people and colours and movement. Cries and shrieks.

'Is she all right?' Zac asks someone. 'Will she be okay? She's not moving!'

I realise he's talking about *me*.

He lays me down on something firm and cold and soft. 'Nina, you'll be okay now. The paramedics are here. I'm sorry. I'm *so* sorry I wasn't here. I thought I'd lost you!'

Something is placed over my mouth and nose and I can breathe better, but it still hurts so much. Like knives in my throat and chest.

'Vanessa,' I croak. But nothing comes out of my mouth. I remember she was upstairs on her own. I wonder if anyone has gone back in for her or if she got out before me. I pull the mask off my face for a moment and Zac leans in to hear me better. 'Vanessa?' I whisper.

'I'll find out,' Zac says. 'The fire service is here now. They'll go in and check. Don't worry, Neens. They'll make sure she's safe.'

But now another thought crosses my mind.

A darker thought.

CHAPTER FORTY-EIGHT

NOW

I let out a low moan. Like an animal. This is like nothing I've ever felt before. It's paralysing. I stagger a few paces away from the back door onto the wet grass. Hot, sharp pain rips through me and I sink to my knees clutching my belly.

It's too soon. Seven weeks too soon. I can't give birth now. I just can't. I grit my teeth and try to breathe, but it's as if the air has been knocked from my lungs. Like some giant being is squeezing the life out of me with its huge fist.

Chris caused this premature labour with his betrayal. I don't think I'll ever be able to forgive him for taking Nina's side. He's my husband; he's supposed to be on my side. And now I'm out here in the cold, alone, having these hideous contractions. If my baby doesn't make it then it's Chris's fault.

Minutes pass and the pain subsides. The relief is like heaven. Maybe they were simply false-labour pains. I hope so.

There's a satisfying orange glow in the kitchen now. It's incredible how quickly those cheap wood cabinets caught fire. Just a few generous splashes of nail-polish remover over a stack of old papers on the stove and the whole thing went whoosh. Good thing I held on to that back door key. I knew it would come in handy one day.

I can already feel heat on my face, even out here. I ease myself backwards, further away from the house just as another contraction *hits. Again, the breath is knocked from my body. I really think this might be actual labour. I can't believe this is happening now on top of everything else.*

One of the kitchen windows shatters, exploding outwards, although I barely register it as I'm gripped by intense pain. It's lucky I moved out of range.

Nina's bedroom is at the front of the house so I'm sure she'll get out before the fire spreads. But if she doesn't… well, there's nothing I can do about it. Not while I'm out here giving birth. Maybe I should call a doctor to help me. But then they'll see the fire and they'll want to put it out. And I can't allow that to happen.

If Nina won't sell the flat to me, then no one will have it.

The whole house can burn to the ground.

CHAPTER FORTY-NINE

The female paramedic's voice fades in and out of my consciousness. Sirens whine as my body sways and jolts. It's too much effort to open my eyes. What I'd really like is to drift off into a warm fuzzy sleep.

'Will she be okay?' It's Zac, his deep voice laced with fear.

I want to reassure him. 'Zac?' I try to mouth. But it's too hard to concentrate on forming the words. There's a sharp pain in my chest and throat. If only I could sleep. The air in my nose is clean and cold, but it hurts so much to take a breath.

'Nina, don't try to talk. They're giving you oxygen to help you breathe. You're going to be fine, okay?' Zac's voice is like a balm. Soothing. He's here with me. I have a vague recollection of him being somewhere else. Of having lost him. But he's really here.

Something happened, but I can't remember what. Something to do with Zac and the flat. It was dark and hazy. Scary. A loud beeping starts up near my head.

'What's that?' Zac's voice is flooded with panic now.

'Nina.

'*Nina.*

'It's okay. You'll be okay.

'She'll be okay, *won't she*?'

CHAPTER FIFTY

ONE YEAR LATER

We reach the boarding gate with only seconds to spare, giddy with relief that we've made it just in time. Our bus from Varca Beach broke down on the way to the airport and we had to wait over an hour for the next one. But we didn't stress about it – it's all part of our great adventure and our promise to live for the moment and not worry about what comes next.

From Goa we're heading north to Agra to visit the Taj Mahal, and then we plan to travel around Rajasthan visiting temples, forts and – for my part – lots of bazaars. I've heard the shopping is amazing.

Zac and I apologise to the airline staff for our tardiness and we race across the hot tarmac to the waiting plane. The air is warm, the sun bright, the ground crew open and friendly. We climb the metal steps of the plane, Zac's hair blonder than I've ever seen it, his skin a gorgeous golden brown. He grins at me and squeezes my hand. It's November in India and we're as far away from the events of last year as it's possible to be.

If I think about it now, it all seems like a bad dream. Mistletoe Lane, the Jacksons, the lies, Edward Newbury, the *fire*… I dread to think what might have happened that night if Zac hadn't shown up at the flat when he did.

He'd had trouble sleeping in Kit and Ben's spare room, and so he got up to make a drink and check his phone. He listened to my distraught voice messages telling him everything I'd discovered about our neighbours, and pleading with him to call me or come over as soon as possible. He realised then that he had to see me. Try to sort things out. When he arrived, he was shocked to see smoke and flames in our flat. Our bedroom was already an inferno, and he'd been terrified that I was in there. That he was too late to save me.

The hall was inaccessible, so he smashed the living-room window and came into the flat that way. The room had been full of smoke, but he'd managed to locate me and lift me to safety. If I'd been in our bedroom, I wouldn't have made it out alive. It was a miracle I had no burns and all I suffered was mild smoke inhalation. It could have been so much worse. Even so, they kept me in the hospital for a couple of days.

Sandra was one of the first people to visit me. She brought me a huge teddy bear and a *Sorry* card. She apologised over and over for not believing me about not having cheated on her son, and said she'd never have forgiven herself if anything had happened to me in the fire. She cried and hugged me, and said that she was so happy that Zac and I had patched things up. She was genuinely devastated that our 'beautiful flat' was destroyed.

As well as Kit, Ben and my other friends, my family also came to visit. Mum was white-faced and shaken while Dad did most of the talking. My brothers teased me affectionately about my whispery, croaky voice, and Belinda was uncharacteristically quiet.

Amy and George went out for their drink the following weekend and, just as I'd hoped, they clicked. They've been an item for almost a year now. I'm so happy for the two of them.

After the fire, Zac said my dad thanked him for saving my life. Said he would never be able to repay him. Apparently Mum kissed his cheek and patted his shoulder, which is some kind of miracle. I told Zac not to expect that to ever happen again. We both laughed our heads off at that.

Dad also asked him about the flat, generously offering to pay for the repairs. Zac thanked him, but said that the insurance would hopefully be sorting it out.

The only rooms in any decent shape afterwards were the living room and the bathroom – they were the furthest from the kitchen where the fire started – but even they were ruined, black with soot. I wasn't allowed inside due to my still-recovering airways, but Zac showed me the video and photos that no longer looked anything like our once beautiful home.

As soon as Zac got me out that night, the fire service arrived. Barry and Sue from over the road had seen the flames and called them. Zac told the firefighters that the Jacksons might still be in their flat. But when they checked, they found the place empty. Upstairs hadn't been as badly impacted as our flat. It was all smoke damage up there.

The fire service put out the flames and found Vanessa crouched in our back garden, freezing and in labour two months early. They rushed her to hospital in an ambulance, but not before one of the firefighters noticed that she reeked of nail-polish remover, which was what they later determined was used to help start the fire.

'Have you got our boarding cards, Nina?'

I realise Zac is speaking. That the air stewards are waiting for me. I apologise, pass them our cards and we walk along the aisle to our seats. I'll be sad to leave Goa. It's been so relaxing and we've met some truly wonderful people. Our beach hut was owned by Jay, who was also the local beach-restaurant owner and looked after us like we were family. We stayed for three weeks – longer than intended – but I felt like I could have stayed there forever. We'll definitely be returning someday.

We quickly find our seats – they're in a row of three, but the third seat is empty, so we'll be able to spread out. Zac lets me have the window seat, which is only fair as he had it last time.

Vanessa gave birth to a premature baby girl that night. Her daughter was kept in the hospital for six weeks until being declared well enough to go home. The last I heard, Chris took his daughter home to his parents' house in Ferndown, where he was staying temporarily until he found a new place to live. True to his word, Chris called Zac the day after the fire and confessed to everything that he and Vanessa had done – the lies, the flowers, the sabotage, *everything*. Zac was devastated that he'd been tricked by him. He felt so bad for not believing me. But I told him that I'd been taken in by Vanessa the same way he'd been taken in by Chris. That neither Zac nor I were to blame. That we shouldn't let their twisted games ruin our relationship.

Vanessa, meantime, suffered a complete mental breakdown. She wanted nothing to do with her new daughter. She freely admitted to the authorities that she had started the fire and why. She also admitted that she knew I was in the flat at the time and hadn't cared if I'd died. When I'd heard that, it had made me feel physically sick. I'd barely known her at school. I couldn't believe I'd had such a negative impact on her life. And that she nearly cost me mine.

How could she have hated me enough to want me dead? Zac reasoned that it wasn't anything to do with me. It was just that I'd been caught up in her obsessions over the house and in her sibling feud. But it's still unsettling to realise that she was so fixated on me. That I'd been plaguing her thoughts on and off all these years.

Once Vanessa had physically recovered from the birth, she was taken into police custody and eventually given a hospital order by the court. She's now in the secure wing of a psychiatric unit and will probably have to stay there for years.

Although the night of the fire was a terrifying experience, there's a tiny part of me that feels sorry for her. She's a very unhappy and troubled woman. I don't know if she'll ever be well enough to live a normal life.

It's ironic that while I was trying to save Vanessa from Chris, it was actually me who was in danger from her. And both of us were being manipulated by her brother Edward.

Edward Newbury did indeed cut off the next stage of investment, but I discovered the main reason for that was due to his company going bankrupt. So, whether my company had failed or succeeded, I would never have received the funding anyway.

Whatever outcome Edward wanted from his terrible treatment of me and Vanessa, I wonder if losing his home and business was worth it. Because, while I can't know for sure how he lost his money, I'm sure his preoccupation with ruining his sister's life didn't help.

As I try to make myself comfy in my plane seat, I wonder why I was so against the idea of going travelling in the first place. These past few months have been the best of my life. All the new places we've seen, the people we've met. We started in Europe and are gradually making our way east. I think my resistance was simply a fear of going against what was expected. I'd been so keen to make a success of my life that I hadn't really considered what that meant.

After the fire, I told Zac that I didn't think I was cut out to run a business. He tried to reassure me that of course I am – that it wasn't my fault I'd been sabotaged by a very disturbed woman and her brother. He said that next time – without Vanessa ruining things – I would make a complete success of it. But I'm not so sure about that.

I realise now that I hadn't enjoyed running my own company as much as I'd envisaged. I hadn't been prepared for all the stress, the sheer hard work, the mini disasters, and the constant firefighting – a bad analogy in light of what occurred. Even without the addition of Vanessa's sabotage, I'm not sure that kind of life is for me. I think I did it more to impress my mother than anything else. To compete with people like Belinda. But I don't want to do that any more.

After everything that happened back home, it's made me understand that I have to try to live the life I *want* to live, not the life I *think* I should live or one I'm *expected* to live. When I found out that the fire had been started deliberately, it pushed me to re-evaluate everything.

In the aftermath, with the police and the fire service and the insurers and all of it, I suggested to Zac that we sell up and go travelling with the insurance money. Zac was shocked by my suggestion. Worried that I'd regret it. He was also worried about what would happen to his plumbing business if we upped sticks and left. But I reminded him that it was his dream to go travelling in the first place and that we probably should have done it years ago. Once he got his head around it, he was the most excited I'd ever seen him. We both were. Our relationship felt brand new again.

Zac suggested setting aside half of the insurance money for when we get back. So we wouldn't return with nothing. It felt nice to have him be the sensible, grown-up one for a change. Perhaps having me relinquish that aspect of our relationship enabled him to take on part of that role. It's freeing to not be so wound up and controlling about everything. To have someone else worry about it for a change.

We sold the flat cheaply as a fixer-upper to the Drapers, a nice young couple from London. I've never been happier to hand over the keys of my once-dream property. More nightmare than dream. But at least I eventually woke up.

Vanessa inadvertently forced me to look at my life and past and see that maybe I haven't been the perfect good person I always thought I was. If I'm being completely truthful with myself, I used to be a little smug, thinking I had the perfect relationship, the perfect flat, the perfect business. I'd always been popular and well liked... until I met the Jacksons.

My dream of being the perfect person living the perfect life was ultimately selfish. Zac had wanted us to travel before settling down, but I'd railroaded him into following *my* dream. Into making my passions *his* passions. I think back to that terrible night when

Chris was yelling at Vanessa about how he'd done everything in his power to help get back her childhood home. That he'd indulged her obsessions, which had ultimately destroyed both their lives. The irony of that isn't lost on me. It was my wake-up call. Okay, so I wasn't anywhere near as fixated on my dreams as Vanessa was on hers, but sometimes you have to take a step back and look at your life and your goals and ask yourself if what you're aiming for is the right thing. The sane thing. The healthy choice for you and your relationships. If it's worth pursuing your dreams to the exclusion of all else.

I've come to the realisation that in order to have a great relationship with the man I love, I need to truly compromise. Not to sacrifice my dreams for the sake of someone else, but to find a middle ground. To not be so rigid. I feel guilty that I allowed Zac's dreams to fall by the wayside to make way for my ambitions. But now, somehow, I've allowed myself to open up to new possibilities, and to combine Zac's dreams and happiness with my own.

While we're on this hiatus, I don't want to think too deeply about the stressful stuff. I'm simply enjoying these glorious opportunities to lie on beaches and stare at nature, wander round historical architecture, or shop at exotic local markets, stepping away from our real lives for a moment in time. Savouring this luxurious freedom because I know it can't last forever.

The *Fasten Seatbelts* sign comes on and the captain starts talking over the intercom, telling us about the flight times and perfect weather conditions. Zac and I buckle up and grin at one another as the plane starts to taxi down the runway. This is my favourite part of the journey. The take-off. When the earth falls away and I get that light sensation in my stomach – nervous, but excited. The start of a new adventure.

EPILOGUE

Liz Draper can't believe that moving-in day has arrived at last. She's also finding it hard to believe that their poky two-bedroom flat in London has bought them this huge family home in Dorset. Granted, the fire-damage was extensive, and they also ended up over-budget converting it back from two apartments into one house. But the stress and debt have been totally worth it. Because here they are, about to move into their dream home by the sea.

'I've got such a good feeling about this place,' she says, putting a hand to her heart and drinking in the freshly painted exterior, swooning over its insane kerb appeal. The white-rendered facade, the red front door, the gravel drive and mature trees. Even now, in late autumn, with everything dying back, with the chilly rain and grey skies, she still thinks it feels magical.

Her husband nods. 'We were lucky to get it for the price we did.'

Liz places a hand on her belly, waiting for the right moment to tell him that they're expecting their first child. As she does so, she catches a movement from one of the upstairs windows. A dark shadow. She shivers and then shrugs off the moment of unsettledness. Must be a trick of the light, a reflection or some such thing.

She sighs again. 'Fifteen Mistletoe Lane. Even the name sounds idyllic, perfect. I can't wait to get inside and start making it our own.'

'Are you coming, then?' Her husband is already at the front door, impatient.

She gives herself a shake, and follows him in…

A LETTER FROM SHALINI

Thank you for reading *The Couple Upstairs*. I do hope you enjoyed Nina's story.

If you'd like to keep up to date with my latest releases, just sign up here and I'll let you know when I have a new novel coming out.

www.bookouture.com/shalini-boland

If you have a few moments, I'd be really grateful if you'd post a review online or tell your friends about the book. A good review makes my heart skip a beat and I appreciate each and every one.

When I'm not writing or spending time with my family, I love hearing from readers, so please feel free to get in touch via my Facebook page, through Twitter, Goodreads, Instagram or my website.

Thanks so much,
Shalini x

ShaliniBolandAuthor

@ShaliniBoland

@shaboland

4727364.Shalini_Boland

www.shaliniboland.co.uk

ACKNOWLEDGEMENTS

So these are my twentieth (twentieth!) set of acknowledgements, and each time the list of thanks becomes longer. I really do owe so many people my gratitude, not least of all my own neighbours who are all really lovely, decent, kind people and nothing at all like the characters in my book – thank goodness!

Thank you to my incredible publisher, Natasha Harding. You always know exactly where to add those suggestions and how to word them so I feel like I can do it. You make brainstorming and editing such a pleasure. I'm a lucky, lucky person to get to work with you.

Thanks also to everyone at Bookouture. Jenny Geras, Ruth Tross, Peta Nightingale, Richard King, Sarah Hardy, Kim Nash, Noelle Holten, Alexandra Holmes, Saidah Graham, Aimee Walsh, Natalie Butlin, Alex Crow, Melanie Price, Hannah Deuce, Occy Carr and Mark Alder. I've named a few of the wonderful and talented individuals, but I know there are many more who helped to get this book off the ground. Hopefully, I'll meet more of you one day soon.

Thanks to my excellent copy editor Fraser Crichton. Thanks also to Lauren Finger for your superb proofreading skills. Thank you to designer Lisa Horton for yet another astounding cover – could this be your best yet? I think it might.

Thank you to the irreplaceable Katie Villa who has narrated all my Bookouture books, under the brilliant production of

Arran Dutton at the Audio Factory and Bookouture's incredible audio manager Alba Proko. You guys always do such an incredible job of bringing my characters to life.

I feel very lucky to have such loyal and thorough beta readers. Thank you Terry Harden and Julie Carey. I always value your feedback and opinions. I haven't been able to include my mum Amara Gillo as a beta reader for these past few books and that makes me emotional. But I like to think she'd have enjoyed this one.

Thank you to my friends and family for your support the last eighteen months. We haven't seen much of one another, but it's been *everything* just knowing you're there. Dan and Billie, Liz and Julian Davies, Neil Nagarkar, John Gillo, Julie Carey, Louise Norman, Sarah Samuel, Kate Aukett, Kelly New, Natalie Milton, Tanja Pepin, Steph Lloyd, my Sunshine group, and my fellow Bookouture loungers. You're all my lifelines and are the absolute best of humanity.

Thanks to all my incredible readers who take the time to read, review or recommend my books. It means more than you can know.

Finally, I want to thank Pete Boland, a talented writer and the most supportive husband in the world.